"Is anything wrong?"

Jack questioned Cassie.

"Should there be?" she answered coldly.

Jack knew that when a woman answered your question with another question it meant you were standing knee-deep in a manure pile.

"I was just wondering if you made it back safe and sound."

"I'm fine, Mr. Merrill. Is there anything else?"

"No, not at all." He backed off toward the shop's door. "Just glad to see that things are going well for you."

Obviously Cassie was having second thoughts about having made love with him. And this wasn't the place to go into that subject.

His aunt was right. Men and women weren't meant to be friends. And he and Cassie apparently weren't meant to be lovers, either.

Dear Reader,

Brides, babies and families...that's just what Special Edition has in store for you this August! All this and more from some of your favorite authors.

Our THAT'S MY BABY! title for this month is *Of Texas Ladies, Cowboys...and Babies,* by popular Silhouette Romance author Jodi O'Donnell. In her first book for Special Edition, Jodi tells of a still young and graceful grandmother-to-be who unexpectedly finds herself in the family way! Fans of Jodi's latest Romance novel, *Daddy Was a Cowboy,* won't want to miss this spin-off title!

This month, GREAT EXPECTATIONS, the wonderful new series of family and homecoming by Andrea Edwards, continues with *A Father's Gift.* And summer just wouldn't be right without a wedding, so we present *A Bride for John,* the second book of Trisha Alexander's newest series, THREE BRIDES AND A BABY. Beginning this month is a new miniseries from veteran author Pat Warren, REUNION. Three siblings must find each other as they search for true love. It all begins with one sister's story in *A Home for Hannah.*

Also joining the Special Edition family this month is reader favorite and Silhouette Romance author Stella Bagwell. Her first title for Special Edition is *Found: One Runaway Bride.* And returning to Special Edition this August is Carolyn Seabaugh with *Just a Family Man,* as the lives of one woman and her son are forever changed when an irresistible man walks into their café in the wild West.

This truly is a month packed with summer fun and romance! I hope you enjoy each and every story to come!

Sincerely,
Tara Gavin, Senior Editor

Please address questions and book requests to:
Silhouette Reader Service
U.S.: 3010 Walden Ave., P.O. Box 1325, Buffalo, NY 14269
Canadian: P.O. Box 609, Fort Erie, Ont. L2A 5X3

ANDREA EDWARDS

A FATHER'S GIFT

Kelly —
Hope you
And the gift of
enjoyment here,
Andrea
Edward

Silhouette ®

SPECIAL EDITION ®

Published by Silhouette Books
America's Publisher of Contemporary Romance

To Dad for his gifts of acceptance, understanding and
mostly for his unconditional, always evident love.
Thank you.

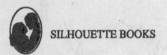 SILHOUETTE BOOKS

ISBN 0-373-24046-5

A FATHER'S GIFT

Copyright © 1996 by EAN Associates

This edition published by arrangement with Harlequin Books S.A.

® and TM are trademarks of Harlequin Books S.A., used under license.
Trademarks indicated with ® are registered in the United States Patent
and Trademark Office, the Canadian Trade Marks Office and in other
countries.

Printed in U.S.A.

Books by Andrea Edwards

Silhouette Special Edition

Rose in Bloom #363
Say It With Flowers #428
Ghost of a Chance #490
Violets Are Blue #550
Places in the Heart #591
Make Room for Daddy #618
Home Court Advantage #706
Sweet Knight Times #740
Father: Unknown #770
Man of the Family #809
The Magic of Christmas #856
Just Hold On Tight! #883
*A Ring and a Promise #932
*A Rose and a Wedding Vow #944
*A Secret and a Bridal Pledge #956
Kisses and Kids #981
†On Mother's Day #1029
†A Father's Gift #1046

Silhouette Intimate Moments

Above Suspicion #291

Silhouette Desire

Starting Over #645

*This Time, Forever
†Great Expectations

ANDREA EDWARDS

is the pseudonym of Anne and Ed Kolaczyk, a husband-and-wife writing team who have been telling their stories for more than fifteen years. Anne is a former elementary school teacher, while Ed is a refugee from corporate America. After many years in the Chicago area, they now live in a small town in northern Indiana where they are avid students of local history, family legends and ethnic myths. Recently they have both been bitten by the gardening bug, but only time will tell how serious the affliction is. Their four children are grown; the youngest attends college, while the eldest is a college professor. Remaining at home with Anne and Ed are two dogs, four cats and one bird—not the same ones that first walked through their stories but carrying on the same tradition of chaotic rule of the household nonetheless.

Once upon a time, there was a beautiful young princess who loved a tall, brave warrior. Their love was so great that the whole village rejoiced when they were wed. Then one day the little village was attacked. The tall warrior fought bravely to keep the attackers from crossing the river, but he was killed, his body slipping beneath the waters. Though she was brokenhearted, the princess fought in his place, turning back their foes when it got dark. She mourned the whole night, crying for her love. The next morning the attackers returned, but a fiercely beautiful white swan was on the river and fought whenever they came near. No arrows could touch it, and the attackers finally went away in defeat. For years the fierce white swan stayed near the village, protecting it. The princess would feed the bird and talk to it, and when she grew old and died, she had the other villagers bury her near the river. The next morning a young female swan appeared. Together the two birds swam down the river and were never seen again.

Prologue

July, twenty years ago

Cassie climbed down through the weeds. She was getting closer to the lake, but still couldn't see Juliet. Cassie had never seen the pair of swans apart from each other in the two weeks she'd been coming to this stupid camp. Yet there was Romeo, all by himself, down the lake a ways.

A funny feeling took hold of Cassie's stomach, twisting it like when their social worker got all chummy. Something was wrong.

She turned around and trudged back to the playing field where all the other nine-year-olds were. Nobody'd noticed that she'd left the group, not that she'd care if they did—Juliet was more important. The other kids were still horsing around while the counselor was writing stuff on his clipboard.

"Jeff!" Cassie shouted. "Hey, Jeff."

The tall, thin counselor turned toward her, smiling. But then he was always smiling. It was enough to make a person barf. "Cassie. Hey, I got you down as captain today."

Cassie hesitated. If there was one thing she really liked, it was being in charge of things, but Juliet was in trouble. Cassie knew it, sure as—

Actually she wasn't sure of too much these days. Mainly just that Daddy had lied to her, big-time. Now he and Mommy were dead, and Cassie was figuring everything he'd said had probably been a lie. So she wasn't wasting her time caring about anybody anymore.

Except Juliet, of course. Juliet was different. She was special.

"I have a stomachache," Cassie told Jeff.

He frowned at her, then began erasing something from his clipboard. "Okay." Probably forever wiping out her name as captain. She would be lucky to be put in charge of table cleanup after this. "Go see the nurse."

Cassie left the playing field, acting like she was going to head up to the nurse's tent. She didn't care what yucky job Jeff gave her. She had to find Juliet and make her okay. That was all that mattered. When Cassie got into the woods, she took the fork that led to the lakeshore path.

His Little Warrior Princess. That's what Daddy had called her after she'd fought with some kids who were making fun of Fiona. He'd said she was always fighting for what was right. But that was before. Lately there hadn't seemed to be much right to fight for, but she fought anyway.

As luck would have it—although Cassie wasn't sure whether it was the good or bad kind—she spied Fiona walking down the path. She was almost glad to see her sister, even dopey as she was. Fiona would help her look.

"Fiona. Hey, Fiona." Cassie put on a burst of speed and joined her sister. "Juliet's missing."

"Missing?"

Cassie gritted her teeth as Fiona threw her hands up to her mouth. All the people that got born in the world and she had to be stuck with Little Miss Perfect for an older sister. Fiona didn't act like she was ten years old.

"Maybe she and Romeo are on the other side of the lake," Fiona said, her voice all shaky.

"Romeo's over here. And you know he never leaves her." Straight A's and her sister was still as dumb as a stump. "Come on." Cassie grabbed Fiona's hand. "We gotta go look for her."

Fiona didn't move. Not an inch. "We should tell Mrs. Warner," she said. "She'll know what to do."

Cassie could hardly keep from gagging. "Don't be so dumb," she snapped. "Grown-ups don't care about birds or kids or anything small."

She could see her sister's face kind of fade back and she knew that she had her. Fiona didn't like to argue with anybody, not even with the boys. And boys were always wrong.

"Miss Kerns likes kids," Fiona said. "She'd help us find Juliet."

Oh, right. Sweet-as-sugar Miss Kerns who was afraid of bugs and snakes and frogs and anything else that crawled around camp. Cassie could only roll her eyes. "I'm going to look," she said. "You do what you want."

Cassie just walked away. All Fiona worried about was getting in trouble. Well, trouble was Cassie's middle name. Even the Scotts, their current foster parents, knew that. They thought Samantha was the cutest thing around and of course, Fiona was so perfect, what adult wouldn't like her? But Cassie was always doing something wrong, always getting into a fight with somebody even when she tried to be good. The Scotts would never adopt them, no matter what they were saying, and it would be all because of her.

Suddenly she felt a burning in her eyes and she started to run. It wasn't like she was going to cry. She was just sick and tired of everybody. Everybody except the swans.

Heavy footsteps sounded behind her and Cassie quickly rubbed at her eyes.

"Aren't we supposed to be playing kickball?" Fiona asked.

"I said I had a stomachache. Jeff told me to go see the nurse."

For once, Fiona didn't argue with her. She just followed along as they crossed the little sandy beach. Cassie slowed a bit so Fiona could keep up with her.

"Where are you guys going?" a voice behind them called.

Oh, no. That was all she needed—a six-year-old tagalong. Cassie stopped and turned to their littlest sister. "Go back to camp."

Seeing the stubborn look on Samantha's face, Cassie didn't stay to argue. She'd let Fiona deal with Sam. Neither of them ever listened to her anyway. She started into the weeds at the far end of the beach, when she suddenly saw movement in the water near her.

Juliet!

"There she is!" Cassie shouted as she rushed toward the water's edge. "There's Juliet."

The poor thing was in among some fallen branches at the edge of the water, half flapping her wings. Cassie began to wade out toward her.

"Cassie, you can't go in the water!" Fiona cried. "There's no lifeguard around."

Cassie clenched her fists and settled for a quick glare at Fiona before wading in farther. But not too much farther. The closer she got, the more frantic Juliet became. She flapped her huge wings but still couldn't rise out of the water.

"She's trapped!" Cassie yelled. Her stomach twisted into a knot of fear as Juliet fell back, exhausted. The swan's head hung down and her wings drooped. Romeo swam closer, making worried sounds as Cassie bent to peer under the branches into the water. What she saw filled her with rage and drove the fear out of her body.

"Her foot's caught in one of those plastic ring things from pop cans!" Cassie shouted.

"We need to tell Mrs. Warner."

"She won't do anything." Cassie splashed back to shore. "You know how she went on and on that first day about swans being mean. She won't let anybody near them. She'll just call somebody and Juliet will die before they get here."

"She might not."

"Come on!" Cassie yanked on Fiona's hand. "We can help her. We just need something to cut the plastic."

But Fiona had taken root again. Probably scared somebody would catch them and she wouldn't be Little Miss Perfect anymore.

Cassie jerked harder and Fiona came forward. "You stay here," Cassie told Samantha. "Keep Juliet company."

"Me?" Samantha cried. "What am I supposed to do?"

"I don't know, Sam," Fiona said. "Sing to her. Read her a story. Show her what's in your knapsack. Just stay out of the water."

Then, before Fiona had a chance to take root again, Cassie hurried her up the path. They crossed onto the little beach. So far, no one was in sight. Once they cleared the beach, though, they could hear the kids at the playing field—and see Miss Kerns and Mrs. Warner at the arts-and-crafts tent. Cassie pulled Fiona to a stop.

"I could ask Miss Kerns for a scissors," Fiona said.

Cassie clenched her teeth. How could anyone who knew the names of all the presidents be so dumb? "No," she snapped. "She'll just ask you what you want them for. I'll go talk to Mrs. Warner. When they're looking the other way, you take one."

"Why can't I talk to them?" Fiona whined. "And you get the scissors."

"Because you're not cool," Cassie replied.

You could stick her sister in a barrel of ice and she still wouldn't be cool. In school, Fiona would confess to things she didn't do just so there wouldn't be any trouble.

Cassie waited as Fiona bit at her lip. The older girl didn't move. "Fiona," Cassie finally hissed.

"All right. All right, already."

Fiona slunk off, skulking from tree to tree. She looked like some kindergarten kid playing secret agent. Cassie shook her head before taking a deep breath and walking slowly toward the counselors.

"Hi, Mrs. Warner," she said as she got near. "Hi, Miss Kerns."

Cassie clenched her fists as both women turned toward her. Fiona was crawling on the ground toward the tables. A blind person could see that she was up to no good.

"You know, Mrs. Warner." Cassie stretched her lips into a smile until it almost hurt. "I was thinking. Could we have an all-star kickball team? The good kids never get a chance to play on the same team."

"It wouldn't be fair if they did," Mrs. Warner answered.

"Oh, I know." Cassie put on her most understanding tone, wiping off the smile and looking real serious. "But if we had an all-star team, we could play teams from other camps."

"Hmm." The camp director tilted her head and smiled. "That's not a bad idea, Cassie."

Fiona was now back to dashing from tree to tree, walking funny with her arm stiff down her side. Cassie hoped she'd stolen a scissors and not a paintbrush or something else stupid.

"But I don't think we can do anything about it this year," Mrs. Warner said.

"Huh?" Cassie replied.

"The camping season is half over," Mrs. Warner said.

"Oh, right."

"But it's something to look into for next year." Mrs. Warner came over and patted her on the shoulder. "Thank you for the suggestion, Cassie."

"You're welcome," Cassie said, trying to keep from watching her sister play hide-and-seek among the trees. "I'm glad you like it."

Fiona was now making wild signs with her arms. Oh, man. Cassie knew that if anybody looked at Fiona she would break into tears and confess to three years of sins. Cassie had to get her out of here.

"Well." Cassie jerked herself out from under Mrs. Warner's hand. "I gotta go. Jeff told me to come right back."

"Then you'd better go."

"Yes, ma'am," Cassie responded and ran down the path. Once out of the counselors' sight, she doubled back and found Fiona behind a clump of bushes near the dining tent.

"Let's go." Fiona was breathing real hard when Cassie caught up with her.

Groaning, Fiona hurried along. "What if they call the police?"

"Why would they do that?" Cassie asked, taking the scissors from her sister's hands. "They got so many scissors, they'll never know one is missing." She ran toward the river.

"Samantha!" Cassie heard Fiona shout from behind her. "I told you to stay out of the water."

Cassie looked down and saw Sam in the water. That same old twisty stomach took her breath away. Was she the only one of them with any sense? She raced ahead as Sam got to her feet and walked out of the water, holding a book over her head. She'd been kneeling—not standing—in water over her waist! Cassie felt her fear go, leaving her plenty annoyed. Why couldn't any of them look out for themselves?

"I had to show her the pictures," Samantha said as she came splashing out of the water. "You always show me the pictures when you read to me."

Cassie just gave Sam a look and plunged into the water. Juliet's wings were drooping away from her body. That was a bad sign. It meant that she was about done for.

But she quickly came to life when Cassie got close to the branches where she was caught. Juliet panicked, flapping her wings and lunging about. Cassie had heard enough warnings about those powerful wings and jumped back, even though the branches were protecting her.

She circled around behind Juliet but no matter which way she went, Juliet was able to turn that way—all the while, screeching and flapping those huge wings. Cassie could feel herself growing frustrated. She knew that she had to stay calm. But how could a person stay calm if the stupid bird was going to kill herself?

She was not going to lose someone else she loved!

"Stop it, you dumb old bird." Cassie tried to hold back her tears but they came anyway. "We're just trying to help you."

She tried again—this way and then that way. But it didn't matter how exhausted Juliet looked. Every time Cassie got close enough to reach under the branches, the bird would start thrashing around and waving those big, airplane wings.

Cassie looked toward shore where her sisters were standing. Fiona was right at the edge of the lake and Samantha was a little behind her, clutching her book to her chest.

"Fiona!" Cassie cried out. "I can't cut the plastic away unless she holds still. You've got to come over here and help."

"In there?"

Why couldn't Fiona just stop being such a worrywart, for once? Didn't she see that Juliet needed both their help?

Cassie fought back the tears that seemed to be coming closer and closer, but then suddenly Fiona was in the lake, walking gingerly through the mud as she circled around Juliet. "When she's looking at me, you cut her free," she told Cassie.

Cassie just nodded, afraid that if she spoke, she would really start crying. And she never cried. Never.

Juliet turned to watch Fiona, and as Cassie watched, she felt relief fill her heart.

"Hi, Juliet," Fiona murmured to the swan. "You remember me? I'm Fiona."

Cassie eased closer to the bird and Juliet flicked a worried glance her way. "Don't be afraid, girl," Cassie whispered. "You're going to be okay."

Fiona was still talking and the swan went back to paying attention to her. Cassie sighed and inched forward. Just another foot. She inched closer, then closer still.

Then finally, taking a deep breath, she reached under the branches into the water. A quick snip and Juliet was free. Clutching the plastic in one hand and the scissors in the other, Cassie propelled herself backward. The swan half-swam, half-flew toward Rome .

Cassie watched the bird hurry away, feeling as if her heart might burst. But even as relief and happiness grew inside her, worry started to push in. What if this had happened over the weekend, when they weren't around? What if it had happened farther around the lake, past the point where the camp was? Juliet could have died.

Cassie felt the stinging behind her eyes again. Mad as she was at Daddy for lying, losing Juliet would somehow have been like losing part of him again. The hurt made her mad and she stomped back to the shore, splashing up a storm.

"Look at this stupid junk," she fumed, waving the plastic ringed strip in the air. "People who throw this stuff in the lake ought to be hung by their necks with it."

Fiona climbed out of the water right behind her. "Come on," she said as she took Samantha's hand. "We'll go back to camp by the nurse's office. We can say we went there with you."

"Whatever." Cassie was too tired to care. What was Mrs. Warner going to do to them, anyway, if they got caught—make them weed the woods?

But Cassie just followed Fiona and Sam along the shore. They were just about to start up through the trees when an old woman came toward them.

"I saw what you did," she said.

"So?" Cassie was in no mood to apologize to anybody. She could feel Fiona pulling at her but she ignored her sister's hand and glared at the intruder.

"It was my fault," Fiona said, stepping in front of them. "I'm the oldest and I should have known better."

Oh, man. The great confessor was at it again. "Gee, Fi—"

But the old woman's laughter cut Cassie's words off. "The gods will smile on you," the old woman said. "You fought so love might live. Someday, the spirits will return to fight for your love."

Cassie just stared at the old woman, stunned for the moment. She wanted to say something smart, something that would snap the old lady back on her heels. But what could you say when someone talked so dumb?

Love wasn't good for anything, anyway. You didn't need it to kick a home run, do chin-ups, or come in first in a race. Love was just a big waste of time. Actually, it was worse. All it did was make you cry.

Chapter One

"My, oh, my. Check it out, Cassie. This could be your Romeo."

"Romeo's a swan," Cassie Scott said and went right on filling out her order form. She knew from Ellen's tone that a man had entered her plumbing-supply house but she, unlike Ellen, was interested only in the supplies he'd come to buy.

"Is he or isn't he studly?" Ellen Donnelly said in a stage whisper that probably woke sleeping dogs in Three Oaks, at least an hour's drive from South Bend, Indiana. Ellen was a happily married mother of five who believed every woman needed a guy of her own and had taken Cassie on as a special challenge. "On a scale from one to ten, I'd rate him a twelve."

Cassie knew Ellen would never let it rest, so she glanced up. Her heart stumbled for a long moment before it started to beat again.

The man had taken a turn to his right and was staring at a row of faucet fixtures that hung on the Peg-Board-covered wall. His well-tailored suit did nothing to hide his husky physique. His shoulders were broad, and tapered to narrow hips and long legs. Dark hair just barely curled over his shirt collar, his beard was trimmed short, and his eyes were blue.

"Studly" definitely was an appropriate description. One that Cassie had used herself last weekend when this man, two little girls and an older woman had moved into the house next to hers. However, she'd also used a few other terms—like "dangerous," "poison," and "heartbreaker"—to remind herself that she was perfectly happy with her life as it was.

"Well?" Ellen said, digging a very nonsubtle, uncool elbow in Cassie's ribs. "What do you say?"

"Eight."

"Eight?" The word almost came out in a shriek. "What do you mean, eight? What's wrong with him?"

"I'm not into suits."

"You're not into suits?"

"Guys who live in them aren't my type. They always think they know everything and I know nothing." Cassie went back to her form. He hadn't been wearing a suit when he'd moved in. No, he'd been wearing jeans and a T-shirt that teased her imagination—a fact that she was reminded of every time he'd wandered in and out of her dreams over the past few nights.

"The suits come off, you know."

"Their attitude doesn't," Cassie said, concentrating hard on the form in front of her, hoping against hope that Ellen would take the hint and get back to her own work.

"Attitude, schmattitude. You get down to the basics in the he-man department and who cares about attitude?"

"You women are disgusting." Burt Klinger, a semiretired plumber who worked for Cassie, had stepped in from the storeroom. "All you females think about is sex."

Like Ellen, Burt felt that Cassie needed a man of her own. But they couldn't agree on what type and spent hours dissecting every remotely potential male who stepped into the store.

"Aren't you two about ready to leave?" Cassie asked.

"Sure you can handle things here all by yourself?" Ellen replied with a sly smile.

"I'll wake Ollie up," Cassie said.

"That beast would chase away a saint." Burt grabbed his lunch box from under the counter. "Have a good weekend."

"And be nice," Ellen added and hurried out after Burt.

Cassie turned her attention back to the list in front of her. Some people just couldn't believe it, but she was satisfied with her life. She had a nice little business, a lot of friends, and teams to play on year-round. And in case things got too boring, she had her hot-air-balloon pilot's license, a kayak for slaloming down the course in the East Race, and all the "Star Trek" episodes ever made—from all four series—on videotape. Her life wasn't perfect but it was a heck of lot better than when she had been married.

"Excuse me."

Her gaze flew up. And her discombobulation level went off the scale.

The man's eyes were that soft, cozy kind of blue that made a lady just want to slide down in the hay. But the little lines at the corners of his eyes spoke more of pain than laughter. She found herself wanting to coax a smile out of him, to erase that first image that came to her heart.

"Ma'am? Are you all right?"

Cassie mentally kicked herself. "I'm sorry." It was obvious he didn't recognize her—and why should he, since she hadn't been the one carrying boxes of belongings up the sidewalk all Saturday afternoon?—but sooner or later they would meet officially, and she didn't want him to think she was a complete ditz. "I have to fax these orders before five and I wasn't paying attention to anything else."

"That's okay." He smiled but his eyes still looked like the sky just before a summer squall. And they still had the power to touch something deep inside her. "I just have a few questions."

She put her pencil down, leaned on the counter and waited. She was stronger this time, though. No matter how she trembled inside, she was not going to let those crazy ideas dance in her imagination.

They stared at each other. It seemed like ages before he cleared his throat and spoke. "Maybe I should wait for that older gentleman."

She paused for a long minute, conscious mostly of an overwhelming sense of disappointment. He was a typical suit guy. She'd been hoping he wouldn't be, but he was. Why it mattered, she didn't know. Just because she hadn't seen evidence of a wife, it didn't mean that there wasn't one.

"What did you want Burt for?"

He looked like he'd wandered into a field he hadn't meant to visit. "I have a plumbing question."

"So?"

"So it's technical."

Cassie glanced at her watch. She was going to have to cut this short if she wanted to get her orders faxed in on time. If she missed the five o'clock deadline, she couldn't get the order in until Monday.

"Look, mister. This is my place. I own it and know every part we have. Why don't you quit wasting everyone's time and tell me what you need?"

His lips twisted slightly. "My faucet leaks."

"Your faucet?" Cassie deliberately let her eyes look around the showroom at the various displays of fixtures. "That really narrows things down a lot."

"Okay." He took a deep breath. "It's a kitchen faucet with a long neck that swivels around. And to make the water come out, you fiddle around with a thing that looks like a joystick."

"That's very technical. I can see why you wanted Burt to help you."

He shrugged. "Hey, I'm a lawyer."

"That's too bad." Cassie let her own smile shine. "But don't worry. We don't discriminate against anyone here."

"Am I going to have to listen to lawyer jokes?"

"Only if you're too obvious with your biases as to what women can and cannot do."

"How about having children?" he said. "Women are the only ones who can do that."

Some women. Not all.

She was tired of this little game all of a sudden. She would let him be the victor.

"Wait a minute." She went halfway down an aisle, past bins of ell and tee joints in three-quarter-inch and half-inch copper, to the boxes of cartridges. Picking one up, she brought it back and handed it to him. "There you go."

He stared at the package like it was something manufactured on Mars with instructions written in Sanskrit. "This doesn't look simple. I thought when your faucet leaked, it was something easy, like changing a washer."

"Not for yours."

"How do you know what kind of faucet I have?"

She took a deep breath and wondered how much longer before she would have to admit she lived in the bungalow to the west of his house. Or how much longer before she had to address the question of why she didn't want him to know. She wasn't scared of him, wasn't worried that a superstud lived next door to her.

"You described it to me," she just said and pulled her order sheet in front of her. "Anything else that I can get you?"

He was staring at the cartridge.

Cassie closed her eyes and counted to ten before she opened them again. She had to get her wobbly heart under control. She had lots of customers come in with no plumbing experience. She didn't take all of them under her wing. There was no reason to want to do so with this guy.

"You do know what to do with that, don't you?"

"Sure." He put it back on the counter with a grimace. "Give it back to you and call a plumber."

If this weren't Friday and if her soul hadn't been on a roller coaster since looking into his eyes, she might have been stronger. At least a little. But she was tired, and that shadow hiding in his eyes was so hard to ignore.

"Getting a plumber out on the weekend'll cost you a fortune," she told him.

He frowned at her. "I can afford it," he said. "Better than letting Aunt Hattie get more upset."

"Aunt Hattie?"

"She washes the dishes in the kitchen sink."

"Aren't you married?" Cassie blurted out, then wished she could hide. Where had that question come from? She didn't care if he was married or single, engaged or on the rebound.

He looked as startled as she had been by the question, but it did worm a slight smile out of him. And that smile sent shock waves clear down to her toes.

"No, I'm not married," he admitted. "How about you?"

"No," she said in what she hoped was a distant, business-like tone. She feared it came out more breathless, though. "What I really meant to ask was, why is Aunt Hattie washing the dishes? Don't you have a dishwasher?"

"It doesn't do the job."

Cassie frowned at him.

"According to Aunt Hattie."

She didn't want to know anything more about his life. She didn't want to start wondering about him. She didn't want her stupid mouth to go blurting out any other questions. Right now, she would be satisfied to just get through the next few minutes until she could close up the shop.

"See that rack over there?" She pointed to the far wall with its array of books, pamphlets and photocopied instruction sheets. "There're do-it-yourself booklets that will show you how to install this cartridge. It's real easy."

She leaned forward and tried concentrating on her list but he was one of those big guys who filled the space around him and crowded everything else out, including the air. Especially since he didn't move.

She looked back up slowly. Reluctantly.

His eyes held an intensity that surprised her; that reached out to her and held her prisoner. "You know how in high school some bigwig know-it-all decides whether you're going into the college prep courses or trade school?" he asked, his voice a feather that tickled her spine.

She just nodded, unable to find her voice.

He leaned his arms on the counter and somehow she was swept with him back to his past. "Well, I didn't like the decision made for me." He took a deep breath before going on.

"See, we didn't have much money and nobody in my house had finished high school by the regular route, but my parents had always encouraged me to dream." His voice had grown soft, but the tension was there and growing. "When Mr. Lincoln told me I was taking shop and basic math my freshman year instead of Latin and algebra, I blew up. He said that given my background, I probably wouldn't even finish high school but if I did, I'd at least have a trade."

The air seemed to quiver around him. The hurt pride and anger of that young boy came back to touch her. She wanted to share his anger and outrage. She wanted to help him slay his dragons. She wanted to take him in her arms and tell him that that was in the past and he should let it go. But she knew he was looking for none of that. Not even her sympathy.

"Anyway," he went on, "I vowed then and there that I was never taking a trade course and would be so successful that I could hire someone to fix even the smallest thing I needed fixed."

She frowned at him, more in an attempt to chill the growing warmth that she was feeling toward him, than in reaction to his words. She wanted to shake off those strange reactions and find herself again. The *real* her—strong and cool and unattached.

"Are you saying you hire someone to change your light bulbs?" she asked. "Or tighten loose handles on saucepans? Or hang pictures in the living room?"

"No, I do simple stuff myself. Just like I would have tightened some fittings or cleaned a filter on the faucet. But bigger stuff—" he nodded toward the cartridge "—I hire somebody."

"So you don't care how easy this is to put in," Cassie said. "You'd rather pay someone sixty dollars than do it yourself."

Something flickered in his eyes. A certain defensiveness?

"You think it's stupid," he said. His voice said he was ready for a fight. "Didn't you make any vows when you were a kid?"

No, she didn't think it was stupid. She understood completely because she'd made her share of vows. And was still making them. "A ton of them," she admitted. "Never let 'em see me cry. That was the first."

"And did you keep it?" he pressed.

She looked away from the persistence of his eyes. Away to the past when she'd made that promise. She'd kept her feelings secret when she'd been a kid starting in yet another new school; when she, Fiona and Sam had waited for the adoption to be official; when she'd had to draw a stupid family tree in junior high and made up all the names. She'd still been keeping that vow a few years back when her marriage had failed and Ron had left her. No one had known how that had hurt.

"Yeah, I did," she admitted slowly.

"Then you understand."

But she didn't want to get into that. Before Cassie had to answer—or give in to the urge she had—she heard a shuffling behind her and saw Ollie come ambling out of the storeroom where he'd been snoozing. After a stretch and a shake and a wag of his tail in her direction, he jumped up, putting his front feet on the counter so he could look over.

"Holy cow!" the man said. "What the hell is that?"

Cassie rubbed Ollie's fuzzy head. "He's an Airedale." And her best friend.

"Dogs don't get that big, not even Airedales."

She just slipped her arm around Ollie's shoulders, needing his closeness to counteract her strange reaction to this guy. But it didn't seem to work. Her heart was reaching out to the man, the way a drowning man reached out frantically for a life preserver.

"Why don't I just fix your faucet for you?" she found herself saying.

The man frowned at her.

"For Aunt Hattie's sake," she explained. "It'll only take me a few minutes."

The man came a few steps closer and extended his hand to let Ollie sniff him. The dog wagged his tail like the guy was a long-lost buddy.

"I know you two, don't I?" the man asked slowly, coming even closer so that he could scratch the top of Ollie's head, although his gaze was on Cassie. His eyes were dark with thought and a touch of suspicion. "You live next door to me. My twins are dying to meet you and your dog."

"Oh, yeah?" She sounded almost cool, almost collected.

His gaze softened just a bit. "I've been wanting to meet you myself."

"Oh, yeah?" A little tremor washed over her. Fear or excitement? It had better be just another row of bricks being added to the wall protecting her.

"I want to get those trees trimmed along the property line," he said. "There's a lot of dead branches that need to be pruned before a storm brings them down, but I'm not sure who owns the trees."

Her heart relaxed. There was nothing to fear here. "I'm not sure, either. Maybe we could split the cost." He looked surprised and perversely she was annoyed. "Did you expect you were going to have to take me to court? You lawyers are suit-happy."

"Not me," he said. "I specialize in hereditary law. A lot of what I do is finding lost heirs or ancestors, not taking people to court."

It was her turn to be surprised. "Really? That sounds like a good thing," she admitted, conscious that her mind was losing reasons to dislike him. And her heart was not making it an offhanded victory. "I take back all my lawyer remarks."

His smile seemed genuine this time. "It's rare to find someone who'll admit they were wrong."

"You can do your admitting when you see how easily I fix your faucet."

But then his frown came back. "I can't let you fix it."

Damn, but he was rigid. Well, so was she. And she wasn't going to let this man with the sad, shadowy eyes beat her. "I can't let you hire somebody and pay weekend rates when it's such a simple job."

"Then let me pay you."

"No way. This is just a good-neighbor thing."

"Then I'll feed you."

She felt a sudden, deeper-than-for-food hunger but refused to examine it, knew somehow that it would be fatal to her peace of mind to do so. "Whatever."

The man stuck his hand out. "Jack Merrill."

She took a deep breath as her hand touched his, not allowing any reaction to well up inside her. And almost succeeded. "Cassie. Cassie Scott," she said. "Just let me finish up my order and fax it in. Then I'll close up here and drop Ollie off at home."

He gave her a quick nod and Cassie went back to the storeroom to settle her nerves in private. Her agitation meant nothing. Just stress after a busy week. Just a touch of spring fever— a little late, she granted, coming in mid-May instead of mid-April—but she'd always marched to her own drummer.

And fixing the faucet was the neighborly thing to do. No need to worry that she was breaking the latest of her vows—not to get involved.

"Daddy, why are you staring at Cassie's feet?"

Startled, Jack came near to swinging on the fluorescent lights on his kitchen ceiling. He took a deep breath and tried to look sternly at his twin daughters, standing side by side in the kitchen doorway, but he wasn't able to hold on to the frown.

"Miss Scott is being nice, fixing that leaky pipe as well as the faucet. I just want to make sure that nothing happens to her. You never know what kind of monsters there might be under the sink."

"Oh, sure," Mary Louise said.

"Really," Mary Alice added.

He cleared his throat, painfully feeling the loss of his yesterdays. Last year, when the girls were five, that monster story had worked just fine. Now it had no more impact on them than the news that Caesar had conquered all of Gaul.

"Why don't you guys go see what Aunt Hattie is doing?"

"We're not guys," Mary Alice said.

"Thank you," Jack said. "I forgot."

"You're welcome," the girls replied.

His eyes wandered back down toward Cassie as laughter floated up from under the sink. He'd been telling the truth when he'd said he wasn't staring—he'd actually been thinking how easy it had been to talk to her. He'd been in her presence for only a few minutes and he'd told her about high school and his vow. In the three years he'd been with Daphne, he didn't think he'd ever told her that story. And in the five years since she'd left, he knew he hadn't told a soul. Hadn't even come close to telling anyone.

What magical powers did Cassie Scott have? And how could he keep them from affecting him again?

He turned to the girls before they accused him of staring again. "When Miss Scott is done, we're going out for dinner."

They looked at each other and then down at their denim jumpers. "We hafta change our clothes."

"Then you'd better get started. I think the restaurant closes at midnight."

They moved quickly enough but their giggles hung in the air like the expensive perfume their mother used to wear. He frowned. Maybe still wore, for all he knew.

"Having a little problem with control, there?"

Cassie had slid out from the cabinet and was now sitting on the kitchen floor, her arms loosely wrapped around her knees. Her grin almost mirrored the same mocking attitude he'd seen in his daughter's faces. Did all women have this need to squash down the men who wandered into their lives?

No, that wasn't true. Daphne had never mocked him; he'd been a star she could hook her wagon to. Of course, he hadn't known that until he'd blown his knee out in the preseason and had called it quits. Then she had left, furious because he'd refused the tryout with the Raiders that she'd claimed he "owed" her, and hitched herself up with an actor. Her refusal to be tied down by marriage suddenly made sense.

She'd never looked back, called, or anything. Maybe she'd thought he would come chasing after her, but he would have been damned first. Jack Merrill didn't crawl, beg or plead. And he paid his own way.

Something Cassie needed to understand.

"Everything shipshape under there?" he asked.

"Yep."

"You were down there awhile."

"It didn't take me more than a minute or two to tighten things up. I was just waiting for you to get things under control out here."

His eyes took in her athletic build, sparkling eyes and short curly hair that made a dusty brown halo around her head. Beauty and high spirits—a combination that could make a man swim the rapids. Well, he'd given up swimming. He walked over to where she sat.

Cassie started to gather her tools from under the sink, then stopped when she saw his extended hand. "I'm not helpless, you know," she said. "I can get myself up."

"I don't doubt that," Jack replied, still holding out his hand. "I'm just trying to be a gentleman."

"That's just a nice-sounding word for 'control freak.' " She made a face and pushed herself upright.

"Now what?" he snapped.

"I know how that scam works. It starts with a hand to help you out of a car or opening the door for you. Pretty quick it moves into giving you all kinds of rules that you have to follow in order to be a proper lady."

Independent, as well as ornery. And with enough fire in her blood to keep the world in chili pepper until the Second Coming. It teased at him, tempting him to look closer. But he could fight it. He had no interest in love and the way it chipped away at your pride until you had nothing left. He would pay Cassie back for her trouble and that would be that.

"And you don't need to take me out to dinner," she said. "This wasn't enough trouble to be called work."

"No way. I pay my debts. And I owe double since you fixed the drain, too."

She frowned at him. "It wasn't a big deal."

"My daddy didn't raise no welchers."

"I never said he did."

"He taught me not to be beholden."

"Beholden?" she repeated.

"You can take a boy out of the hills, but you can't the hills out of the boy," he said. "And it doesn't matter how I say it, I don't like owing."

"What is this?" she mocked. "Some guy honor thing?"

"What's wrong with paying your debts?" He knew he was getting hyper about it, but he couldn't help it. He didn't need or want her charity. Then another thought struck him and his annoyance fled. "Unless you have other plans."

"Not really," she admitted slowly. "But your family might not want to have some stranger butting in...."

He suddenly saw the light—she didn't like kids. Who cared how intriguing she seemed at first blush? "Well, fine," he snapped and grabbed his checkbook from his suit-coat pocket. He would pay his debts one way or another. "I'll have you know they're very well-behaved and a joy to be with, but if you don't—"

Cassie pulled his checkbook away from him and threw it on the table. "What are you talking about? I wasn't insulting your kids. I just assumed that you might want to spend the evening alone with them."

"Oh." His anger deflated. This woman had a strange power, a knack for knocking the underpinnings out from under him. Another reason to stay away. He ran his fingers through his hair and sighed. "Look, I'm sorry for blowing up. The finer points of social interaction sometimes elude me."

"That's all right," she said, her voice soft.

She was smiling at him and he didn't feel so much like a fool as a junior-high kid—tongue-tied and spellbound. There was such a strength about her, such a beauty that shone through those eyes and her smile. He wanted to say something clever and witty, but all he could do was gape. Where was all his great determination? His ability to block out distractions and focus on his goal?

The girls came to his rescue as they clattered down the stairs.

"Girls, girls." Aunt Hattie's words fruitlessly chased after them. "Ladies do not run."

The girls rushed into the kitchen. "We're ready, Daddy."

"Yeah, and we're really, really hungry." The kids had shed their jumpers for matching striped overall shorts and ruffled blouses.

"You put shorts on?" he asked. "I thought you were getting dressed up."

"Aren't we going to Pizza Playland?" Mary Louise asked.

"Remember?" Mary Alice asked. "You promised us this morning we'd go there for dinner."

Aunt Hattie had followed the girls into the kitchen, radiating disapproval as if she'd been storing it up for the past fifty-six years. "You're thanking this young lady for fixing our faucet by taking her to the Pizza Playland? That's like paying your debts with play money."

"We're going to Pete's Patio," he told them. He'd dined there while looking for the house and had found it to be a comfortable combination of casual dress and gourmet food.

"Pizza Playland is better," Cassie said, then smiled down at the girls. "That's where the girls and I want to go, right?"

"Right!" they agreed loudly.

Jack just frowned as the three of them walked toward the door. This was supposed to be a dinner to pay Cassie back, and pizza and popcorn didn't do that. Didn't she take this debt seriously? Well, Miss Cassie Scott was going to learn that Merrills didn't take charity.

After giving Aunt Hattie a nod, he caught up with Cassie outside. The girls were rushing over to his minivan. "I owe you three now," he told Cassie under his breath. "Three decent paybacks."

"Jack—"

"Us Merrills pay our debts," he said. "Three paybacks it is."

"Fine," she snapped. "Far be it from me to taint the macho Merrill honor."

Her voice was like a match striking the flint of his soul. He could have sworn that sparks flew between them. He could almost smell the burning in the air and hear the sizzle as the sparks tried to ignite his heart.

To no avail, though. His heart could sizzle all it liked. His head ran the show.

* * *

"Daddy, would you watch our shoes, please?" one of Jack's daughters—Cassie couldn't tell the twins apart—asked him as they put their shoes on the bench.

"Sure thing, pumpkin," Jack replied.

"And don't tell Aunt Hattie," the other girl implored her father. "She don't like us to take our shoes off."

"My lips are sealed."

After getting Jack's assurances, the girls dashed off to a playroom filled with plastic balls. It was a very popular place, filled with laughing kids—a fact that Cassie appreciated greatly this evening. These were the perfect surroundings to fight off that strange instant attraction she'd felt to Jack at her store. No one could have romantic thoughts while resting their arms in the sticky remains of spilled pop.

She turned back to Jack, but found a new danger. He was watching his daughters with so much love in his eyes that it hurt her to see it. She had to look away. It made her all too conscious of what her life was lacking.

And what it would always lack.

She sipped at her iced tea for a moment, tracing a pattern in the plastic tablecloth with one fingertip, then looked back up at Jack once her pitiful emotions were under wraps. "Sounds like Aunt Hattie is one tough lady," she said.

Jack brought his gaze back to hers. His eyes had a faint wariness in them that seemed to dance around with her heart.

"She grew up in a two-room cabin in the hills and didn't get her first new pair of shoes until she was twelve years old," he said, wiping up the crumbs near his place with a paper napkin. "She has trouble with the concept of dressing down."

He turned to watch the girls throw themselves into the playroom, so Cassie followed suit. Her thoughts were traveling another route, though. It was funny how things from your youth stayed with you all your life. Her father had lied about where he and their mother had been going just before they'd died, and now Cassie half believed everyone was lying to her.

Even finding out last month that her father had been ill and probably seeking medical help hadn't made much of a difference. He could have told them; he *should* have told them. The twenty years between the lie and the truth couldn't be erased, and neither could the feelings of inadequacy that that time had built.

"Next time we're going to a real restaurant," Jack said suddenly, pulling her from her thoughts.

Cassie wanted to say there would be no next time, but he seemed to have this obsession about paying what he perceived as his debts. She wasn't up to another argument over it and just asked, "What's wrong with this place?"

"I said I'd feed you in exchange for your plumbing services. This doesn't count."

Come hell or high water, there would be no next time. Relationships weren't her strength and she was smart enough now to avoid the things that got her into trouble. Even if they had the most tempting blue eyes. "Don't be ridiculous. I like pizza. I come here all the time."

"You have kids of your own?" He suddenly looked concerned. "We could have brought them along."

"No, I don't." For some reason his look made her nervous, like he could somehow see into her soul. Another reason to avoid him. "I'm not married anymore."

"I've never been married and I've got two kids." A dark cloud filled his face. "I'm sorry. I'm not bragging. I'm just pointing out the obvious."

"Which is you don't have to be married to have kids."

He nodded and Cassie turned back to look at the twins. The flip side of that truth was that being married did not ensure that you would have children. She felt the gloom wanting to descend, the storm clouds wanting to expose the misery that lay all too close to the surface.

"Daphne was—and probably still is—very ambitious."

Cassie looked back at Jack, relieved to have the subject changed. He was staring at a point someplace behind her left shoulder. Even without the eye contact, it felt like they were very much alone together. Which was crazy, considering the hordes of laughing kids and weary parents all around them. Which was dangerous, considering the fragile state of her common sense this evening.

"I used to play pro football," Jack said. "And she thought being with me would help her get noticed by some Hollywood producer, agent or something."

Cassie played with her drink, slowly spinning the glass around. She tried running through the names of pro football players she remembered but his didn't ring a bell. But he looked like a professional athlete; his body was lean and tight as if the years of training couldn't be wiped away that fast. If only her heart was that disciplined.

Jack went on. "I'm sure, from Daphne's point of view, the girls were an accident, but she never said as much. Then I tore up my knee and lost my spot in the limelight."

"And she left?"

He nodded. "Daphne's one smart lady. She knew her wagon wouldn't go anywhere if the horse was lame." His words were said in an offhand way, but there was no hiding the darkness that filled his eyes. Was he still pining for her? Maybe that was the reason for the shadows she'd sensed around him earlier.

"Has she made it?" Cassie asked.

"Not that I've noticed." He took a moment to watch his children. "I called in some markers and got her an audition with a reputable agent out in Los Angeles, but I don't know what happened. Certainly no big starring roles."

"Hasn't she been in touch with the girls?"

He shook his head. "I'm not a sports-page item anymore, but we haven't been hiding, either. She could find us if she wanted." He shrugged. "I don't know. She doesn't seem to have any feelings for her kids...."

Cassie wanted to take his hands and hold them tightly. She wanted to say something wise or understanding or even witty. Something that would ease that knot of hurt that seemed to be growing bigger before her eyes. But words eluded her. She wanted to make his pain go away, even for a few minutes, but her mind was frozen with the sense of loss and rejection both he and the kids must feel. Just went to prove how lousy she was at this whole relationship business.

"Your turn."

She blinked.

"Hey, I gave you a snippet of my life's history. You have to give me yours."

Give him her life's history? No way. It seemed cold in the room all of a sudden. Cold and threatening. She shook her head. "I don't have to—"

"Fair is fair."

She glared at him, clinging to the surge of anger with relief. "What are you? A Boy Scout full of pithy little sayings for every occasion?"

He seemed startled by her vehemence and pulled away. "Hey, no big deal," he retorted. "I was just making conversation."

She saw his pride throw up a screen for him to hide behind and realized this guy was pricklier than she was. Her refusal to share had hurt him, made it seem that his confidences weren't important. It only took a moment of weighing to decide which was more important—her need for privacy or his need to feel accepted.

After a long sip of her iced tea, she looked straight across at him. "It's an ordinary story. I got married in college. We grew up and didn't love each other anymore. Divorce seemed the best for everyone."

She looked away then, almost afraid that somehow he would be able to read the rest in her eyes, that he would see all the doubts and fears and accusations. Her doctor hadn't found a reason why she hadn't been able to get pregnant, but they hadn't found a problem with Ron, either. More tests—that was what they had wanted. More tests, further blood work, additional X rays. They'd all seemed so certain that if they just looked at her long enough and hard enough, they would find the answer. All so certain that she was the one who was defective.

Her gaze stopped at the kids in the playroom, laughing and pushing each other. She hated losing a ball game, even a stupid pickup game. Failing at being a woman had hurt almost more than she could bear; she was never going to risk that hurt again. She found Jack's eyes on her and sought to divert them. She couldn't take the chance that he would catch a glimpse into her soul.

"What position do you think your kids will play?" she asked. "Linebacker?"

He turned and frowned when he saw the shoving match they'd gotten into. "I'd better get them out of there," he said, getting up. "Aunt Hattie gets upset if they come home too high. She says ladies are always under control."

Cassie just watched as Jack rounded up the girls. She didn't find Aunt Hattie's reactions strange. Given what Jack had said about her upbringing, she probably was going overboard to keep the girls' childhood from being anything like hers. Sometimes the best you could do was keep those you cared about from sharing in your hurt. That was all that she was trying to do in avoiding a relationship—keeping someone else from the pain of her lacking.

Jack came back with the girls and they waited while the twins put their shoes back on. It had been a pleasant evening, but Cassie wasn't all that sorry to see it end. She was feeling a little too warm toward Jack. A little too willing to think chances could be taken when they couldn't. When they shouldn't. It was time to—

"Cassie?"

"Hey, Aunt Cassie, hi!"

She spun and found herself facing her adopted brother Bobby and his three kids. "Hi, everybody," she said, although her heart was sinking. If this didn't beat all. The one time she was out with a guy—through no fault of her own—she had to run into the oldest and bossiest of her siblings.

"What are you doing here?" her nephew, Timmy, asked.

"Thought you had softball Friday nights," Bobby added.

She sighed and waved her hand at Jack and the girls, introducing them to her family. Bobby's jaw dropped.

"Jack Merrill?" he shouted as he pumped Jack's hand. "*The* Jack Merrill?"

"Man," Timmy was saying. "I don't believe it. Can I have your autograph?"

Cassie just frowned at them all. Apparently, Jack's name meant something to them all.

"Don't you know who this is?" Timmy asked.

"Just *the* Jack Merrill," Bobby answered before she could even shake her head. "One of the greatest running backs that ever played for the Chicago Bears."

"That was ages ago," Jack said. "When dinosaurs roamed the earth."

"Steeplejack Merrill," Timmy said.

"Steeplejack?" Cassie almost burst out laughing at the embarrassed look on Jack's face.

"He was called that because he never tried to dodge a tackler," Bobby explained. "And when he hit them, they heard bells."

This time Cassie couldn't restrain her laughter, shaking her head as she did.

"Hey," Jack protested. "It wasn't my doing. A fella can't always choose his nicknames."

"Poor baby," Cassie murmured.

Suddenly his baby blues turned dark like Lake Michigan in a storm. The laughing voices of children floated off into the sky and a whole range of desires and delights raced across her soul. She saw passion that could make her come alive again and sorrow that she could wipe away with the touch of her hand.

By sheer force of will, she looked away. It was time for her to go home. Before she got into more trouble than she could handle.

Chapter Two

A certain wide smile seemed to dance in Jack's thoughts as he unpacked boxes in his new office. A certain laughter seemed to echo in the air. It was too quiet in the building, he decided as he stacked books on a shelf. That was all. If it were some day other than Saturday, there would be lots of distractions and he wouldn't be thinking of Cassie at all. Of how beautiful her eyes were or how relaxed he had felt with her.

He wasn't in the market for a relationship. Probably never would be. He stopped unpacking with a frown and stared out the window at the grassy expanse between buildings.

Not being in the market for a relationship made him sound like a coward, and Merrill men weren't cowards. Generations of them had left the family farms in the hills and gone to war. They were factory workers, like his father, fighting poverty and boredom to take care of their families, or miners, braving the dangers of the earth to earn a living. He himself had fought on the gridiron, facing three-hundred-pound linemen without flinching.

No, this wasn't fear in his heart. It was wisdom. It was knowing his limitations. It was realizing that love was a monster that hid under the bed until you were feeling safe and cozy and almost asleep. Then it reached out and grabbed you and made a fool of you, set you up for laughter and ridicule—something that was never going to happen to him again.

He turned from the window. He might as well give this up and go home. He would get the girls and they would do something with the afternoon.

He drove home and parked the car in the drive. Although his feet wanted to hurry up his front steps, his gaze strayed over to Cassie's house. It was smaller than his, with a tiny yard, but it had charm and a quiet beauty that somehow seemed to match Cassie.

But even as his eyes admired her house, his heart felt a certain sinking. Her yard was empty. Her doors were closed to the warm spring air. She wasn't home.

Which shouldn't matter to him in the slightest. His only interest in her was as a neighbor. And in paying her back for her help last night.

He hurried up to his front door and pushed it open. "Hello!" he shouted. "I'm home."

The only sound that answered him was the piano moaning in pain and pleading for mercy. He made his way to the living room.

"Hey," he said. "You guys are starting to sound good."

Blessed silence descended from the heavens as Mary Louise stopped beating on the keys. His aunt and two daughters turned to stare at him, eyes hard. Probably because he'd gone and used the G word—guys—again.

"You just about done practicing?"

"Uh-huh," Mary Alice said, jumping down from her spot on the end of the bench.

"Ah, I was just thinking..." There was something this weekend down at the mall on the south side of town, something with animals. "I was thinking of taking the girls down to the mall. They have something called Ag Days this weekend."

"Ag Days?" Two pairs of blue eyes, both filled with suspicion, stared at him.

"Farm stuff," Jack said. "Cows, horses, rabbits, tractors."

"Horses?" Mary Alice asked, her eyes suddenly springing back to life.

"Bunnies?" Mary Louise began jumping up and down with excitement. "Little baby bunnies?"

The girls looked at each other and the identical pink dresses they wore. "We can't go like this," they said. "These aren't farm clothes."

Oh, Lord. Jack felt his shoulders drop into a small slump. There were times when it seemed his kids needed about ninety-nine different outfits. It wasn't that he wanted to deny them anything, but he wasn't comfortable with their fixation on clothes.

"Can we wear jeans?" they asked. "That's what people wear on the farm."

"Yeah," he answered. "Jeans are fine."

That sent them dashing upstairs.

Jack sank into an easy chair and looked around the room. The house was about eighty years old, but well kept up and with a quiet elegance. There was a sense of permanence here that he hadn't had most of the time when he was growing up. Then, his father's search for work had taken them from town to town—just as Jack's stint in pro football had taken him all over the country. He preferred permanence; knowing that this would last and last and last.

"The faucet doesn't leak anymore."

Jack was so intent on his thoughts, his aunt's words took him unawares. Turning, he just stared at her.

"That young lady is very competent," his aunt said.

"Cassie?"

"Cassandra. That's such a pretty name." She nodded and smiled slightly. "And dignified. A proper name for a lady." His aunt nodded again. "Don't see much of that these days."

Jack found himself swirling in a pool of fantasies. Cassie dressed casually in jeans and a knit shirt, but looked like a million dollars. Cassie crawling around on the floor fixing sinks, and making him feel she could fix anything. Cassie with her hair cut short and her eyes glowing, daring him to reach for love again. He fought to surface from his thoughts.

"She looks like a strong young woman," Aunt Hattie said.

"Yeah," Jack replied. "Wrestling with pipes and tools all day would probably do that to a body."

"Jimmy Jack Merrill."

He could feel his cheeks warm. The only people living who knew his given name were himself and Aunt Hattie.

"You know damn good and well what I'm talking about. There's other kinds of strength besides muscles."

"Yes, ma'am."

"She's one a body could count on in a pinch."

He just sighed. This wasn't the first time they'd had this conversation. "I'm not looking for someone," he reminded.

"The girls need a mother."

"The girls are fine."

"You need a wife."

"I'm fine."

"Hiding from love isn't fine," she informed him. "That Daphne was a selfish little twit. You can't live with your head buried under a bushel basket because of her."

"I'm not hiding from anything," Jack insisted. "The perfect woman for me doesn't exist."

"There isn't any such thing as a perfect man or woman," Aunt Hattie snapped. "You just need to find someone who comes close and compromise the rest."

"No one comes close," he declared.

"Of course not," Aunt Hattie said. "Not with that stiff-necked pride of yours."

Two sets of feet were clattering down the stairs and Jack sighed in relief. Escape was at hand.

"We're ready," the girls cried.

"All right." He got to his feet. "Last one to the car gets mud in her ice-cream cone."

The girls raced off, and he followed, conscious of Aunt Hattie's knowing gaze on him the whole way. She really didn't understand. He wasn't looking for perfection. He wasn't looking for anybody. But if he was, he'd be looking for someone who would accept him as he was. Not someone who wanted to own him or to make him jump through hoops. And he didn't think such a woman existed.

"Daddy?" Mary Alice said as they reached the minivan.

"Can Cassie come with us?" Mary Louise asked.

"I don't think she's home."

"Go see." They both pointed at the house next door.

Jack glanced at the house, then back at his daughters. There was a little part of him that wanted to go over to ask her to come along, but it was easy to stomp down. "A man can't just ask a lady out at the last minute," he said. "It's not polite."

"Why not?"

"It's like assuming she doesn't have anything important of her own to do."

"But she might not know about the bunnies."

"I'm sure she does." They were like this with every woman that he showed half interest in. Did they miss a mother's care so much that they were willing to accept anyone as a substitute? But then they usually calmed down once the women started fawning over them.

"But what if she doesn't?"

Jack sighed. "I just can't—"

"I know," Mary Louise said as the two girls took off running toward Cassie's house.

"Hey!" Jack cried.

"We're not a man," Mary Alice called back to him. "We can ask her."

"I don't think—" But just as they neared the house, Cassie's truck pulled up in front and he hurried after the girls.

"Hi, Cassie," the girls were calling, hurrying over to the passenger side of the truck to wave through to her.

"Hi," she called back and got out, a grocery bag in her arms.

She walked around the truck and smiled at Jack. His silly brain forgot all his apologies and explanations of why the girls had come over. All he could do was feel the warmth of her smile down into his toes.

"You all come to help me carry in my groceries?" she was saying, her voice filled with laughter. "Sorry to disappoint you, but I've only got one bag."

"I can take it," he offered, reaching out for the bag, but she dodged his outstretched arms.

"We're going to see the horses and bunnies," Mary Alice said.

"Do ya wanna come along?" Mary Louise asked.

"Daddy said you'd be busy."

That was all he needed—for Cassie to think he didn't want her to come. "That's not exactly what I said, girls," he told them, still reaching back for the grocery bag. Cassie stepped away. "I meant she might have other things planned."

"Actually, I do," she said. "I'm really sorry. Maybe some other time."

"That's all right." Although he was absurdly disappointed. Not that he ought to be. He should be relieved, glad even that the girls' little scheme wasn't going to throw him and Cassie together.

"Where's your dog?" Mary Louise was asking.

"Can we come and play with him sometime?"

"Sure," Cassie replied. "He likes to play."

"Girls, it's not polite to invite yourselves over," he scolded lightly. He took each of them by the hand. It was time they let Cassie go inside and got on their way themselves.

"We don't got a dog," Mary Louise said. "We got a piano."

"We should be going, girls," he said gently and nodded at Cassie. "See you around—"

Mary Alice dug her feet in and refused to be pulled toward their house. "Do you wanna come to a picnic with us? It's on Morial Day and for the school where Daddy's gonna teach."

"Girls!" He was appalled at their invitation. Appalled at the surge of hope in his heart.

"She said, 'Another time,' Daddy," Mary Louise reminded him.

"So I did," Cassie admitted with a laugh.

"It's okay that she comes, isn't it, Daddy?" Mary Alice asked.

He could feel three pairs of eyes staring his way and he gave in. Caved in. Rushed in to grab hold of the hope like a balloon he was afraid would be blown away.

"Sure," he said heartily. "If she wants to."

"Daddy said it's okay," Mary Louise told Cassie, as if she might not have heard.

"And it won't count for what Daddy owes you," Mary Alice added.

Cassie just laughed—a sound that danced on his heart and brought a smile to his lips. "I wish I could," she said. "I really do, but I already promised I'd go to someone else's picnic."

"Aw." It was the girls who said it aloud, but the disappointment was echoed in Jack's heart.

It was just as well, though, he told himself. It would be nice to be friends with her—good neighbors, as it were—but a dating relationship would just change all that. No, this definitely was for the best.

"Well, we should be on our way," Jack said, this time not getting any resistance from the girls. "And I haven't forgotten that I owe you."

"Oh, I haven't, either," Cassie said with a laugh. "I'm compounding the interest daily."

She could mock all she liked, but he was paying that debt. And soon.

"I can still see that game," Bobby was saying. "There was no time left on the clock and they were down by four. It was a touchdown or nothing."

Cassie rolled her eyes in response, but since Bobby was on the phone, he didn't even pause in his recital. She glanced out the side window at the rain. It seemed to be slacking off. The storm must be just about past.

"He broke one tackle after another...."

She'd had calls from Bobby all weekend. And when it wasn't him, it was Larry or Adam. They even had Fiona call the store after she got home from school. All with questions and comments and information about Jack.

"And you wouldn't believe how..."

Cassie went over to the back window. Leaves and small branches were strewn across the backyard, presents of the thunderstorm that had rolled through about an hour ago. She wished she could change her family's attitude as easily as she could clean up after a storm. Their persistence was the reason why she'd turned down Jack's invitation to accompany him to his picnic. Well, one of the reasons. The main one was that she just didn't want to get involved. Not now. Not with anyone.

"So, are you bringing him to the picnic?" Bobby asked.

Cassie woke from her thoughts in time. "We had dinner together once," she informed him. "We are not dating."

"You really ought to bring him," Bobby went on, as if she hadn't spoken.

Wasn't this just like the past twenty years? She would talk and Bobby or Larry or Adam would ignore her. "Ollie needs to go out," Cassie said. "Talk to you later."

She hung up, but even before she could waken Ollie and take him outside to prove she wasn't lying, the phone was ringing again. It was Larry this time.

"Hey, sis, you bringing Steeplejack to the family picnic?"

"No, I'm not. I—"

"'Cause, there's this guy at work who wasn't doing anything...."

Cassie fought back the urge to scream. "Do *not* bring a date for me," she said through clenched teeth. "I don't even know if I'll be there myself."

"Sure, you will. You've never missed a Memorial Day picnic," Larry said with a knowing laugh.

"Ollie's got to go out," Cassie said and hung up before she threw her phone across the room.

Her family was just too much! She didn't need their help with her social life. How was she ever going to convince them to butt out?

She hurried Ollie out the door into the light drizzle, then stopped on the step. Two massive branches from the old oaks between her and Jack's houses had come down in the storm, one landing in her driveway and just missing her garage by a few feet.

Cassie walked slowly over to the fallen branches. She would have to move that one in the drive or she wouldn't be able to get her truck out in the morning. She tugged at the branch, but it didn't budge. She kicked at it but it didn't move. It looked like she would need to cut it up with the chain saw. She looked at the branch, easily thirty feet long and a good ten inches in diameter at the thickest part. She was in for a long night.

She felt unbearably weary all of a sudden; unbearably alone, although she told herself she was being silly. If she wanted help, all she had to do was call her brothers. They would be over within minutes. And this was just part of being independent, just part of being—

"What a mess."

Cassie looked up to see Jack on the other side of the fence. For one split second she thought she saw something new in his eyes. Some hunger or longing or need that was somehow reflected in her own heart. But then a curtain seemed to fall over his eyes and all that she saw was the same, slightly distant Jack. It was probably all in her mind. Probably a trick of the gloom left behind by the storm.

"Anything damaged?" he asked.

She shook her head. "Nope. I'll have to get this branch moved, though, or I can't get my truck out."

"I can help," he offered.

"That's okay." Her mouth said the words quickly, before her heart could get involved. "I was going to call Bobby and Larry."

"Boy, you are stubborn," he said. "How come you can help me but I can't help you?"

"You couldn't fix your faucet. I can fix this."

"I could have hired someone."

"Well, I can get my brothers over."

"Hey, I ought to be helping," he said. "It's partly my fault that the branches are down. I talked about getting them cut but never called the tree service to set it up."

"I could have called, too, you know."

"Why don't we argue about it while we're cleaning it up? Let me change into something a little grubbier."

Before she could argue further, he turned back to his house. The girls had come outside and were standing in the middle of the yard. Dressed in bright green rain slickers with pink umbrellas, they looked like little flowers. Jack stopped to talk to them and Cassie could hear their voices on the evening breeze. She watched for a long moment, her heart feeling a strange longing at the sight of them together. Even Ollie was sitting and watching, as if there was something in that neighboring yard that would never be in theirs.

She tried to ignore the emptiness in her heart, the sense that she was drifting without purpose, and turned toward the house.

"Standing around getting all moony isn't going to get this branch moved," she told Ollie. "It's stopped raining, so I might as well get started."

She got her chain saw out of the basement, along with a pair of safety goggles and a long extension cord. Beginning with the smaller side branches, she lopped them off one by one, tossing them into a pile to one side of the driveway. She had no idea what was with her this evening. It wasn't like her to get all mopey and discouraged when some unexpected chore came along. She'd handled that broken water pipe last year just fine. And when the boiler in her last house broke in the middle of winter, she coped very well. So why was her practical nature on vacation now?

Jack came up next to her, dressed in jeans and a sweatshirt. And looking all too appealing. "Want me to do that?" he asked, nodding toward the chain saw.

She glared, angry at him for being so near, so willing for her to lean on him. "Why? Is this another thing women can't do?" She didn't wait for an answer, but sliced off another branch—the din of the machine made conversation impossible.

"I just thought your arms might get tired and I could take a turn," he said when she paused between cuts.

"My arms are just fine, thank you."

She concentrated on cutting off another branch and watching it fall to the rain-wet driveway. She knew she was acting like a jerk, but she couldn't help it. He was too damn nice, too damn good-looking, with too damn much of what she wanted from life. All she had to do was weaken a hair, just the tiniest bit, and she'd be setting herself up for pain.

Jack didn't keep up the argument, but just carted the branches she cut off to the pile over at the side. Unfortunately, his silence didn't mean he was invisible. She was all too aware of him as he came near for the next branch, as he held aside the spread of leaves so she could see to make a cut.

He made her feel small—an unusual feat since she was fairly tall. Small and able to be protected. She hadn't felt that way in ages. But then it had been ages since she'd been willing to loosen the reins of control enough to let someone in.

But Jack was different. He could tackle the hard times, she thought suddenly, and not be thrown by them. He wouldn't be one who would run at the first sign of trouble.

But what did that mean to her? Did it mean she should relax and see where her emotions took her? But what if they took her close, really close? When was the time you stopped to confess failings?

"Watch it!"

She stopped instantly, her heart in her throat. She'd almost cut through the extension cord. She hadn't been paying close enough attention and had almost made a rookie mistake that could have been really dangerous.

Jack carefully took the saw from her suddenly shaking hands. "Maybe we should switch for a little while."

His voice was so gentle, so nonjudgmental. She felt as if everything inside her were melting. All her fears, all her worries, all her well-made defenses. She felt as if she had no strength left, no energy to fight as the enemy slipped behind the walls and laid siege to her heart.

She handed Jack her safety goggles and he just began to saw, leaving her to haul the wood in peace. The air was damp, ripe with the scent of the wet earth and spring. The storm in the sky had passed, leaving the fading light of day to stain the few remaining clouds. The storm in her heart was just starting to rage. Should she stop fighting this attraction or should she put up more barricades?

Jack paused, laying the saw on the driveway and wiping his forehead with his arm. "Thing's starting to get hot," he said. "Thought I'd give it a chance to cool off."

"What?" The word came out more as a yelp than a simple query.

Jack gave her a strange look. "The saw," he said, pointing down at it. "I was afraid it was overheating."

"Ah." She nodded her head wisely. "Right. Good thinking."

"You okay?" he asked, sitting on the wide expanse of branch.

"Sure. I'm fine. Great." Except that she was babbling like an idiot. "Why do you ask?"

"You stopped arguing, for one thing."

"Hey, I may be stubborn but I'm not stupid. This is a lot easier with help."

"So you admit I was right," he said. "A victory for the men of the world."

Suddenly the air around them changed. There was a headiness, an awareness of Jack that caught at Cassie's breath. Her gaze was captured by his, and her eyes drank in a shadowy world of riches and splendor, of sparks and fires, of desires that would never be left unfed. She had such an urge to lean forward, to slip into the world that Jack's eyes promised existed.

Instead she looked across at Jack's yard. A wooden play set was in back of the house, with swings and a slide and a clubhouse above a cargo net set up for climbing.

"That's a nice play set you've got for the girls," Cassie said. "We had one of those metal swing sets when we were growing up. It got lots of use, but that looks like a lot more fun."

Jack's gaze followed hers. "One of the places I lived as a kid was just down the street from a park. They had this metal climbing tower that I loved. I'd climb to the top and somehow, ten feet or so above the ground, I could dream of all the great things I was going to do."

"Cure cancer? Win the lottery? Be the number-one pick in the pro football draft?" Cassie guessed.

"Beat up Billy Cooper for making fun of my dad." Jack's eyes were on his yard. Or maybe on his past. "Get the only A in the class on a math test so that my name would be the only one on the math stars' list on the bulletin board. Buy my mom some real jewelry instead of the stupid flower pins we made out of the pop tops from soda cans."

Cassie was touched by the glimpse into his childhood. "I see," she said softly. "Real things."

Jack just shrugged as if he'd said too much. "Oh, I don't know how real they were. Maybe it shows I wasn't into big dreams."

"Did you ever do them?"

He concentrated on the chain saw, as if checking to see if it had cooled. "Naw. Billy Cooper moved away. My fourth-grade teacher wasn't into singling out students. I did get my mom some better jewelry once I was in college, though." He laughed. "Though she still kept wearing those stupid flower pins."

"I think moms really believe it's the thought that counts," Cassie noted.

Jack glanced up, his gaze resting on his house for a long moment, then he looked back down at the saw. "Maybe some mothers."

Cassie let the silence descend. There wasn't much to say about the twins' mother. Nothing positive, anyway. But if Jack was still in love with her, anything Cassie said would be wrong.

"I was wondering about the picnic," she said instead. "The one the girls mentioned on Saturday."

Jack looked away for just a moment. The undercurrent she'd just felt was still present but subdued, hidden for the moment. "It's just something the law school is putting on," he said. "It's going to be at Clements Woods. There'll be boating, swimming, beach volleyball."

"Am I still invited?" she asked. She wasn't sure why she was asking. She sure was fed up with her brothers, but that didn't mean she ought to be rushing headlong into Jack's invitation.

Something sparked in his eyes for just a moment. "Sure," he said. "What happened to your other picnic?"

She shrugged with a slight smile. "It's at my dad's house and we have it every year. This time my brothers are driving me crazy. I think they're preparing a highlight film of your playing days."

He just laughed. "And you're willing to miss that?"

"I've never been impressed with past exploits," she said. "Just what kind of magic can you work now?"

Her words seemed to surprise him as much as herself. Where had they come from?

But Jack seemed to recover faster than she did. "If you're talking about football, I'm afraid I'm pretty much out of magic."

"What a shame." Her voice sounded strained and unlike herself. But maybe he wouldn't notice. Maybe she needed to keep her heart from noticing things about him. She looked around at the shadows in the yard that were rapidly swallowing up the last few patches of sunlight. "It's starting to get dark," she said. "Think we can finish this before nightfall?"

"Sure." He got to his feet and picked up the saw. "Just a couple more cuts. The pieces will be big, but we should be able to manage them together."

Together. Just what her foolish heart was crying for and what her past experiences were shouting for her to avoid. But how could she not carry the logs with him? What was her alternative? She had to get her truck out in the morning.

By the time she'd carried the rest of the little branches over, Jack had the main part of the limb cut into pieces and was waiting to carry them.

"The kids'll be glad to hear you're coming to the picnic with us," Jack said as they lifted the first one.

"You want me to bring anything?" she asked.

"Heck, no," he replied. "The law school is springing for the whole thing. The food's going to be catered."

"Okay." They tossed the log to the side and went back for another one. "You have much storm damage at your place?"

"Just little stuff down in the yard."

They got another log and carried it over to the pile. The silence seemed to grow as heavy as the log.

"I really appreciate your help," she said as they went back for another. "I guess we're even now."

"Oh, really?" he said. He was closer to her than she had expected and his voice tickled the side of her neck. "As I remember, I owed you three and this is just one. One that I'm not even sure should count since these very well could be my trees."

His tone started something smoldering deep in her heart, something that sent little flickers of warning all through her. She wanted to play a teasing game, to flirt and laugh and give him knowing looks. But suddenly all she felt was that emptiness deep inside her; that bit of her womanliness that failed. If she gave in to the teasing, played that little game, one day she would have to confess the truth. One day she would have to admit to being a failure as a woman. Maybe he wouldn't care. But maybe he would. It was too great a risk to take.

"So, what do you think?" Jack asked. "What do you say we all go swimming?"

"Sounds good to me," Cassie said, although she knew Jack was talking more to the twins. They'd been at the picnic for an hour or more now and from the comments made, she knew the girls were not enthusiastic about swimming.

"Uh-uh," Mary Louise said.

"We don't wanna," Mary Alice added.

Jack was fighting to keep an aren't-we-having-fun smile on his face around all the other law-school families, but Cassie saw something desperate and confused in his eyes. He looked like Ollie did when the big dog was at Fiona's apartment, being played with by her sister's cats. Apparently, old Steeplejack didn't run over every obstacle that he encountered.

Cassie's heart softened at Jack's vulnerability and she felt her newly repaired defenses slip slightly. Big and strong as he was, he looked lost. She wanted to take care of him, promise him everything would be all right. Which was absolutely crazy. He had fame and fortune and good looks. He didn't need anything from her.

"We'll just go in a little," he told the girls. "Just enough to get your feet wet."

As if hearing the same cue, both started crying and ran to the back of the beach. The twins appeared to be terrified of the water.

"I don't think you should force it," Cassie told him softly. "I used to teach swimming at the YMCA and it never works to force kids into the water."

He sighed and then nodded as he walked over to where the girls were. They had him on the ropes and the look he gave Cassie pleaded for help. It caused a strange and heady sensation in the region of her heart, his looking at her like they were part of a team. She told herself she was foolish, but she liked the feeling nonetheless.

"Ollie likes to swim," she told the girls as she sat down next to them. "He was scared when he first tried, but now he has lots of fun in the water."

"Did you teach him to swim?"

"Kind of."

Mary Alice looked up at her father. "Can Cassie teach us to swim, Daddy?"

"Yeah, Daddy," Mary Louise echoed. "Can she?"

Cassie just laughed at the trapped look on Jack's face and found herself rescuing him once again. "I think it's almost time for the nature walk," she said.

"Oh, boy."

"Let's go."

Jack and Cassie followed the girls across the beach and into the woods. Jack was busy answering their million-and-one questions about the people at the picnic while Cassie just let the peace of Clements Woods bring back her common sense. She came here once or twice a month, mostly to check up on Romeo and Juliet, but also to put things into perspective. Since rescuing Juliet all those years ago, she'd felt she could see things more clearly here. See what was really important and what didn't matter.

But somehow her common sense wasn't rushing back as she'd wanted it to. Instead of concentrating on how full her life was and how she didn't need to add anyone or anything, she kept thinking how delightful the girls were. And how Jack was an old softy who wore his heart on his sleeve when it came to his daughters. Cassie liked that; liked that he wasn't ashamed to let everyone know how much they meant to him.

Then her thoughts were running off in even wilder patterns. Why hadn't he ever married? If Daphne had left when the girls were one year old, he'd had five years to get over her and find someone else. Hadn't he gotten over her? Or was he just not interested in marriage?

Not that the answers were important to her, she assured herself. She didn't care if he spent his life pining away for Daphne, or if he thought marriage was a plague to be avoided at all costs. This was just a friendly outing, not the start of anything.

"You know," Jack said, slowing down to let the girls go on ahead. "There are times I wish the girls were two-hundred-fifty-pound linebackers."

Cassie wasn't at all loath to leave her thoughts. "Why?"

"Then I could make them do what I wanted."

She made a face at him. "Linebackers are usually the meanest and toughest guys on a football team and you were able to make them do what you wanted?"

"You don't think I could?"

"Oh, I believe you." And actually she did. He was lean but not thin. He was more like a panther, the explosiveness of his strength visible just beneath the surface of his skin. That was not exactly a neutral, uninvolved observation, though.

"I just thought if we played around a little they'd see how much fun it was."

"Sometimes that works, sometimes it doesn't," she said. "For the most part, parents aren't the best teachers for their kids. Even if they're experts in the field."

"Which I'm not, anyway. I can swim enough not to drown, but I'd never try teaching them." His laugh was honest and straightforward but almost held a touch of panic. "I just wanted them to play in the water a little. I thought it would show them there's nothing to be afraid of."

"But only if they're willing to go in the water."

He nodded and they walked a bit farther. "It's really nice here," he said, glancing around at the woods that surrounded them.

"Yeah, I like it."

"I hear there's even a pair of swans that live on this lake," Jack said.

"Yep." She squinted through the trees out at the water but all she saw were a few boaters on the serene surface. "I think there're too many people around for them to come over here now."

"I suppose."

Would he appreciate the swans as she did? Would he see their magic and majesty?

A young couple joined them, much to Cassie's relief, and then a few law students. Just as well, Cassie thought. She had been about to tell him about Romeo and Juliet, about how special the swans were, and she should know better. Or at least, her head should. Opening yourself up to someone else, telling him all the little secrets of your soul, just gave him more ammunition when expectations weren't met.

Not that she was going to be around Jack long enough for there to be expectations. Her reticence was just a habit. A good habit. A safe habit.

They reached the brick shelter where the kids' nature walk was starting from. There were probably ten kids, ranging in age from about five to twelve, as well as a park ranger and two of her college-age guides.

"You gotta stay here," Mary Louise told Jack.

"It's just for kids," Mary Alice added.

"Cassie'll take care of you," Mary Louise said, then the two of them ran off.

Just what did that entail? Cassie wondered, but said nothing as they watched the kids get separated into smaller groups and paired with a guide. She and Jack stayed until the kids were all trooping off down another path, then he turned to her.

"I think volleyball's next up," he said.

"Great." That was what she needed—some invigorating exercise that would wipe all the silly dreams from her head and replace them with weariness. But they'd only taken a few steps toward the volleyball pit when she noticed he was limping. "Your knee hurting you?"

"Why? Am I limping?"

"A little."

He shrugged. "Things have been a little hectic the past month or so, what with the move and all. I kind of slacked off on my exercises."

"That's not a good idea," Cassie replied. "One way or another, your body will make you pay."

"Yeah, I know." He stopped and glanced down at her left leg. "You've had some arthroscopic work," he said, obviously noticing the tiny scars on the side of her knee.

"Yeah." She nodded. "I had some damaged cartilage removed when I was in college. No major injury. I guess I was luckier than you."

He frowned. "I don't know about your luck in the past," he said. "But I think I'm much luckier than you, right now. I've got a full-on view of your legs and you don't. And let me tell you, they're a mighty fine pair of stemware."

His compliment took her by surprise; he hadn't seemed to be into joking and teasing. She felt a sudden warmth fill her cheeks even as pleasure filled her heart. She felt like a woman, an attractive woman. It felt good, but it also felt dangerous. It felt like she was leaving herself exposed to attack. She wasn't good at this repartee stuff like Sam was. And she was absolutely terrible at handling compliments.

"They keep me from falling over," she said, trying to hide her embarrassment. "And they get me from here to there."

Jack laughed. "I imagine that's what the warranty says they're supposed to do."

What a dumb remark she'd made! She wished she could hide in the bushes. She felt more like a junior-high kid than she had when she'd been in junior high. It wasn't really true that she couldn't handle compliments. People were always complimenting her. *Nice catch. Good save. Great shot.* But the people who did compliment her didn't make her heart start sprinting.

She tried to regain her composure as they walked the rest of the way over to the volleyball pit, but rather than join the crowd that was already splitting into teams, Jack just shook his head.

"I think I'll sit this one out," he said. "My knee is thinking of locking up."

"Are you sure?" Cassie asked. She was disappointed that they wouldn't be competing together although, for a moment, it felt like more than that. It felt like disappointment that she wouldn't be with him. She really needed the volleyball to start.

"You go ahead," he said.

Her feet wouldn't move, though. Part of her wanted to go play, but it was the part that had been so uneasy at his compliments. It suddenly felt cowardly to play. And rude.

"Want to take one of the pedal boats out instead?" she asked.

"Pedaling around the lake'll certainly keep my knee from locking up," he said sarcastically.

"I can do most of the pedaling," she assured him, although she wasn't sure where the suggestion had even come from.

A few minutes later, she and Jack were sitting side by side in a little molded plastic boat, pedaling in unison as they eased their way out into the lake. It was pleasantly warm out on the water; the sun seemed to spark across the surface while glittery fish darted almost within reach. Jack's thigh came close to hers with each downward stroke, and his arm had no place to go except around her shoulder.

Maybe this wasn't a good idea, she told herself. But the air was sunny and mild and the lake so peaceful and quiet, it seemed crazy to worry.

"So were you as ornery as your kids when you were little?" she asked him.

He looked startled, then began to laugh. "Hardly. My parents were as strict as could be. I had to toe the line."

"Somehow I can't imagine you not slipping just a bit." He gave her a strange look and she started to laugh. "Don't all kids? I know I wasn't perfect. I was always catching hell for something."

"Me, too," he admitted, then turned a touch more serious. "Not so much from my parents, though. From teachers, other kids, their parents. I guess I had a chip on my shoulder the size of Montana. If anybody looked at me cross-eyed, I was sure they were putting me down. If they mentioned my parents, I was convinced they were mocking their lack of education or their low-end jobs. If they asked where I was from, I was certain they thought they were better than me."

"You were a proud little boy," she said.

"Yeah." He looked away and again she got the sense that he had said more than he'd wanted. "Probably too much."

"I think it's nice," she told him. "A lot of kids would be ashamed of their parents or where they came from. Shows you have real strength."

He looked at her then, his eyes alive with some sort of fire that touched a hidden spot in her heart. She felt for a fleeting moment that she could bloom and grow in the heat of that gaze, that the walls around her heart would willingly fall. But then he looked away and common sense came back.

"All that fighting actually helped me out, though," he said. "In junior high, the football coach caught me in a brawl and invited me to come out for the team. I started out as a lineman, banging heads, but discovered soon after, that what I didn't have in bulk I had in speed. They made me a running back and let me run with the ball as well as crash into people."

"But you still have the chip on your shoulder," she said.

He looked at her. Hard and deep. "Yeah," he said after a long minute. "But I thought I'd camouflaged it some."

"A bit. Or maybe I've got one, too, and it makes me good at seeing others'."

"Kindred spirits."

She just shrugged and they sat in silence for a little while, drifting with the gentle current. A few ducks swam by while dragonflies with iridescent wings hovered above the shimmering water. She was feeling too close to Jack and too certain that she would regret it.

So what if they had a lot in common? It didn't matter a hill of beans in the long run. She was alone and better off that way, even if Fiona liked to remind them of the old woman's prophecy when they'd rescued the swans. Fiona had gotten all moony since meeting Alex.

Jack shifted in his seat, brushing her leg with his, and she awoke from her thoughts. The silence had grown too long.

"How come you're so easy to talk to?" Jack asked. "I haven't ever told anybody all that stuff about my childhood."

She shrugged and looked at him. His eyes seemed to want to capture hers, and she turned away. "I think it's Ollie," she said. "He put a hex on me."

"I knew he wasn't an ordinary dog," he said with a laugh.

His laughter disarmed her, caught her crazy heart off guard and she tried to reclaim her common sense. They were too alone here, sitting too close together. Next thing she knew, all sorts of dancing dreams would start weaving through her thoughts, making her lose sight of the shore.

"We ought to be getting back," she said. "The nature walk will be over soon."

"Sure thing."

They pedaled back toward the dock while Cassie told herself she was being silly. She could be alone with a handsome man in a tiny boat and not lose her heart or her head. Maybe she played too many sports; she always thought in terms of winning and losing. She could just be here and enjoy a new friendship. She might even find somebody she could talk to about her past, and about her father.

They got the boat to the dock and, while a park employee grabbed hold of it, Jack climbed out, then reached back to help Cassie.

"Am I allowed to do this?" he asked. "Or will you accuse me of controlling?"

It took her by surprise, his remembering her earlier words. But, given the fact that she had said them in an attempt to ward off her attraction to him, she would rather he hadn't.

She held out her hand out to him and found his touch was

welcome and warming, somehow sneaking all the way into her soul.

"I'll allow it this once," she replied.

"You're too kind," he said.

That was something she'd never been accused of before, but the laughter on her lips died when she turned to face him. There was a fire in his eyes that startled her, heated her, caused a delicious tingling in the deepest part of her.

He leaned closer, his lips brushing hers ever so gently. It was over almost before it began, so light and so fast that she might only have dreamed it—except for the yearning his kiss awoke inside her, the hunger for his touch, the need to come alive again. The memory of loneliness slipped away as the promise of sunshine beckoned.

Where had these feelings come from? How could just one light touch destroy all the years of careful guardedness? This wasn't what she wanted. This wasn't what she was looking for. She was happy just the way she was. Wasn't she?

She pulled back and caught his eyes, so like the waters of Lake Michigan. Right now, they weren't a calm blue, but halfway between gray and thunderstorm black. She saw all her own questions and confusion agitating the surface, and felt her own worries hanging in the air around them.

"We'd better get over to that shelter," she said quickly. "The girls could be back."

"True."

She hurried off the pier and onto the path as if a fire were pursuing her, nipping at her heels and threatening to engulf her if she slowed even a step.

Chapter Three

" ' 'And Mr. Bear lived happily ever after.' " Jack closed the storybook and the girls both sighed, leaning against him.

"That was so good," Mary Alice said.

"Read it again," Mary Louise added.

This was a game they played every night, trying to postpone bedtime. He just put the book on the nightstand. "You guys should be tired," he said. "You had a busy day."

"The picnic was fun."

"I like Cassie."

He felt their eyes on him, expectantly waiting for his response, and he looked off across their room. Shelves of stuffed bears and dogs and cats were staring back at him. They were all waiting for an answer, mocking his hesitation, smirking at the worries in his soul. Yes, he liked Cassie, all right. Maybe too much for his peace of mind.

"Don't you like her, Daddy?" Mary Louise asked.

"Sure. Yeah. Of course," he said quickly.

"You acted funny when we took her home," Mary Alice told him.

"Like you did when you had a toothache."

Like when he had a toothache? "How did I act then?"

"All funny," Mary Alice said.

"Yeah. Frowny and funny."

"I was frowny today?"

"Kind of."

"And you kept looking at her."

"Like she took your ice cream."

"But she didn't."

"'Cause you didn't have no ice cream."

He hoped the girls were exaggerating. Yeah, he hadn't meant to kiss Cassie. And he certainly hadn't expected to feel so drawn to her—that was the last thing he wanted. But he hadn't wanted to be unfriendly or rude. He just wanted to be careful.

"She's not like Tiffany," Mary Louise said, sticking her nose up in the air in imitation of Tiffany's unfriendliness.

"Or Zelda." Mary Alice puckered her mouth up and began kissing the air.

Zelda had been a little overdemonstrative, Jack was willing to admit, and Tiffany hadn't been too interested in the kids, but he'd only dated them a few times each. He was surprised that the girls remembered them.

"Cassie's not all fakey," Mary Louise said.

"No, she isn't," he agreed slowly. Was that it? Was that why he was so drawn to her, because he felt he could trust her?

It wasn't something that he wanted to think about, wasn't something to ponder. It didn't matter if he could trust her; he wasn't looking for someone to trust. He wasn't looking for someone, period.

He would never forget that feeling of devastation when Daphne had left, that overwhelming anger. She had used him and then expected him to come crawling back, ready to do anything not to lose her. But he wouldn't. He couldn't. He had learned his lesson, though, and speaking of lessons . . .

"You know, I was thinking about the summer," he said. "Some of the other parents at the picnic were talking about day camps. I guess there're some programs around that are pretty good, that have horseback riding and arts and crafts—"

"And swimming?" Mary Louise demanded suspiciously.

"We don't wanna swim," Mary Alice added.

"We don't wanna get drowneded."

This was getting tiresome. "Girls—"

"Cassie could teach us to swim," Mary Louise reminded.

"She wouldn't let us drowned."

This was getting scary. "Girls!" This was getting out of hand. "She can't teach you two to swim," Jack said. "She's got other things to do."

"You could ask," Mary Louise suggested.

"You could say please," Mary Alice added.

Jack slid off the bed and turned back Mary Louise's bedcover. "Come on, hop in. You two should have been asleep ages ago."

Mary Louise trudged over to her bed and slid under the covers. "You really could ask her, you know," she coaxed.

He pulled the covers back on Mary Alice's bed and she climbed in. "Don't you think she likes us?"

Jack sighed. "I'm sure she likes you. It has nothing to do with that. She's just a very busy lady." He kissed Mary Alice good-night, then Mary Louise.

Mary Louise sighed loudly and turned on her side as he walked to their door. "I guess we ain't never gonna learn to swim."

"It's okay, Lou," Mary Alice called over to her sister. "We'll just get drowneded together."

Jack stopped at the door, his hand on the light switch. When had they learned to play hardball like this? He didn't have a chance. "Fine," he said. "I'll ask her. But if she says no, I'm signing you up for lessons at the YMCA."

"She won't," Mary Louise sang out.

"She's nice," Mary Alice added.

"Good night." Jack pulled the door until it was almost closed.

How was he going to be able to drift away if he was having to ask Cassie for more help?

* * *

Cassie pulled out the last of the weeds and sat back on her heels, admiring her results. This bed almost looked perfect, with its impatiens and pansies and azaleas. All that was missing was time for the plants to grow to full size. Of the three houses she'd rehabbed over the past six years, this one had the best yard. As she gathered up her bucket of weeds, Ollie suddenly sat up, woofing suspiciously.

Cassie turned around. A man was walking up the front walk—Jack. Her heart skipped a beat, but she forced a frown onto her face as he got close. Ollie stood, and woofed more definitively, then trotted over to meet him.

"Hi, Ollie," Jack said as he looked up at Cassie. "Hi."

"Hello." She knew she sounded unfriendly, but she couldn't help it. She needed to keep her heart in line.

Ollie greeted Jack like a long-lost friend, jumping, panting, woofing until Jack bent over and scratched the animal's fuzzy head. He sent Ollie into a delirium of happiness.

Cassie walked down to join them. "You're spoiling him, you know."

"I'm sorry," he said, taking his hand away from the dog's head. Unfortunately, Ollie wasn't about to give up the attention and he bumped Jack's thigh with his head until Jack went back to his scratching. "He's too big to argue with."

"And I thought you were so tough," she mocked. His eyes seemed to have a definite gleam today, and she felt a little tremor of concern. She would need to be extra strong. "So, can I do something for you?"

"Uh, I'm not sure," he said.

He wasn't sure? "Did you want that wood after all?" she asked. "Watson's came yesterday and cleaned it all up. I'd told them there was no hurry and that they should do the other storm-damage work first."

"No, that wasn't what I came about." He took a deep breath as if preparing to jump into deep water. "Is there some place we can talk?"

She just paused. This sounded more serious—or more personal. She told herself not to be such a chicken and nodded. "We can go out back."

She led him around the house. The yard was small, but private. A picnic table sat in the shade of an old elm tree.

"Want a soda or something?"

"No, thanks anyway."

They sat at the table. The breeze carried the scents of summer on the air as well as the sounds—lawns being mowed, kids playing baseball and birds celebrating the day. Ollie wandered off, sniffing the bushes as if checking for intruders that might have snuck in during the five minutes he was away.

"So, what can I do for you?" Cassie finally asked.

Jack looked her straight in the eye. "I'm trying to convince the girls to take swimming lessons."

"They have to want to," she said.

"That might not be until they're forty," he said. "They keep turning me down."

"Like I said," she told him. "They have to want to learn if it's going to work."

"They are willing," he said. "But only if you're the teacher."

Her heart turned fearful. "How did I get into it?"

"You said you'd taught swimming."

Ollie came over as if on some invisible leash, resting his head against her arm. She petted him slowly, but was almost suspicious of his presence. He was liable to play some trick on her and get her involved with Jack again.

"I'm not sure this would be any wiser than you trying to teach them," she said. Seeing Jack often wouldn't be, she was sure of that. "The Y has any number of programs. They can help you."

"They don't have anything until the end of June. I checked."

"That's less than a month from now."

"I was hoping you could give them a head start. You know, just take the two of them and show them how much fun they can have."

She needed to stay separate in order to stay safe. "I know the director of education at the Y," she said. "I'm sure I can get her to recommend one of her regular instructors."

"My kids want you."

"I haven't done any instructing for a few years now."

"That's okay," Jack replied. "I don't want anything fancy.
If they'll get their feet wet without screaming, I'll be happy as
a pig in slop."

She wanted to laugh, but knew better. "You really have a way
with words," she said.

"It's that chip on my shoulder, always sticking its head out
and daring someone to start a fight."

"Well, I'm sure not looking for a fight." She wasn't looking for anything even if her heart was saying the opposite. She
wrenched her gaze away from him and turned her attention to
the dog at her side.

"I know you're busy," Jack said. "But I'll pay you whatever you want."

Cassie let her eyes go back to his. A sudden thought snuck
into the light. "I don't need any money," she said slowly. Here
was her chance, if she dared take it. He was a lawyer. And he
specialized in finding ancestors. "But there is something...."

"Sure. Anything."

She stopped petting Ollie and closed her eyes, gathering all
of her strength, before rushing ahead. "You said you specialize in hereditary law and learning about ancestors. Well, I want
you to help me find out who my father was."

"Are you adopted?" he asked.

She opened her eyes and looked his way for the briefest of
moments. Concern was there, and compassion and a something else she couldn't define. But it was the past that had a
hold on her. It was weighing down so heavily that she could
barely breathe, and somehow she knew it was time to ask for
help.

"Yes, but I know who my biological father was."

Suddenly she shook her head. She sounded like a lunatic and
took a deep breath. "It's coming out all mixed up. My biological parents died when I was eight. I know my father's name.
What I don't know is where he came from, what his background was, or anything like that. I've found out that some of
the things he told us weren't true."

Jack frowned. She knew just what he was thinking. She could read his reluctance in his eyes, but she had gone beyond all these arguments already. She'd had twenty years to argue things out with herself.

"People hide things for good reason," he said. "Usually because the things hidden have the power to hurt. Maybe it would be best to leave well enough alone."

He didn't understand. No one could—not unless they lived along an emotional fault line with a crumbling foundation beneath them. "There're things I need to know."

The tension was almost thick enough to see. She could hear Ollie panting beneath the table and the sound of traffic out on the street, but mostly she could hear Jack's silence. He had to help her; she had to make him understand that she needed the truth.

She wanted to tell him more, but she hadn't opened herself to anyone in years. She'd never even told Fiona or Sam any of this, yet now the words wanted to pour out to a relative stranger.

"We were close," she said slowly. "Fiona had Mom to talk to. I had Dad. I could tell him anything and he never made me feel stupid or silly or incompetent. One day after I got in a fight with some neighborhood kids who were making fun of Fiona, he called me his Little Warrior Princess. Said I was the strongest of them all, and that I should never change."

"It sounds like he loved you a lot." Jack's voice was quiet, a gentle balm on stinging wounds.

She was tired of hurting. "He lied to us." She whispered the words, but knew he heard them. "He said he and Mom were going to Milwaukee about a job, but they died in a car accident in Minnesota."

Jack said nothing. Thankfully, not even the old, *You must have misunderstood.*

Cassie went on. "Alex—that's Fiona's fiancé—found out Dad was sick and thinks he was going to the Mayo Clinic for treatment. Some co-worker of Dad's said Dad told him he was going to get his heart healed."

"And lied so you wouldn't worry." Jack nodded. "That makes sense."

She gave him a look and he backed down. "The people he was supposed to be descended from had no descendants," she said. "He never talked about his childhood or his family or where he went to school. It was like he didn't exist before he came here."

Jack sighed and reached over for her hands. His hold was tight and secure, as if he was willing his common sense into her. As if he were trying to hold her down to earth and reality.

But she'd had a long tiresome dance with every version of reality over the past twenty years. What she wanted now was the truth.

"Maybe he didn't exist before," Jack said. "Maybe he'd been in some kind of trouble and wanted to put it all behind him. Can't you accept him as the man he was to you, not the stranger he was before?"

"I've thought of all that," she assured him. "I realize he might have a prison record, or maybe was on the run, or all sorts of things. But I still have to know. I have to know who he was to know if all the things he said were the truth or a lie."

Jack just sighed and she knew she'd won. She felt no sense of winning, just a deep certainty that somehow now she would know. A stillness settled on her soul.

"What do you know about him?" Jack asked.

"His name—Joe Fogarty—and social security number."

He nodded. "That's good enough for a start."

"Great." She hoped her voice sounded livelier than her heart felt. It was a trade-off—her need to know for her need for privacy—but it was a trade that had to be made. "When do you want me to start the swimming lessons?" she asked. "How about tomorrow evening?"

"That should be fine," he said. "You can use the swimming pool at the university. It has a shallow end for little kids."

"Seven o'clock okay?"

"Sure." He paused. "You know, looking into your father's past will be like cutting open a feather pillow in the wind. Once it's done, it'll be impossible to put things back together the way they were before.''

"I know." She nodded. "I'll pick the girls up and take them myself. Probably best if you're not at the pool.''

"Okay."

She had this urge to flee, to run from those blue eyes that were churning with her troubles. She didn't want to see her secrets in his gaze, didn't want to hear the sympathy in his voice. She didn't want to feel so vulnerable and exposed. Those dark corners of her heart had been hidden for so long, just the very brightness of his gaze hurt.

But she was good at pretending. She smiled at him and tossed a ball for Ollie as if the world wasn't spinning the wrong way. Jack could be trusted. He wouldn't turn on her, wouldn't use her weaknesses against her. But even as she smiled and walked back to the front of the house with him, her heart was frozen with fear.

Jack stopped at the edge of his property and, for some reason she didn't understand, she stretched up and brushed his lips with hers. Maybe it was to prove how unaffected she was by their conversation or by his presence, but it didn't quite work that way. Somehow it rocked Cassie right to the very core of her being. There was such gentleness in his touch, such respect and kindness and even a hint of something like awe. It felt like the beginning of something. Like the sprouting of a tiny acorn that would grow into a majestic oak.

Like she needed a good night's sleep and the return of her common sense.

Jack couldn't sleep. He was tired enough, but somehow sleep wouldn't come. Moments from the past weeks kept replaying through his head. Cassie at her store with that annoyed little gleam in her eye when he'd wanted to talk plumbing with a man. Cassie at the pizza parlor. Cassie at the picnic. Cassie at her house. Every scene ending with his lips on hers—even the ones that hadn't ended that way.

He heard a truck with a bad muffler go down U.S. Route 31 at 1:34 a.m., then the ConRail train in the distance at 2:02 a.m.

Two cars were drag racing down O'Brien at 3:14 a.m. and an ambulance went speeding off to a rescue at 3:54 a.m.. When the first twitterings of the birds sounded soon after 4:00 a.m., he gave it up and got out of bed. He slipped on some shorts and his running shoes and let himself quietly out of the house; then over to the deck where he couldn't see Cassie's house. An invigorating run would do him wonders, he thought, and leaned against the deck railing to stretch the backs of his legs.

The day was just starting to come alive—just as he was starting to come alive when he was around Cassie.

It was a disquieting thought; one that seemed to jar with the peace of the morning. He already was alive, he told himself. He didn't need one certain woman to make him more so. Besides, how could you be more alive? Alive was alive; there was no more-or-less.

Yet his heart beat faster when Cassie was near. His smile seemed nearer and the world brighter.

Hogwash.

He straightened. The hell with stretching. He would just let a gentle jog stretch things out for him and he started down the driveway, determinedly keeping his eyes from the dark house next door.

It was just moving to a new place, that was all. Everything was unsettled so it was hard to sleep. Things would settle down in a few weeks.

He turned up the street—away from Cassie's house—and enjoyed the early-morning solitude. The birds' singing had grown but the light was only beginning. Fingers of morning were just starting to reach out across the dark sky. He waved at a sleepy-looking man in a van, stopping at occasional houses to deliver the newspaper, and then at a dog in a backyard who took offense at Jack's freedom.

Cassie would be coming by tonight for the girls' first swimming lesson. He needed to figure out his strategy before then. He turned down a side street and smelled bacon cooking. He passed a house with warm light spilling out of kitchen windows, then slipped back into the shadows. With each step he took, he felt a growing sense of confidence. He was in control of his life.

It didn't matter how much he and Cassie were thrown together; he was in control of his feelings. His heart wouldn't go soft and tender anymore. It wouldn't fall for a laughing smile and chocolate-brown eyes.

He had nothing to be afraid of. Love held no attraction for him anymore. He had seen it at its worst and knew he wanted none of it. He would be Cassie's friend. But that was all.

Around another corner and suddenly he was back on his own street. The day was coming faster now; there was no stopping it. Like a dam bursting, the morning sun was cascading into the shadowy dawn and sending the darkness away.

He slowed to a stop as he neared his house, an uneasiness catching up with him again, now that he could see her house ahead of him. He could also see Cassie's smile in the sunshine and the glow of her eyes in the coming day. He could hear her laughter in the song of the birds and taste the softness of her lips in the morning air. Her image in his mind was playing hardball.

But then as he stomped up the walk, he knew the answer. This was all because he hadn't paid her back. If he would pay his plumbing debts, he would be left in peace. It was just that simple.

Cassie rang Jack's doorbell and then looked around the yard as she waited. She'd spent a restless night, regretting confiding in Jack, yet knowing that she'd had no choice. So now what? Were they close friends now that he knew the secrets of her soul? Or were they only business acquaintances who just happened to know a little about each other? Cassie was going to opt for the latter.

"May I help you?" Aunt Hattie's gray hair was pulled back in a bun, giving her face a severe expression that her voice didn't dispel. She looked like an aunt who knew that she would never make grandma.

Cassie quailed slightly. "I'm here to pick up the girls," she said.

"Yes, I know."

Cassie's stomach danced nervously. Aunt Hattie seemed to know a lot, but it didn't look like she agreed with any of it. What was bothering her? Did she object to Cassie, to the swimming, or to all of the above?

"Won't you come in, please?" Aunt Hattie stepped back from the doorway to let Cassie in. "My nephew and the girls will be here in a moment."

Cassie walked into the foyer and stopped there.

"Won't you sit down, please?" Aunt Hattie had waved toward the living room. "I'll tell them you're here."

Cassie looked into the living room. All neat, everything in its place, and not a speck of dust. Even the throw pillows were straight. Walking in there would be like sending Ollie into an operating room.

"I'll just wait out here," Cassie said.

"Very well," Aunt Hattie replied, before disappearing up the stairs.

Cassie waited until the woman's skirts disappeared from view before leaning against the wall and breathing a sigh of relief.

Aunt Hattie reminded Cassie of their first foster mother—a stern woman who believed that the world was divided into ladies and gentlemen. The woman had respected Fiona and doted on Samantha but had kept telling Cassie that she acted like a wild animal, had kept insisting Cassie would have to acquire some manners if she hoped to find a good husband. The woman's attitude had made Cassie act up all the more; but deep down, even though she hated to admit it, Cassie had always been intimidated by the Aunt Hatties of the world.

"We're ready," Jack said, hurrying down the stairs. His daughters trailed along behind, as eager as a pair of puppies going to the vet. "Let's go."

Cassie felt her heart suddenly lift and a smile break out on her lips. "We?" She laughed. "Do you need swimming lessons, too?"

Jack stopped, lines of confusion wrinkling his brow, while his daughters giggled. Cassie grinned at them, then shook her head at Jack, a strange lightness coming over her like the strings of a hundred balloons had been let go.

"Sorry," she told him. "Union rules. No parents allowed while swimming lessons are in progress."

"I thought I could wait in the lobby."

"We'll be all right, Daddy."

"Yeah. And we'll tell you all about it."

A smidgen of uncertainty remained in Jack's eyes, and she wanted to reassure him. She wanted to ease those worries and bring his smile back. And most surprising of all, there was no panic in the realization.

"They'll be fine," Cassie told him. "I promise."

His eyes met hers and a bond seemed to form between them. A slow dance, a waltz where they moved in time to the same sensuous beat. A delicate lace woven of hopes and dreams and desires. Time seemed to stand still for one sweet moment when all things were possible and all fears disappeared as easily as dew in the morning sun.

"I know," he said. His gaze was somehow saying other words, though, singing other songs. Then he slowly, reluctantly, looked back at the girls. "I'll carry your bag out to the car."

"That's okay, Daddy."

"We can take it."

"You guys sure know how to make a guy feel wanted," he said.

"We're not guys," they chorused.

"Don't worry, they want you. They just want you where they say." Cassie smiled at him. Something was happening here; something unexpected, something she ought to be fearful of.

"Hard being a guy in the nineties," he said.

Aunt Hattie came down the stairs, bringing reality in her wake. "You girls be careful," she said.

The woman was talking to the twins, Cassie knew, but there was a warning there for her, too. Why was she suddenly getting all wimpy and weak, and forgetful of all the lessons she'd learned the hard way?

"Come on, gu—" Cassie quickly swallowed the end of the G-word. "Let's go. My truck's out front."

"A real truck!"

"Wow!"

The girls ran out, the carryall bag swinging awkwardly between them. Cassie looked back at Jack.

"Thanks," he said.

It was suddenly stuffy in that big old foyer, like all the air had been sucked out. Thunderclouds rolled and twisted in Jack's eyes, making them seem almost black.

"We'll be back in an hour," she said, grasping at the last tattered remnants of her common sense as she hurried out the door.

"This is gonna be fun," one of the twins said.

"Yep," the other one agreed.

"How do I tell you two apart?" Cassie asked as she helped them up into the truck.

"Mary Alice has a loose tooth," the one near the door said, pointing to her sister who demonstrated the tooth's looseness.

Cassie climbed into the driver's side. "Great," she said. "So all I do is reach into your mouths and wiggle your teeth. Sounds easy."

The girls dissolved into giggles and Cassie laughed with them. The evening air helped her heart slow down and her breathing return to normal. Teaching the girls to swim would be fun, and seeing Jack occasionally would be no problem.

She smiled over at the girls. "I know you're scared of swimming and I'm not going to make you do anything," she told them. "But sometimes, if you try what you're scared of, you might find out there's nothing to fear. If you never try swimming, you could be scared of it all your life and miss out on all sorts of fun."

Suddenly the words seemed to echo in her heart. She saw herself in a mirror and knew that she was just as guilty as the girls of running away. But instead of running from swimming, she was running from love. From friendship, even.

She was thoughtful as she coaxed the girls to the edge of the pool and into the water, and quiet as she took the girls home.

Once they ran off to tell Aunt Hattie about their swimming lesson, Jack walked out to her truck with her. It was just starting to get dark and there was a stillness in the air that said the night was waiting. Maybe the way she was waiting, poised to let her life begin again.

"So how did they really do?" he asked.

"Just fine," she said. "It's going to take time, but they'll be having fun in the water by the end of the summer."

"Hard to believe. They were so scared just last weekend."

She opened the door of her truck, but only leaned against it. "We probably should go swimming at least once a week," she said. "Maybe more, if life ever gets less hectic for me."

"If you can spare the time," he said, then put his hand on the truck to her left. "I've put some feelers out about your father, but I haven't learned anything yet."

She nodded, trying to concentrate on his words. But he seemed close, too close, for her peace of mind. Her eyes kept lingering on his lips, her heart kept racing when his hands moved slightly.

"I imagine it'll take some time," she said.

"Doesn't everything?"

Moving into his arms would take hardly no time at all, she thought, the idea racing through her mind and catching her by surprise. She tried to stamp out the panic that followed in its wake and found her fears weren't as strong as she'd thought they were.

Jack took a deep breath. "So you're busy this week," he said.

"Yeah," she answered slowly, uncertainly. She searched his eyes for reasons, but the shadows of the night were creeping too close. "If you think the girls should go again this week, I guess I could rearrange some things."

"I wasn't thinking about the girls," he said. "I was thinking about me."

Her heart faltered. Her mind said to run, but her feet didn't move. "Oh?"

"I still owe you three decent meals," he reminded her. "My conscience is bothering me about them."

She swallowed hard. This was one of those flirty, teasing situations she was so bad at. She tried to think of what Sam would say. Or Fiona, now that she had Alex and was able to flirt with him at the drop of a hat.

"If we go out, will your conscience leave you alone?"

"That mean you'll find a time for me?" he asked.

"Sure." Having dinner with him didn't really mean anything, she told herself. It sure didn't mean they were going to have any more of a relationship than they had now—casual friends who did each other favors. "Maybe next week sometime."

"Great."

He leaned forward suddenly, like he was breaking free of some invisible bonds, and brushed her lips with his. Sparks seemed to shoot down her spine, sending out waves of energy that moved her closer to him. His arms slipped around her, pulling her nearer, into a place she found so warm and welcoming that her heart never wanted to leave. Her hands slid around his waist.

There was a magic in the air that must have snuck up with the darkness. She felt no worry, no fear, no desire to hurry away and pretend life was fine. His lips on hers brought only wonder and surprise and delight. It was like being at the top of the Ferris wheel with the world spread out below her.

When he pulled back slightly, she was barely able to breathe. She needed time to think, time to put things back in order.

"I'll give you a call," he said. His voice was ragged and told her he was having the same trouble finding air to breathe.

"Okay." She climbed into her truck, relief mingling with regret. He closed the door for her. After sending a weak little smile his way, she concentrated on backing out the drive. Given her present state of mind, it was lucky she only had to drive a few feet.

Chapter Four

"Do you think they'll let us do that?" Fiona asked. "If all the guests want to feed the birds, that'll make for a lot of stuff on the water."

"We're talking about throwing bread on the water," Cassie reminded. "What the swans don't eat, the ducks and fish will."

Cassie leaned back on her sofa and took a long drink of her soda. The three of them were in her living room, going over the plans for her older sister's wedding. As usual for these sessions, they were dressed in their grubbies, their feet were bare, and they were imbibing pizza and soda.

"I don't know," Fiona said, shaking her head.

"Trust us," Samantha replied. "It'll be a nice touch. And what's the point of having the wedding at Clements Woods if we can't have Romeo and Juliet there?"

Reaching for another slice of pizza, Fiona just grunted. Ollie hovered near, as if he was hoping the pizza would get rowdy and need to be subdued.

"Don't worry about it, Fiona," Cassie added. "If anybody's nose gets out of joint, I'll straighten it for them."

Fiona was the worrier, Samantha always made sure that everyone was happy, and Cassie was the enforcer. She was the muscle for the three of them; it had been that way for as long as she could remember.

"Want to split that last slice?" Samantha asked her.

Cassie frowned at it. The last time she'd had pizza, she'd been with Jack. Now, why had that thought come to mind?

"No, thanks," she said.

Samantha took it with a definite smirk on her face. "Cassie just doesn't want to be the old maid," she said to Fiona. "She's got a guy and doesn't want to jinx it."

Cassie felt as if she were tooling along the highway and a rock had suddenly fallen in her path. Her mouth opened and she fought for air. Not a lot of air, just enough to scream.

"Oh, yeah?" Fiona turned toward Cassie. "Who is he?"

"I don't *have* anybody," Cassie protested.

"He's a lawyer," Samantha said. "A new professor at the law school."

"Wow," Fiona said.

Cassie finished her soda and stood, feeding a pizza crust to Ollie before she picked up the empty pizza box. "Let's not go spreading any rumors. Especially ones that aren't true."

"Is he handsome?" Fiona asked Samantha.

"Pure, one-hundred-percent stud," Samantha replied. "At least, so I've been told. He lives next door, though, so we could go over and check for ourselves."

Fiona turned and grinned up at Cassie. "Think we ought to, Cass?"

Cassie just rolled her eyes and took the box into her kitchen. Ollie trailed along behind her. "Go over if you want, but you'll just be wasting your time. I am not going with anyone," she called over her shoulder. "He came into my place and I sold him some plumbing parts."

"She had dinner with him at that pizza joint on McKinley," Samantha said. "You know, the one with kids' games and stuff."

"Uh-huh," Fiona said.

"She went there with Jack—his name's Jack Merrill—and his twin girls. They're about six, aren't they?" Sam called this last out to Cassie.

"You'd think I never went out with a guy," Cassie grumbled to Ollie. She fed him another crust just to ensure his loyalty, then grabbed up a couple more cans of soda and went back into the living room.

Samantha and Fiona were watching her, goofy smiles on their faces. "It wasn't a date," Cassie told them. "I did some plumbing work for him and he bought me dinner."

Her sisters blinked at her, like two cats watching a mouse. Cassie felt like squeaking. She put the extra cans on the table, opened one for herself and flopped onto the sofa. "So, who's going to double-check with the rental place about chairs?"

"What about that picnic you went to with him?" Samantha said.

"What are you doing, spying on me?" Cassie opened her eyes to glare at her little sister.

"The sister of one of the women at the library works for the catering firm that did the law-school picnic." Samantha turned toward Cassie, flashing that sickeningly sweet little smile of hers. "You were wearing that red-and-black bathing suit of yours."

"Oh," Fiona said knowingly. "That one."

Cassie glared at her sisters while they just laughed. "Aren't you supposed to be meeting Alex at the tux shop?" she asked Fiona pointedly.

Fiona just kept on laughing as she stood. "I think it's just great," she said. "And really nice that he has kids. Now it doesn't matter if you can have any or not."

"Thanks a lot," Cassie snapped. What did that mean? That Jack wouldn't care that she was less than perfect? But Cassie didn't ask the question aloud, knowing Fiona hadn't meant it that way.

But it reminded Cassie of all the old problems. All the reasons for staying apart, for staying safe. No one got hurt that way, especially herself.

It reminded her of all the old doubts, all the old fears that she was lacking—as a woman. She'd never admitted any of that to anyone; not to Fiona or Sam, certainly not to anyone she dated. But suddenly all the fears were here again, swirling around and daring her to find someone who wouldn't care. Someone who wouldn't find her wanting.

Samantha opened herself a new can of soda once Fiona had gone. "You think she suspects about the shower?" she asked.

Cassie tried to shake her gloom. "Since you were so busy making up stories about me and Jack, she probably never gave it a thought."

Sam just gave her a look and pulled some papers out of her purse. "Well, I do think it's really great that you found somebody," she said, acting like Ollie when he had a squirrel treed. "Now you can have the family you've always wanted."

Cassie just sighed. "I have not found *somebody*. We are not dating."

Her little fantasy was over. Reality was back and it was time to call a halt to everything before anything started.

Jack held out his hand and Cassie walked through the night toward him, the light of the moon bathing her in the softest of glows. She was exquisite. There was such life, such vitality about her.

When her hand touched his, he swung her into his arms, laughing aloud with pure joy. She smiled down at him and his heart wanted to burst. Ever so slowly, he put her down but pulled her closer even as he did. His lips hungered, his body ached, his soul sought its mate. She would be everything to him.

He bent down, the fire about to consume him, and let his mouth—

Jack sprang up. He was alone in his living room, some late-night talk show was on the TV, and his book lay on the floor where it must have dropped when he'd fallen asleep. He felt foggy and disconnected and put his feet on the floor, rubbing his hand over his face.

"Damn," he muttered. This was getting ridiculous.

He turned off the television with the remote control, put his book on the end table and got to his feet. The drapes on the side window were open and he saw the lights on in Cassie's house across the way. It was late and he wondered what she was doing. Was she a late-night person like himself? Or were there lights on because something was wrong?

But even as he toyed with the idea of walking over—just to check on her—the lights went off and the house seemed to disappear into the darkness.

He closed the drapes and turned off the lamp. Darkness claimed the room, but a glow from the lamp lingered before his eyes for just a second. And in it he could have sworn he saw Cassie's smile. He rubbed his eyes and the image faded.

"You remember Daphne?" he asked himself. "Are you looking to repeat that?"

The night held no answer and he went through the darkness into the kitchen. The breeze rustling the trees outside seemed to carry Cassie's laughter. He closed the back window with a thud.

"I'm going to pay off those debts," he assured himself. "That'll put an end to all this."

"Jimmy Jack?"

Jack spun even as the kitchen light was flicked on. Aunt Hattie was in the doorway, an old plaid robe wrapped around her and fuzzy blue slippers on her feet.

"Who are you talking to?" she asked, even as her eyes looked around the room. "There ain't no one here."

"Just myself," he said. "I was just reminding myself of some stuff."

Her eyes narrowed. "You fighting with your pride about Cassandra?" she asked.

He made a face that he hoped expressed his impatience. "Come on, Aunt Hattie. There's no reason for me to fight with my pride. Cassie is just a neighbor, that's all."

His aunt's lips were a tight, disapproving line. Her eyes were dark and frowning. "You're asking for trouble, boy," she said. "There's things that just won't be denied."

He would take his chances. "You must have read a different set of neighbor rules than me," he said and reached for the light switch. "You going back to bed now? Or are you staying up?"

She turned and headed back toward the stairs. "I'm going. I'm going." She waved her hands in the air. "I can tell when you're determined to be pigheaded."

"Sleep well," he called after her, then turned off the light once she was at the top of the flight.

The night swallowed him up but he strode briskly toward the stairs himself.

"Good morning," Jack said as he stepped inside Cassie's plumbing-supply store early the next week.

She was standing behind the counter, dressed in her usual jeans and T-shirt, but looking like sunshine come to life. She literally took his breath away and he was grateful when Ollie came running over to greet him.

"Hey, Ollie," he said, rumpling the beast's fuzzy head. "How are you, boy?"

"Ollie." Cassie's voice was sharp and the dog dropped down. "Bad boy. You know better than to jump on people."

"That's okay," Jack said. "I'm sure he knows that I have a treat for him." He pulled a giant dog biscuit out of his back pocket and gave it to the animal. Ollie took it gently in his teeth and scurried over to his spot behind the counter.

"He gets enough to eat," Cassie said. "He doesn't need treats."

There appeared to be a bit of an edge to her voice. Was she having a bad day or irritated because he'd brought Ollie a treat? A young woman came out from the back—a smaller, softer version of Cassie. A sister?

"Hi." The young woman stepped forward, her hand out. "I'm Samantha Scott, Cassie's sister."

Jack shook her hand. "Jack Merrill."

"I know," Samantha replied. "I've heard so much about you."

"Sam's my younger sister," Cassie murmured, her voice as sweet as vinegar.

Samantha obviously felt something negative in the air as she gave her older sister a sugary sweet smile. Jack felt his own smile wanting to slip away. He hoped he hadn't come at a bad time. He wanted to get a day picked for his first payback.

"What can I do for you today, Mr. Merrill?" Cassie asked, her voice all brisk and businesslike. "Do you need a plumbing fixture?"

"Not today."

Cassie just stared at him and Jack noticed that Samantha was suddenly busy tending to Ollie, bending over and talking to him behind the counter so that she almost disappeared from view. He noticed, too, how close Cassie's hands were to his. How he could just reach over and—

Those kinds of thoughts would get him nowhere. "So how about our dinner?" he asked her. "When are you free?"

She frowned. "Look, there's really no need for that."

No need? "I thought we covered all this," he said quickly. "Merrills pay their debts."

"I did you a favor and you did me one. It's over with."

"I owe you for your help. You agreed to let me take you to dinner."

"You can't be this hard up for company," she snapped. "Every woman in the Western Hemisphere probably wants to go out with you."

"Apparently not every one," he said.

"So, every one except me. You've got a lot to choose from. All sorts of perfectly great women."

"I don't owe any of them for fixing my plumbing."

"So, I transfer your debt. Take out Sam. Take out Princess Mishawaka."

"Who?"

She ignored him. "Take out Juliet."

"That's a swan," Samantha said, suddenly there again and giving Cassie a knowing smile before turning back to Jack. "You don't want to take her out. Or Princess Mishawaka, since she's been dead a few centuries."

"I see." Although he didn't.

"Cassie's always been stubborn like this," Sam went on. "She doesn't mean what she's saying."

"I do, too."

Sam just smiled at Jack. "Are you doing anything this Friday night?"

He stopped. Was she asking him out? She seemed nice enough, but it was Cassie he had to pay back, not Sam. It was Cassie who lingered in his dreams. Cassie whose laughter was a web he was caught in.

"Uh, no," he answered cautiously. "I think I'm free Friday."

"Good," Samantha said. "Then you can come to the party we're having for my sister Fiona and her fiancé."

Be at a party with Cassie? But from the way she was frowning at him, she didn't seem to be thinking party thoughts. At least, not the kind of parties he went to.

"It would be nice if you could come," Samantha said. "We have a big crowd coming and it would be great to have an extra hand or two."

Oh. That was it. They needed help and Cassie hated to ask. It was a chance to pay her back.

"Sure," he replied. "I'd be glad to help out."

"Great," Samantha said. "See you Friday around seven. Cassie will give you directions."

"Super." But Cassie didn't look like she thought anything was great or super or even okay. Was she upset about Samantha's invitation, his acceptance, or both?

Maybe she didn't even want him for a friend. The thought hurt, like a quick stab whose pain comes only when you look at the wound.

Cassie parked her pickup in front of Jack's house, cut the ignition, and dropped her head on the steering wheel. Why couldn't she have been an only child? Jack didn't know how lucky he was.

She'd been all set to wring Samantha's neck yesterday, but her sister had been out the door, saying she had to get to work at the library, before Cassie could get her hands on her.

Jack had no interest in coming to the shower. That was as obvious as the muscles in his chest. Just as it was obvious that he had a life of his own and didn't need another family horning in on his time. The fact that she occasionally wished circumstances were different was of no importance.

Sighing, she pushed herself away from the steering wheel. Lordy, what had she got herself into? she wondered as she dropped down onto the street. She should never have promised to teach his kids how to swim. She should have sold her house and moved away as soon as she saw him unloading his van. Unfortunately, she seemed to have lost all power of reasonable thought over the past few weeks.

Cassie wrestled her feet onto the sidewalk and up the steps to Jack's house. Her hand twitched and flittered about, but she finally made it ring the bell. The door opened before she could turn and run.

"Hi," he said.

He was wearing a knit green shirt, jean shorts, and sandals. The outfit went very well with his deep voice and showed off his muscles better than anything he'd worn so far. All he needed was a petite blonde at his side, one of those with big blue eyes and long, wavy hair who could give him a houseful of kids if he wanted them. Not some tall, gangly woman who—

"Come in, please. The girls will be down in a minute."

Cassie nodded. She stepped into the foyer and stopped there.

"Let's go in here and sit down," he said, indicating the living room with a sweep of his arm. "I'll get you something cool to drink while we're waiting."

"No, I'm fine. I'll just stay right here."

"Okay." He leaned against the doorframe, folding his arms across that broad, deep chest of his. "Your sister is very nice. She seems like a lot of fun."

"Yeah, she's a riot."

He turned away, but not before she could see his grimace. This whole thing was a disaster. She should just give him the names of other swimming teachers, people much more competent than her, and get out of his life. Run, not walk, to the nearest airport, and take the first plane out. Disappear forever in the depths of some tropical jungle. She would forget her silly dreams about him in time—maybe after a century or two.

"What do you have planned for today?" he asked, turning back toward Cassie.

"More of what we had the last time—playing, splashing around, getting comfortable in the water. And I'm hoping to get them away from the side a little."

"When are you going to get into real swimming?"

"When they're ready," she snapped.

They turned away from each other. This was going to turn into a fight. She could feel it in her bones.

"The girls should be down soon."

"That's all right," she said. "We have plenty of time."

He brushed back his hair and sighed. They shared another couple of decades of silence.

"I could bring the girls over to your place on lesson night," he said.

"That's okay," she replied. "I've got the car out anyway. It's no big deal to drive here."

"No, you're doing us the favor."

"I said it was no big deal, so let's just leave it as it is."

"Fine."

"Good."

The air around them turned a bit more dense and Cassie found it necessary to clear her throat. It appeared to be bothering Jack also, as he suddenly began coughing. That done with, they both settled into silence again and took turns looking up the stairs.

Darn, those girls were slow. She never took that long to dress. Of course, she never thought it made any difference anyway. And it still didn't. Another way that she didn't—wouldn't—fit in here.

"I don't have to come to the party," he said.

"What?" Cassie quickly went on before he could answer. "You don't have to come, if you don't want to."

"I didn't say I didn't want to come. I just didn't want to force myself on you."

"You're not forcing anything," she retorted. "I just don't want you to feel obligated to do something you didn't want to do in the first place."

"I never said I didn't want to come."

Cassie could feel her eyes rolling toward the skies. Samantha did that all the time and she hated it.

"Look," Cassie said, trying to be as reasonable as the circumstances allowed. This was as bad as when her brothers brought a date to the family Memorial Day picnic for her. "You won't know anybody there. And it's a gift thing. Why should you be forced to buy a gift for somebody you don't even know?"

"Buying a set of steak knives isn't going to send me into bankruptcy."

She just stared at him. He made it sound all too reasonable when it wasn't.

"All right." He glanced quickly up the stairs before turning back to her. "It's up to you. If you want me to come, I will. If you don't, I won't."

Those big blue eyes had turned dark, like a sea in a storm. Cassie found a need to swallow hard. "If you want to." She shrugged. "If you want to, it's fine with me."

His chest grew about a mile in circumference as he took a deep breath. "I want to," he replied quietly. "The question still before the jury is, do you want me to?"

He was handsome. He was funny. He was an all-around nice guy. And she spent most of her nights dreaming of him. Of course, she wanted him to come. "Yeah." Cassie could feel a smile tugging at her lips. "I wouldn't mind if you came."

He glared at her.

"All right," she snapped. What had he been in a former life—chief torturer at the Inquisition? "I'd be happy if you came."

He continued looking at her.

"But it counts against my plumbing work," she added quickly. "You come and help out and we're even."

"We are not."

Suddenly his eyes were a deep blue and a brightness filled his face, as his lips turned up into a small smile. He stepped forward and she gave up, letting her own lips curve into a smile. She tilted her head back, just slightly, so that they could better research each other's eyes.

"We're ready."

The words rolled down and echoed around the foyer. Two pairs of little feet thumped down the stairs. Instead of the dress shoes they'd worn last time, the twins each wore a pair of sports sandals, probably bought specially for their swimming-lesson trips. They skipped the last three steps as they jumped down to the floor with a solid thump.

"Hey!" Jack shouted as he scooped them up, one in each arm. Cassie almost thought she could feel relief in his voice. "Don't wreck the joint. We have to live here, you know."

"Daddy, put us down."

"Yeah, we gotta go swimming."

"Okay." He let them slide down to the floor "Now give me a kiss."

They gave him a smack, each on the cheek nearest them. Cassie felt a little lump working to bubble up in her throat. "We'd better get going," she said. "Or there won't be any water left for us."

"Will too," the little girls shouted in unison.

They tumbled out of the house, riding a cloud of good cheer, as they skipped out to her truck. Cassie tagged along after them.

Mary Louise turned to Cassie as she climbed up into the truck. "We don't got a mommy, you know," she said.

"But everybody's supposed to have one," Mary Alice said.

"We got Aunt Hattie, but she's not a mommy."

Cassie got in the driver's side, pretending to concentrate on buckling up everyone's seat belt. "I bet she really really loves you, though," she told them.

"You want to be our mommy?"

"We'd let you."

Cassie just looked at the girls, not sure what to say. Not sure what her heart was telling her. "It's not that simple," she said slowly. "It would be something that would be up to your dad and me."

"Daddy likes you," Mary Louise said.

"Yeah," Mary Alice said. "He was really grumpy before you came."

"And then you came and he was all happy."

"I think we'd better get going," Cassie said and started the truck.

This was all crazy. She doubted that Jack was grumpy all day, or that he had suddenly gotten happy when she'd arrived. Of much greater concern to her was the fact that she had gotten happier when she'd seen him. Definitely not a good sign for someone who prided herself on staying detached.

Chapter Five

"I can take care of myself," Jack told her. "Honest."

Cassie just gave him a look and returned to her conversation with Samantha. That was all right with him. It gave him a chance to catch his breath. Somehow, being around Cassie, working next to her setting up the bar in the dining room and helping to carry chairs from other parts of the house, had affected him. It had been harder than running wind sprints in preseason had been.

His eyes just couldn't keep from following her around, from letting his gaze linger on her slender form. She was in dress slacks this evening, with a silk blouse that clung in all the most alluring places. He tried to force himself to look around the room, to watch Fiona and Alex mingling among their guests, but his eyes refused to obey. After a quick scan of the party crowd, they were back on Cassie.

"I need your help for just a few minutes," Samantha was saying to her sister. "Then I can take care of things from there on."

"That isn't fair," Cassie insisted. "The two of us are responsible for this shower. I can't leave the work up to you."

"But somebody has to take care of Jack," Samantha replied.

"Why don't we let Jack take care of Jack?" he said. And he might be better off if given a task far away from Cassie. Maybe he would learn to breathe again. "He is a big boy."

They were treating him like he was Cassie's date—something he wasn't. He was just a friend there to help out.

"I know," Cassie said, obviously agreeing with Samantha that he needed a keeper. "He doesn't know a single soul here."

"Just don't tell anybody he's a lawyer," Jack whispered. "And he'll be fine."

Cassie gave him one of her instant frowns. There was something so sweet and fiery about her. He had a sudden urge to sweep her into his arms. It caught him by surprise, slipping in under his defenses and stealing what little bit of his breath was left. He looked away for a moment to steady himself.

"Wait!" Samantha exclaimed. "Daddy."

"Good idea," Cassie agreed.

Jack just shook his head. "Why do I need taking care of?" he asked, even as they were waving their father over. "I'm supposed to be helping."

Cassie glared at him. "You're done helping," she said.

Her glare didn't do anything to dampen the fire that was starting to smolder inside him. "Done? I worked about ten minutes."

"About the length of time I spent on your sink," she returned with a definite smirk on her face. "So we're even."

"I think not," he said.

"Daddy, keep an eye on Jack, will you?" Cassie asked, patting her father on the arm. "I'll be back later."

"Is that a threat or a promise?" her father asked.

"Jack can take it any way he wants," Cassie said, giving her father a peck on the cheek.

Jack waited, his breath caught somewhere between his lungs and his distant hopes, but she just turned and hurried off with Sam. Just as well, Jack told himself as he turned toward Dan

Scott. A little time alone and he'd be in control of himself again.

"Great girls," Dan remarked.

Jack just nodded his head. His eyes followed Cassie, unable to let her go.

"My wife and I had three boys," Dan said. "Having the three girls join our family kind of evened things up."

"They were lucky to find you," Jack said.

"Naw," Dan replied. "We were the lucky ones. They brought a lot more to the table than they took."

Judging from Dan's words and Cassie's attitude, the adoption had been successful, but that didn't mean she didn't need to know more about her biological father. Jack wondered if Dan knew of Cassie's search.

"The three girls are different but the same," Dan went on. "It's hard to explain."

Jack nodded. He knew exactly what Dan was saying. The twins, being identical, were a whole lot the same. But once you got to know them you could see little differences that made each one unique.

"And Cassie's the toughest," Dan said.

"I learned that when we first met."

Dan shook his head and chuckled. "If I had me a dollar for every time I had to go to school because of some fight or other, I'd be a rich man now."

"I imagine she had a temper when she was a child."

"As a child?" Dan repeated with a laugh. "How long have you known her?"

Jack shrugged. "All right, she still has one."

Dan nodded, but his eyes had taken on a distant look. "But of the three of them, she has the softest heart."

Jack remembered how Cassie's dark eyes could look like softened chocolate kisses. How quickly she had agreed to teach his girls how to swim. And the absolute and total devotion she commanded from her big, fuzzy dog. There was no doubt that she had a tender heart.

"That's why she acts so tough," Dan explained. "Without that tough exterior, she'd live in constant pain."

Jack nodded.

"Care for a beer?" Dan asked. "I think they're going to start opening gifts soon."

"Sure."

They got two cans from an ice-filled tub in the dining room. Cassie was herding everybody over to the chairs, while Samantha was getting Fiona and Alex set up near the presents. Maybe it was best this way, that he was not all that close to Cassie. Maybe this way he could build up an immunity to her. Maybe this was the way to fight his dreams.

He and Dan found some seats at the edge of the crowd. "You don't have to baby-sit me, you know," Jack said.

"Hey, you trying to get rid of me already?" Dan laughed as he settled himself in the chair. "Everybody else has already heard all my stories at least ten times. I don't have anyone left to talk to."

"Okay." Jack took a sip of his beer. "I'm glad to help you out. I just don't want you stuck on my account."

"Naw, I'm fine." He took a healthy pull on his can. "Besides, if we can't think of anything else, we can always talk about your football career."

"Not much there," Jack said. "They'd give me the ball, I'd run, and then some really big guys would come and knock me down."

"You made yourself a good career out of that," Dan said. "For a few years, at least."

Jack shrugged. "Injuries are part of the game. If you expect them, you won't be disappointed."

"Isn't that a description of life?" Dan asked. "Things are bound to go wrong once in a while. Accept that and you can spend the rest of the time being happy."

Jack let his eyes stray across the room while the other man's words sank into his thoughts. Was all that with Daphne just something "going wrong"? Was he being foolish in seeing it—and everything—as a challenge to his pride? His gaze rested on Cassie. Was there happiness waiting for him there if he just had the guts to try for it?

"We always called her our little warrior," Dan said. "The only time she really seemed comfortable was when she was saving some creature or other."

"Big dogs like Ollie?" Jack asked.

"Everything," Dan replied with a laugh. "If it looked the slightest bit in need, she was going to rescue it."

Jack frowned. What did that mean in relation to him? Did she see some vulnerability in him and was that why she took care of him at times? But he wasn't needy or vulnerable. He watched as Fiona opened a big box. Towels. She went into raptures over them while Alex made some wisecrack that had those close to them laughing.

"Cassie ever tell you about the swans?" Dan asked.

Jack turned to the older man. "No, she hasn't."

"The summer before the adoption was final, we sent them to a day camp," Dan said. "Cassie was nine. And these two swans lived on the lake there. Romeo and Juliet. Or still live there, for that matter. Cassie said that swans can live for thirty years or more, and they mate for life."

"A little more faithful than us humans," Jack said, Daphne once more creeping into his thoughts.

"Well, one day Cassie notices that the male is the only one hanging around. She figures something's got to be wrong, so she and her sisters go looking for Juliet and find that she's got her foot caught in one of those plastic rings that hold pop cans together. Cassie decides that they have to rescue her."

"That can be dangerous," Jack observed. "Swans are big birds."

"And they can be mean," Dan added. "But they leave Samantha to watch the birds, run back to camp and get a pair of scissors, run back to the lake, and Cassie cuts the swan free. The girls told us about it years later."

"Gutsy." Jack looked toward Cassie again. She was laughing at something Fiona had opened. Cassie was so beautiful. So very much alive, like she held the sun in her hand and doled out joy to the world. "And lucky."

"A warrior," Dan said.

Jack continued watching her. Somehow all the pieces seemed to fit together. No wonder they seemed so right together at times. They were so alike, wanting the world to be fair and just and kind. Wanting to trust, to find someone they could be safe with, but knowing all too well how rare that trustworthiness was.

He began to see Cassie in a new light. A trusting light. A light that beckoned his heart closer. What if it wasn't his conscience bothering him about his debts, but his soul telling him that she was the one person he could trust with his heart?

"Here," Jack said. "Let me take that."

"I can carry a bag of empty pop cans," Cassie insisted, wishing he'd go into another room. It was too much—having him here, acting like they were a couple. "It's about as heavy as a box of toothpicks."

"I'm supposed to be helping," he said.

"I told you that you didn't have to stay," she said. "Didn't I?"

He just looked at her as if he could see past all her objections and pretenses and subterfuges, and look straight into her soul. Like he could read her fears and knew the answer to each and every one of them. An answer that was found in his arms. Or was that her own crazy heart telling her where to go?

She deposited the bag just outside the back door. "We've been cleaning up after parties and picnics ever since we were kids," she said. "We've got the routine down pat."

"I can see that," he said. "But another body can't help but make things go faster."

"It's not that simple."

What wasn't so simple was her feelings, Cassie thought, and picked up a sponge. Jack was a nice guy, a great guy. Just standing near him made her heart race and her thoughts get all jumbled up like tangled spaghetti. He deserved better than her, she told herself. She should send him on his way—not just tonight, but completely. Trouble was, she was just too damn weak.

"Here, let me wipe down these counters."

Turning completely spineless, Cassie let him take the sponge from her grasp. She looked into his blue eyes and decided that was all she was giving up.

Fortunately for her, he applied himself to cleaning the countertops, saving her from the need to fight for her principles—not something she was up to doing at this hour of the night. Not when she was starting to doubt their value.

"Boy, Cassie." Her father laughed as he stepped into the kitchen. "You're a real slave driver."

"I didn't tell him to stay."

"Cassie." Fiona had followed along after their father. "Jack's such a gentleman. Why do you have to be mean to him?"

Because she couldn't afford not to be. Her defenses were so weak; the only way to keep him at a distance was to take the offensive.

"Here." Fiona stepped forward and took the sponge from Jack. "Let me do that."

"Am I fired already?" Jack exclaimed. "What did I do wrong?"

"You're not doing anything wrong," Fiona replied as she wiped the cabinets. "Guys just never wipe counters right."

Jack frowned. "Not only am I a failure, but so is my whole gender."

"Cassie," Samantha hissed.

"I didn't fire him and I didn't insult him," Cassie retorted, glaring at her sister. "Fiona did."

"Well, you know how fussy Fiona is," Samantha said. "You should have stopped her."

I didn't tell him to stay! Cassie wanted to scream out, wanting to fling the words until they bounced off her sisters' heads, but they stayed buried in her throat. And that was just as well. Because they would have been a lie. She did want him to stay. Not just here to help, but at her side. A crazy, dangerous thought.

She was tired, that was all. She would think more clearly in the morning.

"Looks like everything's under control here," Cassie said. "I think I'll head for the barn."

"You should have let me drive you," Jack said, suddenly at her side again. "Then you wouldn't be driving home alone."

"That's okay," she replied. That would have been all she needed, cooped up with him in a car. She would never start thinking clearly. "I had to come earlier than you. But thanks anyway."

Her brother Bobby had just come in, his hands all greasy, and she handed him a paper towel. Somebody must be having a problem with their car.

"I'll follow you home," Jack said.

Right. And then, once they got there, he would have to walk her to her door. Where they would talk and she would be in Jack's arms in about two seconds flat.

"There's no need for that," Cassie told him. "We're even."

"It would be a challenge to find another route," Jack said. "And we aren't even."

"No, thank you. And we are."

"You never heard of interest?" He frowned at her. "Actually, I have to follow you. I get lost real easy. Especially when I'm driving around in a new town in the dark."

"Ask one of my brothers for directions," Cassie snapped. "They know these streets better than I do."

The skin grew tight around his eyes for a moment and Cassie felt sorry about her sharp words. But damn it, this was for the best. She had her life the way she wanted it and she wasn't looking for any changes. No matter what her silly heart wanted her to believe.

They shared a long silence; Jack's blue eyes slowly faded to black. She wanted to look away but wouldn't be the first one to do it.

"Why don't I walk you to your truck?" he suggested quietly.

"Sure," she said. What would be the harm in that? It would be rude to refuse all his offers. Turning to her siblings, Cassie said, "Good night, all."

"Boy, is it that late?"

"We have to get going."

"Yeah, we promised the baby-sitter we'd be home early."

"Good night, Dad."

Cassie frowned at her brothers and sisters. They usually dribbled out when leaving an affair. And it wasn't all that late—only about ten o'clock.

"Isn't there some cleaning up to do yet?" Cassie asked. "I could stay and help."

"Oh, no," Samantha insisted. "There're just a few things."

"Are you sure?" Cassie asked.

"Yes," her sister said firmly. "Now go. All of you."

Once they stepped out into the hall, Jack took her arm and the rest of the tribe trooped out after them, down the stairs and out onto the sidewalk.

As they reached her truck, Cassie slowly withdrew her arm. It took more effort than she'd expected but then that was the way things sometimes went. Especially on a warm Indiana night in June, when the sky was dark with the promise of rain and the humid air was soft like velvet.

Cassie stopped for a split second and fought the inclination to run, screaming, down the street. What was wrong with her? She'd never been poetic in her life. She hated poetry.

"Thanks for inviting me," Jack said.

Cassie couldn't help laughing. She never was too good at pretending that things were different than they actually were.

"All right," he said. "Samantha invited me. But you agreed."

"Yes, I did." She could feel her face fall into a soft smile. "And I'm glad you came."

"Even if I wasn't needed?"

"You helped," she said. "And your willingness to help more counted a lot."

They were drawing closer and closer. Her heart was starting to race and her breath was ragged. Where were all those principles she'd been protecting? She couldn't find them, and didn't care. She was so tired of being lonely, so tired of fighting to be strong. So tired of telling her heart not to care. She leaned—

Something was wrong. Cassie pulled away from Jack and discovered that everybody was still hanging around. They should have been in their cars by now. Even Sam and Dad had stepped out onto the porch. What the hell were they doing?

"I have to go." Cassie's voice was brusque and her movements quick. She was inside her truck in one flash of a bunny's tail, slamming the door and rolling down the window. "I'll see you Tuesday evening for the twins' swimming lesson."

He waved and stepped back.

Cassie turned on her lights, put the key in the ignition, and turned it.

Nothing happened.

She tried again.

Still nothing.

"Damn," she muttered under her breath. Now what? She leaned out her window. "Bobby!"

He ambled over at the same rate of speed he'd used when their mother called him back to clean up after himself. Was it her or was her whole family developing an attitude?

"Yeah?" he asked.

"My car won't start," Cassie replied. "Nothing's happening."

"Your lights work, so the battery's okay."

Cassie nodded as she released the hood latch. Bobby was good, the best. He'd have her going in a matter of minutes.

"I don't know." He rubbed his chin. "Could be complicated."

"Could be a lot of things," she told him. "Why don't you lift up the hood and look?"

"Too dark."

There was a streetlight right in front of them. And she knew that among them all, they had enough flashlights to illuminate half of St. Joseph County.

"I remember you fixing cars by candlelight," Cassie snapped. "Besides, I know that you guys all have flashlights in your cars."

"Too much glare."

"Aw, come off it, Bobby. Quit jerking me around and fix the damn thing."

"I'll look at it in the morning," Bobby said. "Besides, I've got a feeling that I'll need parts."

"How can you tell?" she asked. "You didn't even lay your hands on the hood."

"Now don't get testy, sister, dear. We'll get you a ride home."

Cassie threw herself back on her seat. She didn't want a ride. She wanted to drive home herself—drive to her house, take Ollie for his walk, and plop into bed. She didn't want to put up with another human being until morning at the earliest.

"Anybody got room for Cassie?" Bobby asked.

There was a rumble of words that she couldn't make out but she certainly sensed their negative tone. What the heck was with them? She knew they had room in their vans or cars.

"I'll be glad to take her home."

It was a male voice, but not one of her brothers or her father.

"Hey, that'll work." Bobby leaned his elbow in her open window. "Jack will take you home, Cass."

"How convenient."

"Now, don't be getting hostile here," Bobby whispered to her out of the side of his mouth. "He's a nice guy and the only one making the offer."

"This whole thing feels very well rehearsed to me," she hissed back.

Bobby shook his head before pushing off and opening her door. "She's a little out of sorts, but don't pay her no mind," he murmured to Jack. "She gets really attached to her trucks."

Damn it. Cassie kicked her door right into Bobby. "Oh, excuse me," she said, trying to force sugar into her tones.

They were ganging up on her—not that it was the first time. She would have appealed to her father, but for all she knew he was involved in this charade, too. If it weren't so dark and if she wasn't so tired, she would have taken the time to find the wire that she was sure Bobby had pulled. Or would have walked home. It wasn't all that far.

"You can leave your car right there, Cassie," Sam said. "We'll look out for it."

"I'll come by and look at it first thing in the morning," Bobby assured her.

"Don't forget to leave your keys with Bobby," Fiona warned.

Cassie wished she were ten years old again, then she could scream and kick the stuffing out of her siblings. Being an adult wasn't all it was cracked up to be.

But this wasn't the end of it. She would go home, rest and be ready to fight another day. Jerking the truck key off its chain, she slammed it into Bobby's hand. She hoped it stung him as much as it did her. Then she turned and stalked toward Jack's car, presuming he would follow.

Neither said a word as Jack opened the passenger door for her. Cassie climbed up into the minivan and sat in the passenger seat. Jack closed her door, then came around to the driver's side, quietly getting in himself. Cassie leaned against the door as he pulled away, letting the farewells of her sappy siblings fade away behind them.

It was several blocks before Jack broke the silence. "Your family is very nice," he said. "I enjoyed meeting them."

"They're sneaky, conniving, scheming twerps," she declared. And nice.

Although Cassie wasn't in any mood to admit it. But, yeah, they were nice. Nice, caring, and loving. They were all kinds of things, positive and negative, rolled up into one big, lumpy, asymmetrical ball.

"Kind of makes a person wish they'd come from a big family themselves."

Surprised, Cassie realized for the first time that Jack might be lonely. She had never thought of him in that light. All she saw was his successful professional career, his beautiful children, and the fact that just about everyone in the world, or at least the male half, knew who he was and wanted to be his friend. The women just wanted *him*.

"Not that I'm complaining, mind you." He flashed that little-boy grin of his. "Daddy always said to play the cards that were dealt you and don't complain. Said the Lord doesn't like whiners."

They fell into another silence, broken only when he pulled up in front of her house and turned off the ignition.

"I like your house," he said. "Have you lived here long?"

"About a year."

Cassie's inclination was to get out and run in, but Jack seemed to want to talk. She held herself still, figuring she needed to quit running from him. Or maybe it was more a case of running from herself. She sighed.

"I buy old houses and refurbish them while I live in them. This is the third house I'm doing, but I'm almost done with it."

"Looks like you've got yourself a full life," he said.

Cassie shrugged. Yeah, it was full—full of things, mostly. Although she did have her sisters, brothers, and father. There really was no need to complain. Fate had dealt her a more-than-reasonable hand.

"I should be getting in," Cassie said. "Ollie's been locked up for a while now."

"Look, we really have to have dinner," he said. "A real dinner that I pay for."

"You're looking into my biological father for me," she reminded. "That's—"

"That's for the swimming lessons. What I'm talking about now is the plumbing gig."

"The pizza was fine," she replied. "And you helped with the tree and tonight. You don't owe me anything more." She opened her door.

"Go out with me tomorrow night. Someplace nice. Just you and me."

Cassie hung out there in space, half turned around in her seat, left foot in the car and right partway to the ground. She didn't like being backed into a corner, but she also didn't want to be mean to Jack. He was just trying to be nice. Wanting to give her a meal for a teeny little job.

"We'll go anywhere you want," Jack said. "As long as it's nice."

Cassie could feel a cramp coming on in her leg so she jumped out of the car. Just then, Ollie's deep bark rumbled through the walls of her house, rolling down the sidewalk and out onto the street. Hot dog! Saved by the woof.

"I really need to get in and let Ollie out," she said, turning to Jack. "He's been cooped up too long."

"Cassie."

His voice was firm and demanding. Her cheeks warmed as she thought of Jack being that way in other circumstances. Fortunately, Ollie barked again.

"I'll call you," Cassie said hurriedly. "In a half hour."

"Cassie."

"I promise. If I don't let Ollie out, he'll tear the place to pieces." She slammed the car door and ran for her house. It might be cowardly but it was safe.

Ollie greeted her enthusiastically, barely giving her a chance to open the door. Holding him back with one hand, she waved with the other to Jack, indicating that all was well inside. Cassie didn't breathe until his taillights disappeared up his driveway.

Jack put the cordless phone on the kitchen table and opened the metro section of the newspaper, scanning the page for some article he hadn't read earlier in the evening. Cassie wouldn't call; he knew that. But just in case she did, he ought to be close to a phone. He read about a giant garage sale being run by a local church and a report from a city council meeting before he glanced up at the clock. He'd been home ten minutes.

By the time he finished the accident reports for both South Bend and Mishawaka, it was fifteen minutes. Time enough to read the obituaries and the want ads, then to switch over to the entertainment section and a review of a new album by some group he'd never heard of. Two movie reviews and the announcement of a new restaurant opening were followed by a summary of local festivals—an egg festival in Mentone, a blueberry festival in Plymouth, an ethnic festival in South Bend, and on and on. These Hoosiers sure appeared to be festive folks.

Jack glanced at the clock. Thirty-five minutes. He'd been right. She wasn't going to call. He closed up the newspaper and tossed it back with the other papers, but refused to go to the window and see if her lights were still on.

What was he supposed to do? Hog-tie her and force her to have dinner with him? He could see it now—Cassie tied up and thrown over his shoulder as he carried her into an elegant restaurant. Knowing Cassie, the minute he put her down, she'd be hightailing it to the door, even if she had to hop across the room. Or else, she'd be hightailing it over him, even if she had to hop all over his body to make him black-and-blue.

The phone shrieked at him, splitting the silence of the night. For one endless second, he was frozen by surprise, then grabbed the receiver.

"Merrill here," he said.

"It's Cassie."

"Hi." Brilliant conversationalist.

"Hi."

Her voice did funny things to his breathing, made him want to turn off the lights and sit in the dark, clutching the phone like some high-school kid. He stood and walked over to the window, staring over at her house. The lights were on on the first floor. What room was she in?

"Look, I really don't think we should do dinner," she said.

"Why not?" He flicked the light off so that his reflection wouldn't stare back at him. And so that she couldn't see him.

"Huh?"

"Why not?" he repeated. "Give me one good reason why we shouldn't."

"Give me one good reason why we should."

"Because I owe you, and Merrills—"

"Always pay their debts," she finished for him. "I know. But besides that."

"My conscience says I have to."

She laughed and his breathing grew even rougher. "Sleep with a light on and it won't bother you."

"My conscience is tougher than that," he protested. "So what's your reason why we shouldn't have dinner?"

There was a long silence. Long enough for a car to go down the street, its lights sweeping away the darkness, then letting it fall back in place behind it.

"I just don't want any more complications in my life right now," she said.

"What's complicated about eating?" he asked. "You on some weird diet program?"

She laughed although exasperation came through pretty clearly, too. "I can't explain it," she said. "We're just too different. We probably have all different expectations of life."

"I was just expecting some company for dinner," he said.

"See?" Her voice had a mocking tone, but he could sense something else there, too. "You'd want to eat and I'd want to be swept off my feet with wine and roses and poetry so that we fall in love and run away to some magical land far, far away, where we'd live happily ever after."

"What if I'm willing to do that when dinner's over?"

She laughed, but somehow he knew a door was closing. "We're just not compatible."

This was all a lot of nonsense, he knew that. She wasn't some starry-eyed teenager who was dreaming of love. She was an adult—a clearheaded, realistic woman who would pound the living daylights out of some man who tried to cart her off to some magical land. She would want to walk there at his side.

But still, he had no idea what was really the matter.

"Let's just call it even and say good-night," she said.

"We're not even."

"You'll get used to the idea," she replied and then the phone went dead.

Jack stood there for a long moment, staring out at the darkness and holding the phone at his ear, listening to the mocking notes of the dial tone. After a moment, the lights in her house went out. He felt the strangest sense of emptiness, of loss. It was a weird idea, since he'd never had her in any sense.

He walked slowly across the kitchen and hung up the phone. The house was dark and silent.

She wouldn't even take a damn dinner from him, let alone ask for anything else. And the more she refused, the more deeply he felt in debt to her.

He was going to settle this. He had to.

Chapter Six

Cassie took a quick step back from her shower stall and turned her head to avoid the spray of water as Ollie shook himself. Since he was half-in, half-out of the shower stall, the bathroom walls, the sink and the floor got the benefit of his shaking. Not to mention her.

"Why'd you do that?" she asked. "I'm not the one who needed a bath."

He responded by coming all the way out of the stall and shaking himself again, sending a finer spray of water all over her. It didn't matter, though. She was already soaked from bathing him.

"Come on, boy," she said and draped an old beach towel over him, rubbing him vigorously. "Let's get you dry so I can fix some dinner."

He seemed far less interested in food than in licking her face anytime it got near his.

"You're really determined to clean me up, aren't you?" She stood and looked at her reflection in the mirror. Her T-shirt was soaked from struggling to bathe him, her shorts were damp, and her hair was all stringy and plastered to her face. "I think I look rather glamorous, myself."

Ollie wagged his tail.

"In fact, I wouldn't be surprised if hordes of handsome men were pounding down my door this evening."

She pushed aside the unsettling knowledge that at least one handsome gentleman could have been at her door this evening if she'd let him, and went back to towel-drying Ollie. She'd done the right thing in turning Jack down. Maybe she was a little lonely now and then, but it was the price she had to pay for being safe.

"So what should we have for dinner?" she asked Ollie, although the prospect of an empty evening stretching ahead of her had dulled her appetite. "Grilled cheese or hot dogs? Maybe I should just order a pizza, or I could scramble up some eggs."

Ollie was listening, or at least wagging his tail at her as she spoke, but then he stopped and looked away. After a moment of holding himself still, he ran out of the bathroom and down the stairs. She heard him barking from the living room.

"Must be those hordes of handsome men," she muttered as she grabbed up the wet towels and trudged after him. It was probably Sam wanting to drag her to the movies.

Ollie was frantic at the front door when she finally got there. "Oh, quiet," she said. Sam was hardly reason to get quite so excited.

Shifting the towels so her right arm was free, Cassie pulled open the door. It wasn't Sam standing there. It was Jack, dressed in a suit and with his arms full of packages.

"Hi," he said and moved past her into the house, leaving a delicious scent in his wake.

"Hi," she said vaguely. She closed the door and trailed after him. Actually, after him and then Ollie. Maybe she should show that there was a difference between her and her dog.

"What are you doing here?" she asked with a little bit of oomph in her voice.

He put all the packages down on her dining-room table. "Bringing dinner," he replied.

She frowned at him, trying hard to ignore the seductive smells that had Ollie turning into a quivering mass of terrier. "I was just getting ready to go out," she said.

He looked her over, head to foot. "Logrolling or washing cars?"

Her frown deepened. She'd forgotten how she looked and raked her hand back through her wet hair. "I just hadn't changed yet."

"I see." His gaze lingered—annoying her, teasing her, making her feel alive. "Well, maybe as you're changing, you'll want to nibble on a few things."

"I doubt it."

He ignored her as he pulled over one bag and peered in. "You have your choice of poached salmon with cucumber sauce or beef Wellington. Potatoes are twice baked and I can't remember what the vegetable was. Some kind of green beans with a long fancy name."

Her knees were weakening but she fought it by digging her toes into the carpet. The dinners she'd been considering were just as good. She didn't need him here to feed her.

"I'm not really hungry," she said.

He pulled over another bag and whipped out a bottle. "A fine zinfandel to accompany your choice and—" he reached into his suit-coat inside pocket and pulled out a miniature rosebud that he handed to her "—a flower for the lady."

She had to take the tiny rose—it would have been rude not to—but it wouldn't change her conviction that they were wrong for each other.

"And lastly—" He took a piece of paper from another pocket and began to read: "'Roses are red, violets are blue, I'm pretty hungry and hope you are too.'"

Cassie burst out laughing. "Okay, maybe I am," she admitted. "So what?"

"Want to eat here?" he asked, nodding at the dining table.

She tried glaring at him, but nothing seemed to dim that damn gleam in his eyes.

"Want me to read another poem?"

"Let me get cleaned up," she said with a sigh. "It won't take me more than a minute."

Still clutching her rose, she hurried back upstairs. Her heart was racing, but it had to be from laughing or rushing up the stairs, or from the exertion of washing Ollie. She frowned at herself in the mirror as she stripped off her T-shirt. Face it, she told herself. The racing heart, the shortness of breath, the idiotic grin on her face were all because of Jack.

He was so real, so right, so damn stubborn. If only she had the guts to tell him straight out about her problem. Maybe he didn't want any more kids, so it wouldn't matter. Maybe he knew of some different better doctors who could make things right. Or, most likely, maybe he only wanted dinner so his conscience would leave him alone.

She hurried into her bathroom and took a quick shower, then resisted the temptation to blow-dry her hair or put on makeup. She combed her hair and put on a clean blouse, dress shorts and nixed the shoes. Dinner companionship was what he'd said he wanted the other day, and that was all he was going to get. Not some fashion model to gawk at. She picked up her flower and went back downstairs.

He had the table set by the time she got down there—tablecloth, dishes, silverware and wineglasses. And candles in his hand.

"Ollie told me where everything was," he said. "Hope that was all right."

"Fine," she said and got candleholders from the side cabinet. "Ollie doesn't use candles much so he probably didn't know where these were."

"I suspected he had pyromaniacal tendencies," Jack said.

She laughed, feeling silly and giddy and nervous. She found herself wiping off her sweaty hands on her shorts as Jack put the candles in the holders. Ollie wagged his tail at her. As encouragement, most likely.

"This is just for effect, I'm afraid," he said as he stepped back.

"You're not allowed to carry matches, either?"

"It's light out." He waved his hands about. "We can light them, but I don't think you'll notice much."

"No, I guess we won't."

But it didn't matter. She felt like a little kid who got taken to the circus. She felt like it was Christmas and her birthday and Halloween all at once. She was going to have a good time tonight.

Jack had come around and pulled her chair out. She sat down, conscious of how close he was; of hands on the back of the chair that could be on her if she moved just so. Suddenly she was wishing that she had agreed to go out with him. There was something too seductive, too intimate about being here alone with him.

"So which main course do you want?" he asked.

She shook her head. "They both sound great. Can we split them?"

"A woman of compromise," he said and began opening packages and assembling the plates.

"Not really," she said with a laugh. "Just ask my sisters."

She caught just a glimpse of his quick smile that lit some sparks in her heart and turned, finding herself watching his hands as they opened cartons and distributed the food. They were strong hands, deft and sure. Hands that could be gentle. Hands that could be dangerous if they were allowed to roam where they would. Her skin suddenly felt on fire.

She got to her feet. "I'll open the wine."

It gave her something to concentrate on. Something besides Jack, that is. She opened the bottle and poured them each a glass. By the time she was sitting back down, Jack had the food distributed and a plate at each place. Ollie nudged her hand as if reminding her to share.

"It looks delicious," she said.

Once they were both seated across the table from each other, he picked up his glass of wine. "To repaying one's debts."

It was a safe toast. Better than any her addled brain might have come up with. She raised her glass. "To repaying one's debts."

After a sip of the wine, she took a bite of her food. "Where is this from?"

"The Royal House," he said. "I never ate there, but I was told the food was good."

"I've never been there, either," she said. "But it's delicious."

The mention of The Royal House turned her pensive. She and her siblings had wanted to take Mom and Dad there for their twenty-seventh wedding anniversary some years back, but Mom had gotten wind of what was going on and killed the operation, saying it was too expensive for an ordinary anniversary. She'd said it was for something special like a thirtieth. They'd gone to the Riveria instead. Mom had died a couple of years later, just days before her thirtieth wedding anniversary. It just proved that one shouldn't put off joy when it was offered.

So did that mean she should be accepting Jack's invitations?

Cassie lifted her head and attention back to Jack. His eyes were a soft blue, like the waters of a pristine north-woods lake. Would it be safe to lean on him? Could she let her heart relax just a bit and trust that she wouldn't regret it?

"A penny for your thoughts."

No, better safe than sorry. But "sorry" had a lot of levels and sometimes she was sorry she didn't have somebody just to talk to. Still, she wasn't ready to take a chance.

"Wow," she mocked. "A big spender."

"All right," he said, with a sigh. "I'll go to a buck, but no higher."

As she stared at him, Cassie could see his eyes begin to darken. Should she tell him the story of her mother and how she never got to eat at The Royal House? Part of Cassie wanted to spill the story, but she just looked down at her plate.

"I was just thinking how this is a lot better than grilled cheese."

He laughed. "It certainly beats the grilled cheese I've had so far in my life."

They ate in companionable silence for a time. Ollie sat next to her, his eyes glued to her fork, following its every movement. She smiled at his intensity and felt herself relax. This was nice. One time would be okay.

"Your conscience should certainly leave you alone now," she said. "This is great."

"I don't know. It doesn't feel terribly satisfied."

"Maybe we should review just how little I really did."

"It wasn't the actual work you did," he said, his voice soft and low. "It was that you helped me out, even though I was a complete stranger. I was very impressed."

The look in his eyes made her uneasy, or maybe it was the tingling reaction in her stomach. She sipped at her wine, then sipped again. It went down so nicely and spread a sweet fire all through her blood. She had another sip.

"A lot of people here do that kind of thing," she said. "It's different in a small town than in the big city."

"No. You're different," he said. "You're more willing to help people out."

She laughed, trying to ease the sudden steaminess in the air. "Help them out the door, Sam would say."

"You're not as tough as you pretend to be."

She frowned at her food, wondering how this conversation had gotten so serious. And how to turn it aside before she started baring her soul.

"You want to see 'tough'? You should try giving Ollie, here, a bath. You'd think he was Samson and I was Delilah washing off his hair."

Jack's eyes turned teasing. "Maybe he's embarrassed that his mommy's still giving him a bath."

"Or else it's a guy thing," she said. "And he doesn't like me seeing him in the bathtub."

"Do you hurry him through so he doesn't have time to play with his toys? Maybe he wants time to play with his boats or little duckies."

Cassie laughed. "When we were real little, Fiona and I had to take baths together and she used to drive me nuts. I always wanted to play and splash and put all sorts of soap in our hair to make it stand up straight. She always insisted that we wash first. Like there was somebody going to come and check.''

"You and Fiona seem very different," he said.

Cassie nodded and felt her smile slip slightly. "I really made her life miserable after our parents died. I was always getting into fights and she was trying doubly hard to be good so we wouldn't get thrown out of another foster home."

"Sounds like you each dealt with your grief differently."

Cassie just shrugged. Why did their conversations always turn so serious? Why did she keep getting the urge to confide in him?

"Maybe it overemphasized our most dominant traits," she said. "I was always looking for a fight and Fiona was always afraid to break the rules."

"Her fiancé doesn't seem to be a 'rules' person."

"Alex? No, not at all. He's exactly what she needs. Someone who focuses on the end, not the means."

Jack had finished eating and pushed his plate to one side as he picked up his wineglass. His eyes were on Cassie. "And what are you looking for in a man?" he asked. "Someone to fight against or someone to fight alongside?"

Cassie clutched at her own wine, finding the question a little bothersome. In the deepest, darkest part of the night, she longed not to fight at all, but to have someone she could lean on and trust. Someone who would always be there for her. Always.

"I'm not looking for a man," she said lightly. "I like to go out and have fun sometimes, but I sure don't want another long-term commitment."

"Afraid he won't be there in the long run?"

She almost jumped, wondering if he could somehow read into her soul. "Oh, I don't know. Maybe I don't want to promise 'forever' myself."

He nodded and stared into his glass. "That's being honest. I wish Daphne had admitted she felt that way. Maybe if I had known up front..."

"What?" she probed. "Would you rather have not had the relationship? Then you wouldn't have the twins."

"I guess." He sighed and ran his fingers through his hair. "I just wish I had known. I hate surprises. For years I felt we were a matched pair, and then I found out she had all sorts of different goals. I just want honesty."

"Is that so hard to find?"

"Impossible."

"Maybe you haven't asked the right questions," she said. "Or watched for the right clues. Or else you always gravitate toward the wrong type."

He looked slightly annoyed. "Maybe I just don't like the idea of loving someone who doesn't love me back just as much."

"How can you measure love?" she scoffed. "You got a love scale or do you give a woman a test before you fall in love?"

"I don't need a scale to know when a relationship is one-sided."

"All relationships are one-sided," she said. "At any given time in any relationship, one person needs more than the other. If you love enough, you give what the other needs. Even if it's freedom so they can go after their dream." Or find someone else and have a family.

Jack just stared at her. "So you're saying I didn't really love Daphne because I felt betrayed when she left?" he asked slowly.

"No, I'm saying she might have loved you just as much but knew she couldn't make you happy in the long run."

"That's the stupidest thing I ever heard," he snapped. "If she loved me so much, why was she talking only about her acting career?"

What was he getting annoyed with her for? She was just expressing her opinion. "What's Daphne supposed to say—'I love you, but I can't make you happy if I'm not happy'?"

"So my love wasn't enough." He was growing distant, pulling away from her.

Cassie had never been one to cajole people into better moods. "No one's love is ever enough," she returned sharply. "Maybe if we all lived in a vacuum, it would be. But we're all a product of everything and everybody that we've come in contact with. Maybe Daphne never felt loved when she was growing up and needed the acclaim of lots of people. Maybe you were always so busy seeing an insult in everything people said that you never stopped to consider the idea that someone could find your love was enough.''

He turned from her and she thought she'd gone too far, but after a moment, his gaze met hers again. His eyes were troubled, like the sea as a storm waned, but his lips were trying for a smile.

''Hey, how'd we get so serious?'' He reached over for the wine bottle and refilled their glasses, then took her hands in his. ''What should we do after we clean up the dishes? Want to rent a movie? Take a walk? Or did you have plans?''

Cassie didn't know what to say. She had no other plans for the evening, unless she counted combing Ollie's hair once it was almost dry. But the real questions was, did she want to start a relationship with Jack? Her family certainly would love it if she did, but that was no reason to send him packing. Not enjoying his company because everyone wanted her to was no smarter than seeing him because no one wanted her to. In either case, she would be allowing others to run her life. And it was time she took it in her own hands.

Her gaze fell on his hands—scarred from the years he'd spent playing football—that covered her own. Control was still in her hands, even if her hands were in someone else's. Just like she could enjoy her own happiness even if it made someone else happy.

''Fifty dollars for your thoughts.''

Startled, she looked up into his face. His eyes were near to black. Cassie could feel her pleasant warmth turn to raging heat. Her eyes darted around.

''Let's rent a movie,'' she said. ''Then you can help me comb Ollie. It's a two-person job.''

Jack put the newspaper down and listened. Sure enough, that was Cassie's truck. He got to his feet and hurried to the door. The twins were tumbling out of the pickup and racing across the lawn by the time he got the front door open. Cassie followed them more slowly, the girls' sandals in her hand and a smile on her face that lit up all the shadowy recesses of his heart.

"How was swimming?" Jack asked.

"Wet," the girls answered, then dissolved into giggles as they ran past him.

He let his eyes linger on Cassie as she came to the door. "How's it going?" he asked.

"Their lessons? Just fine. We're making progress." She handed him the girls' sandals.

He wasn't sure that was all he had been asking about, but let it go. He tossed the sandals onto the floor just inside the door. "Aunt Hattie made a strawberry-rhubarb pie. Want a piece?"

"I probably shouldn't," she replied and glanced back at her truck as if afraid it might wander off without her. "I need to water my garden."

"It's going to rain tonight."

She frowned up at him. "I thought they weren't predicting rain until next week."

"Who, the weathermen? What do they know?"

She just laughed at him and started back toward her truck. He didn't want her to go, not just yet, and followed her. She got in, but didn't start the engine. He leaned on the edge of the open window. She was close enough to touch, to let his fingers play with the softness of her curls. He just kept his hands still.

She had been in his thoughts constantly over the past few days. Along with her words. Much as it pained him to admit it, she'd been right about a lot of things. Her analysis of him had been right on. What would be her reading of herself? he wondered.

"I had a good time Saturday," he told her.

"Yeah, it was nice."

"I thought maybe we could do it again. It was nice to have someone to talk to." Maybe he wanted more of her wisdom, or more of her straight honesty.

She sighed and looked down at the steering wheel. "Yeah, it was."

"Want to go to Pizza Playland with me and the girls on Friday?"

"I have softball."

"Want some rowdy fans?"

"Sure, why not?" Her smile was like a spring breeze bringing warmth and joy. "Boehm Park. Six-thirty."

The girls came running out of the house, half racing and half skipping over to the truck. Their hair was still damp from swimming, and their faces flushed with laughter.

"How come you're still here?" Mary Louise asked, jumping so she could put her arms though the open window and hold herself up.

Mary Alice joined her. "Do ya want some pie? It's real yummy."

"I already offered her some," Jack told them. "And she said she had to go home."

"How come?"

"Is your doggy lonesome?"

"We could play with him if he wants."

Cassie just laughed. "How about after my softball game on Friday? We can go over to my house for dinner."

"We're going to your softball game?"

"Are we, Daddy?"

"Sure," he said. "I thought we could go cheer her on."

Mary Louise frowned and looked at Mary Alice. "We're gonna be cheerleaders."

"We don't got no cheerleader clothes."

"We don't got pom-poms."

Jack just groaned and put his head down on his arms as Cassie laughed. "Good thing you have a couple of days to get ready," she told the girls.

"Yeah." They climbed down from the truck and raced away.

Jack lifted his head up. "Where do they get this from?" he asked. "It can't be Daphne. She was hardly around for them, yet sometimes they seem so like her it's scary."

"They're like lots of little girls," Cassie assured him. "Stop seeing problems everywhere and learn to laugh."

He just looked at her—at her dark brown eyes that held so much calm and wisdom. He needed to see more of her, to listen to more of her common sense. But she was leaving.

She started her engine. "See you Friday."

He stepped back. "Right. Boehm at six-thirty."

"With pom-poms or without," she called out as she backed from the drive.

He just waved and watched as she drove down to her house. His heart was telling him something, but not in a language he could understand.

"Go, Cassie!" a little voice called out.

"Go, go, go!" another one sang out.

"You got your own cheering section?" the catcher asked Cassie as she stepped up to the plate.

Cassie waved at the girls in their matching red shorts and white shirts—and red pom-poms—before she took her place. Okay, she waved to Jack, too. It wasn't like she was ignoring him. "Yep, my fan club sends members to all my games."

"Oh, yeah." The other woman glanced over toward the twins in the bleachers on the first-base side. "That stud can belong to my fan club anytime."

Cassie just looked out at the pitcher. "I think your husband would object to that, Stacy."

"Hey, I didn't say I was going to do anything with Mr. Hell-of-a-Hunk. Just let him in my club."

"I see." The first pitch came hard and outside. Cassie let it go by.

"Ball one!"

"Unless you got dibs on him." Stacy threw the ball back.

"We're just friends."

"Girl, you don't have hunks like him for a friend."

"I do." The next pitch was high but Cassie swung anyway.

"Strike one."

That was stupid of her. She should have known better. It was the last inning, and her team was down by six. They needed her concentration if they were going to win.

"I don't think I've ever seen anybody at these games for you," Stacy said.

"I've had fans here before." Of course, it had been Fiona or Sam or Bobby and his kids. The next pitch was low and inside, just where she liked it. She swung hard and connected with a satisfying thud. The ball flew into the outfield as she sprinted for first. She made it with room to spare, but her team was yelling for her to stay put, so she did.

"Wow, that was awesome!"

"It musta gone a mile."

Cassie turned slightly and grinned at the twins. They had come down from the bleachers and were peering through the fence at her. "Hi."

"Daddy said that was almost a home run," Mary Alice said.

"He said you must be really strong," Mary Louise added.

Yeah, but did he consider that an asset? Cassie glanced back up at the bleachers where Jack was sitting. He waved at her, then gave her a thumbs-up sign. Maybe it was good. She waved back.

"Cute kids," the first baseman said to her. "They yours?"

He must have been new to his team this year because Cassie knew most of the members on the other teams. They'd been playing against each other for years. It was a natural question, yet it stung for some reason.

"No," she said, concentrating on Marv up at the plate. "They're the kids of a neighbor."

"Oh."

Come on, Marv. Get a hit.

He got a strike.

"The guy with the beard? He looks familiar. He work at Bendix?"

"No, teaches at the law school."

"He ever play ball for the university?"

"No." Marv got another strike.

"He sure does look familiar."

Marv swung again and this time connected. It looked like the shortstop might get it, but Cassie ran anyway. She slid into second and was deemed safe. Safe, in truth. She was farther from Jack and the girls, and could concentrate on the game.

As it turned out, there wasn't much to concentrate on. The next two batters struck out. And, since the other team was the home team, there was no need to play the last half of the inning. The game was over; Cassie's team had lost. Amid some halfhearted cheering, the players walked back to the dugouts together, more intent on planning their postgame partying than on anything else.

The twins rushed at her. "I like softball," Mary Louise said.

"Will you teach us how to play this, too?" Mary Alice asked.

Jack was close enough to hear that and laughed. "Hey, now, girls. Cassie can't teach you everything."

"But she's so good at it!" Mary Louise whined.

"We like her," Mary Alice added.

Jack was at her side. "Nice game," he said.

"Thanks." She smiled inside and smiled even more when he slipped an arm around her shoulders.

"You coming to Coaches?" someone called over to her.

Cassie shook her head. "Nope. I can't make it tonight."

Amid a spate of hooting, Cassie walked over to the parking lot. Somewhere in the walking, Jack's arm left her shoulder and she felt lonely all of a sudden. What she should be feeling was relieved, she told herself. She didn't need a man's arm around her to walk to the parking lot safely.

"I was really glad you all could come," she told Jack and the girls. "I was the only one there with my own cheerleaders."

"These ain't real cheerleader outfits."

"We couldn't find ones nowhere."

"Aunt Hattie said these shorts would be just fine."

"Daddy said we didn't need pom-poms."

"But he helped us make these."

"See? They're made out of paper."

Cassie looked up from her inspection of the tissue-paper pom-poms. Jack just shrugged when his eyes finally met hers. He was embarrassed about it!

"It was no big deal," he said.

"It was very nice of you." She slipped her arm through his. "And resourceful. How'd you know how to make them?"

"We studied every aspect of the game of football in college," he said and stopped at her truck. "We'll meet you back at your house?"

"I want to ride with Cassie," Mary Louise cried.

"Me, too," Mary Alice added.

Jack frowned at them. "You always get to ride with her," he said in a whiny voice. "It's my turn. You two drive the minivan this time."

The girls just giggled and climbed up into Cassie's truck. Cassie just shrugged at Jack. "See you there," she said and climbed in herself.

"Cheaters," Jack muttered and leaned in through the open window to plant a quick kiss on Cassie's lips.

She felt a rush of heat, a desire to pull him back for a longer, more lingering kiss. His eyes met hers and shared her longing, shared her hungers and needs and worries. But then a group from a passing car called out goodbyes to Cassie and the spell was broken. She turned to wave but when she looked back, Jack was already heading to his minivan.

"Are you gonna be our mommy?" Mary Louise asked.

"No, of course not," Cassie said quickly and started out of the parking lot. "Why would you ask that?"

"You kissed Daddy," Mary Alice replied.

Actually, *he* kissed *her,* Cassie wanted to point out, but didn't. The girls probably were not into such nuances. "Adults kiss lots of times," she said casually as she pulled into traffic. "It doesn't mean anything."

"Oh."

"You could still be our mommy."

"Can you make brownies?"

"Would you make us eat oatmeal?"

"We hate oatmeal."

"Yuck!"

Cassie drove carefully. "Your dad and I are friends," she told them. "He probably has lots of friends, but that's all we are. Friends."

"Don't you want to be our mommy?"

Cassie flashed a glance at the girls and found two pairs of serious little eyes staring at her. "There's a lot more involved in becoming somebody's mom than just wanting to," she answered slowly. "Your mom would also be your dad's wife, so she'd have to be somebody he likes, too."

"He likes you," Mary Louise said.

"Honest," Mary Alice added. "He really does."

Cassie was never so glad to see their street come up. "There's a big difference between liking somebody as a friend and loving them like a wife." She pulled into her drive. "Well, here we are."

Jack's van was right behind her. Hopefully the girls would not rush out and continue this discussion. Maybe if she distracted them somehow...

"Ollie gets pretty excited when I get home after being gone awhile," she said as she helped the girls out. "He doesn't mean to, but he could knock little kids down if they aren't careful."

"Okay."

By the time Cassie had her front door open, Jack had joined them. Ollie was trying to restrain his excitement over having some kids to play with, the girls were dancing around as they oohed and aahed over him, and Jack was trying to say hello himself. Fortunately, there was no chance for any type of conversation, let alone one about mommies.

"Why don't you girls take Ollie into the backyard and throw a ball for him?" she suggested. Once that was done, she turned to Jack and laughed. "Just a little confusion."

"I think they'll want to live over here from now on," he said.

This was too near the "mommy" conversation for her peace of mind. She went into the kitchen. "I was just going to barbecue some hamburgers. That all right?"

"Great. What can I do?"

Soon they were all out in the backyard where she and the girls kicked off their shoes. The twins played with Ollie, while Jack got the grill fired up and she set the picnic table. It felt so very right and comfortable that it was scary. It was like they were a family, like they belonged to each other.

Such a yearning burned in her heart, such a need to be a part of love, that she wanted to run and hide. Why couldn't friendship be simple? Why couldn't anything ever stay simple?

"Got those burgers ready?" Jack asked. "The coals are good and hot."

"Coming up."

She gave him the meat to cook, then tried to stay busy by bringing out the buns and chips and the fruit salad she'd made earlier, but none of it seemed busy enough to keep her heart from feeling. Her life seemed so empty in comparison to this one evening. But it was what she wanted, what she had chosen.

Ollie's barking brought her outside again in a hurry. Her brother Adam and his kids were in the backyard. Great, she thought with a sigh. Just what she needed—her family to start making more plans for her.

"Hi, sis," Adam said when she came out. "Rosemary sent us over to get your card table and chairs if you don't need them."

"Sure."

They went over to the garage and by the time they came out with the table and two chairs, the twins were turning cartwheels across the grass with Missy, and Jerry was at the grill talking to Jack.

"It's really good to see you with somebody," Adam told her.

She thought about hitting him with the chairs. "The girls wanted to play with Ollie, that's all."

Adam just grinned at her as they walked out to his car. "Sounds good."

"It's true." She waited while he put the table into the trunk, then she put the chairs on top of it. "We're just friends."

"That's a good start."

"It's the start," she said grimly. "And it's the finish."

"Oh, don't be so stubborn," he said. "You're not still carrying a torch for Ron, are you?"

If she'd still had the chairs in her hands, she would have hit him. "Ron? You've got to be kidding. I was over him before we separated."

"So?"

"So, what?" she repeated with a frown as they walked back to the garage. "So why haven't I settled down with someone else? Maybe I don't want to."

"Sure, and kids don't want Christmas to come."

"You want the rest of the chairs or not?"

He just grinned, so certain he was right. "We know you, Cass. And we know when you're hiding." He got the other two chairs from the garage. "Come on, kids. Time to hit the road."

Amid moaning and groaning, his kids came along with him. The yard was quiet again—peaceful—with only the people who belonged. She frowned at the thought and went over to the grill. She meant only the people she had invited.

"Girls, run in and wash up for dinner," Jack called over to them. "The hamburgers are just about done."

Cassie brought the plates over. "You didn't have to do the work, you know."

He grinned at her. "Hey, don't you know outdoor cooking is man's work? Standing in front of a barbecue is very manly."

She didn't know about it being man's work, but he certainly looked manly standing there. But then, he always did. No matter what he was doing, there was something about him that took her breath away. It must be a universal reaction—not a sign that her heart was weakening toward him.

"I read about an art fair in town this weekend," he said. "Want to go with me? I have a lot of bare wall-space in my office that needs filling."

"I don't know anything about art."

"Neither do I, but at least you could help me carry stuff back to the car."

She laughed. Such a romantic. He was safe; being with him was safe. "Sure," she said. "If Sunday's okay, I'll be glad to lend my muscles to the cause."

"We're all clean," the girls called out as they hurried back.

"And everything's here that we need," Cassie said.

She watched as they settled around the table. And she felt a strange certainty that her words might be right in many ways. Maybe everything was here that she needed. But did she have the courage to hold on to it?

Chapter Seven

"And they can do the jellyfish float," Cassie said. "Both of them."

Jack steered them around a cluster of old ladies wearing sneakers, floppy gardening hats, and tie-dyed T-shirts that looked to have come from the sixties. He was trying to concentrate on Cassie's words but found it easier to concentrate on her nearness. He was wanting more and more to take her in his arms, to taste the softness of her lips, and to—

He shook himself back into respectability. "Jellyfish float?" he asked.

"You know." Cassie took her hand out of his and bent over slightly, letting her arms hang down. "It's where you stick your face in the water like this and just hang limp."

"They called that the dead man's float when I was a kid."

"We don't use such scary words anymore."

Cassie straightened and he found her hand back in his. It seemed to fit her, this willingness to put her hand in his so easily. It seemed to say that she trusted him, and in doing so, he could trust her.

He and Cassie stopped in front of a table of small pottery—vases, bowls, plates and sculptures. None of which tweaked his interest, so he let his gaze wander over her.

In spite of her strength, there was something so gentle about her. She knew the right words not to scare the kids, the right ways to relax their fears. They really were enjoying their lessons, looking forward to them with excitement. He wasn't sure whether it was the swimming or Cassie, but the girls definitely were losing their fears.

And what about him?

He looked down at his hand in Cassie's and felt the urging of his heart. Hadn't she somehow done the same for him—lessened his fears so that he could look for happiness again?

"Fifty cents for your thoughts."

"Huh?" He found himself staring at Cassie and her impish grin.

"Hey," she said, laughing. "There are big-money people and then there's the rest of us—operating on the fiscally conservative side of the road."

He found himself smiling. His heart had known right from the beginning that he could trust her. His mind had been a little slow to catch on, but eventually he would come to see the truth. She was different from so many of the others.

"I think we need to get out of the way," Cassie said.

Blinking, he looked at the river of people flowing around them. "Yeah." His voice felt rather gruff and he cleared his throat. "I guess you're right. We'd better move on or get trampled."

They started walking again, moving slowly to take in the exhibits, their held hands swinging, like two kids going steady.

The temperature was in the upper seventies, with a soft breeze from the west pulling in cooling moisture off the river and spreading it among the old oak trees. It was a beautiful day. And the park was so large that even today's crowd was unable to overwhelm its comforting sense of greenness. He was glad he'd asked Cassie to come with him; the girls certainly hadn't had any interest in coming.

"Boy," he muttered. "Kids sure grow up quick."

Cassie laughed and hugged his arm. "Poor baby," she crooned. "Are you still moping because your girls wouldn't come along?"

"They didn't really say they wouldn't come. They just preferred to go to the movies with Kristin and her mother." He tried frowning but there was no dimming the twinkle in Cassie's eyes. "Besides, I'm not moping."

"Right." She gave him a quick kiss on his cheek, leaving the spot several degrees warmer than the rest of his face. "Don't worry about it. They're not rejecting you. They're just starting to venture out on their own. You're doing a good job with them."

He squeezed her hand. "I appreciate your vote, but the verdict won't be in on that for a number of years yet."

"Oh, look." Cassie stopped before an exhibit of wildlife sketches, then moved in under the canopy to look at the drawings of bears and wildcats and deer. "Aren't they beautiful?"

Jack followed her. They were nice. In relatively few lines, the artist had captured the essence of each animal. "Think I should get some for my office?"

"I don't know. Let's keep them in mind."

Cassie was taking her job of finding him artwork seriously. She wanted to check everything out before they made a decision. It was all right with him. The more she pondered, the longer they would be here together.

"So," he said, as they moved on to some seascape paintings. "You think that someday my kids won't be afraid of the water anymore?"

"No doubt about it," she replied. "We ended up our session yesterday, splashing around in the pool getting each other's faces wet."

As he looked into her bright smile and sparkling eyes, Jack wondered why she didn't work with kids all the time. She seemed so good at it.

It could be that there wasn't any money in it, but Cassie didn't appear to be the type who would chase the almighty dollar. Maybe it was just something that wasn't as much fun when you did it for a living. In any case, he was damn lucky to have her working with his girls. Good luck seemed to be a major part of his life since he'd met Cassie. Was there a correlation?

He spotted an artist doing pastel portraits ahead of them. "Let's have him draw our portraits."

"Naw," she said. "Whenever people try to do mine, they break their pencil."

"Please," Jack urged.

"No." She pulled at his hand, starting in another direction. "I'd rather see the Indian jewelry over there."

"The girls would really love it," he coaxed.

He could see her wavering. "How about if—"

"Cassie?" A thin, average-size guy had been pushing a stroller, but stopped right in front of them. "Cassie, it is you."

Cassie seemed to freeze. Not visibly, but the air around her seemed to go still like it might just before a storm broke.

"Hi, Ron," she said. "How are you?"

Jack frowned. This couldn't be a friend of hers, not with her voice so stiff and emotionless. Her eyes kept going to the kid in the stroller.

"Great, Cassie. Just great."

She looked like a balloon that had been pricked. All her joy and sparkle had escaped like so much hot air, leaving her limp and deflated.

An anger and protectiveness grew inside Jack. Was this someone Cassie had had problems with before? Well, he'd better not try anything today. If it weren't for the kid, Jack would have decked the guy right then and there.

"What are you doing here?" Cassie asked.

"We're in town to visit Collette's family," the man replied. "She's over there with her mother."

The man indicated a crowd of people off to his left, but Jack never took his eyes off him. Cassie didn't look, either. Collette must not be the problem, but Ron sure the hell was.

"So," Ron said. "I hear you got a business of your own."

Cassie nodded.

"Doing okay?"

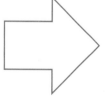

NO COST! NO OBLIGATION TO BUY!
NO PURCHASE NECESSARY!

PLAY "LUCKY 7"
AND GET FIVE FREE GIFTS!

HOW TO PLAY:

1. With a coin, carefully scratch off the silver box at the right. Then check the claim chart to see what we have for you—FREE BOOKS and a gift—ALL YOURS! ALL FREE!

2. Send back this card and you'll receive brand-new Silhouette Special Edition® novels. These books have a cover price of $3.99 each, but they are yours to keep absolutely free.

3. There's no catch. You're under no obligation to buy anything. We charge nothing—ZERO—for your first shipment. And you don't have to make any minimum number of purchases—not even one!

4. The fact is thousands of readers enjoy receiving books by mail from the Silhouette Reader Service™ months before they're available in stores. They like the convenience of home delivery and they love our discount prices!

5. We hope that after receiving your free books you'll want to remain a subscriber. But the choice is yours—to continue or cancel, anytime at all! So why not take us up on our invitation, with no risk of any kind. You'll be glad you did!

"Yeah." She nodded her head again. "It's fine. I'm fine. And you?" The words seemed to come out slowly, as if forced through a net of pain.

The man shrugged. "I'm doing okay."

Jack didn't like any of this and took Cassie's arm. "We need to get going, Cass."

Old Ron gave Jack the once-over, but quickly backed off. He wasn't much shorter than Jack, but he had a lot less beef. "Yeah," he said. "I gotta catch up with Collette. Nice seeing you again."

He nodded but Jack just gave him a hard stare in return.

"Yeah," Cassie responded. "Good to see you, too."

Ron turned and was swallowed up by the crowd, but Cassie kept staring after him. Jack felt as if a lead weight had lodged in his stomach.

"Well," he said, trying his damnedest to sound perky. "Let's get our sketches done."

The silence hung in the air as Cassie continued staring at the space that Ron had just occupied. The lead weight began to grow into fear, but damned if Jack knew of what. He just knew that something was threatening someone who was becoming dear to him.

"Cassie."

"I'd rather not. Not today."

She wouldn't look at him, but her voice sounded so tired. He'd seen her after her softball team had lost and she'd scarcely blinked an eye. She knew how to take defeat, at least in small things. This had to be something major.

"What's wrong?" he asked.

Cassie just looked away as if fighting for control.

But he didn't want her to hide her feelings from him. "Cassie." He took her chin in his hand and turned her head so that she had to look at him. "If that guy's bothering you, I'll—"

"No." She pulled her head away from his grasp. Her voice was sharp. "He's no problem."

"Well, something's wrong."

She gave him a look that said he was pushing too much. "Nothing's wrong," she insisted. "I was just surprised to see him, that's all. I hadn't seen him in four or five years."

"Who is he?" Jack pushed in spite of the warning in her eyes. He couldn't let her retreat inside herself.

She sighed and looked away. "Ron's my ex-husband."

"There's an empty table," Jack said. "Over on the edge, there."

The coffee shop was crowded with people overflowing from the art exhibit, but Cassie didn't care where she sat; all she wanted to do was run and hide. She gazed in the direction Jack was pointing.

"Fine."

He hurried ahead to grab the table while she followed more slowly. She'd felt brittle and about to shatter ever since Ron had pushed that baby carriage in front of her a half hour ago. How was she going to sit here and make polite conversation with Jack? She needed to get home and . . .

And what? Go for a ten-mile run. Spar with the old punching bag for a few hours. Ride her bike down to New Orleans and back without stopping.

"Thought I'd make myself useful," Jack said, dumping the litter into a nearby trash can. "Otherwise someone else would snatch this."

He had the table cleared before she could help and was sliding her glass of iced coffee toward her. She sat down.

"Beautiful day," he said.

She nodded. Jack was just making conversation, trying to perk her up. But like the failure she was, Cassie couldn't even respond to that.

"You don't have to tell me if you don't want to." Jack was staring intently at her; his baby blues were almost black and there was a tightness around the corners of his mouth and eyes. "But is this guy Ron giving you some kind of trouble?"

She shook her head.

"I can take care of it, if he is," he said.

For a moment she thought she was going to cry. It was so nice to have someone concerned about her. She blinked back the sudden wetness in her eyes, willing herself to be stronger.

"Look," Jack said, leaning in closer and taking her hands. "Is he stalking you? We can get the law on him and put a stop to that."

Cassie took a deep breath. Concern was nice up to a point, but then it was time for him to let go. To stop pushing. "It's nothing like that," she assured him.

"Well, whatever it is, I want to help."

"It's nothing," Cassie repeated more sharply. "He's just my ex-husband."

"I see."

Jack turned quiet and Cassie felt her anger subside. He was only trying to help. She shouldn't have snapped at him—not when he was so worried about her. It was just that seeing Ron with a baby had shaken her right to the core. All the old fears had come back; all the old guilts, all the old inadequacies.

"Has he been keeping in touch with you?" Jack asked.

Cassie came back to the present and shook her head. "No, not at all."

Though why hadn't he? Sending her pictures of his child would have been in character for the Ron she remembered. A picture would have been proof that he had been right—that the inadequacy had been hers and hers alone.

"And you wish he had."

"And I wish he had what?" she repeated. Suddenly she stopped, her mouth hanging open. "You think I'm still in love with him? Not on your life. The only feeling I have is regret. And not for what's past, but for getting into the situation in the first place."

Jack relaxed in his chair and took a long drink from his glass. Cassie sipped at hers but couldn't bring herself to the same state of relaxation.

Jack gave off such feelings of strength. A quiet strength. A quiet competence. You could feel his self assurance, his belief in his ability to handle whatever came his way. You felt you could tell him anything and everything and he wouldn't be shocked; he would just take care of it.

But there were some things that couldn't be "taken care of." There were some things that were best left buried. This time the facts carried too many hurts with them and there was no way she could talk about any of it without reliving all of them. She was still too close to the pain of just seeing a pregnant woman. To the instinct that made her turn and head in the opposite direction if she saw someone with a stroller approaching. To the torture of living in two-week cycles—fertility, defeat, fertility, defeat—over and over and over again.

She took a longer drink of her iced coffee this time and willed the past away. "We were just too young," she said.

Jack nodded his head and folded his arms across his chest—telling her to go ahead, he had time.

"When you're young you have such—" Cassie shook her head, feeling at a loss for words.

"Expectations?"

"Yes. Expectations." She felt herself smiling. "Ron and I had different expectations. Different things we expected of the other."

Jack nodded.

"Suffice it to say, neither of us met the other's needs."

"Maybe you guys were just too young."

"Yeah, maybe." Cassie nodded slowly. "I'm sure that's what it was."

"Maybe you'd like another chance?"

"No way." The words came out fast and strong. At least, judging from his expression, that was how they probably sounded to Jack. Cassie was a little surprised herself at their vehemence.

"I mean, not with each other," she said. "Time hasn't made me into what he wanted, and probably hasn't made him into what I want."

"So both of you are ready to push on, then?" Jack asked. "Forge your own trails separate from the other?"

Her vision blurred and she saw Ron's child. It looked like a boy, his soft face all smiles and interested in life around him.

Ron had the family he'd always wanted, and he appeared happy.

Obviously, he had his life together, while all she was doing was running hither and yon. Her life was full of activity, but the bottom line was that all she was doing was treading water. But it was something she was very good at. That and keeping things to herself.

"Hey, that's what I've been doing for the past five years." Cassie slapped a big smile onto her lips. "Blazing my own trail."

"Want to blaze some more by having dinner at my place tonight?"

Her smile tried to waver, but she wouldn't let it. "I wish I could." Tonight was too soon. The pain was too fresh and she would do something stupid like blurt out the truth. She frantically tried to come up with some lie.

"I promised my dad I'd go take a look at a house with him. He's been wanting to start a bed-and-breakfast, and this great old house just came on the market."

Jack frowned at her as if seeing all the holes in her story. Well, there was some truth in it. Dad did want to start a bed-and-breakfast, and he did want her to take a look at this old house he'd seen, but not tonight. Anybody with half a life would have better things to do on a Sunday night than house shop.

"If you're sure," Jack said slowly.

"Hey, I am." She smiled at him, digging up all the bravado she could muster. "I was just surprised to see Ron, that's all. I'm fine now. In fact, I think we should go back to the show and get some of those wildlife sketches for your office."

He just stared at her and she thought she'd gone too far. But then, after a moment, he finished up the last of his iced coffee and got to his feet. "Lead on," he said.

And she did, just as a trailblazer should.

Cassie tossed the bread onto the water and watched as the swans daintily picked at it. "He had a kid," she told them. "A little boy with big brown eyes."

Juliet looked up at Cassie. The bird's dark eyes were watchful.

"All along he said it was my fault we couldn't have kids," Cassie said. "I guess he was right."

She tossed the last of her bread onto the water, and sank down on the log near the edge of the beach. "I just never wanted to believe it," she murmured to the evening air.

Ollie came over and plopped down on the sand next to her, apparently tired of chasing ground squirrels. He eyed the swans briefly, then lay down. Cassie reached over and petted him gently, finding comfort in his steadiness.

"So now what?" she asked Ollie.

He sighed and closed his eyes.

She turned to the swans, hovering out of Ollie's reach in the water. "What do I do now?" she asked them.

But they gave her no answer, either.

Cassie rested her elbows on her knees and her chin in her hands, watching as the birds poked in the water for food. Ever so slowly, they were easing back out onto the lake and away from her.

"Stay safe," she called after them, although they'd never appeared to be in any danger since the time Juliet had been caught in the plastic ring. And the branches where that had happened were long since gone, cleaned out by some Boy Scout troop along with other debris one summer.

Cassie watched them finally swim behind some trees and disappear from her sight. There was such an emptiness inside her, such an aching void for the children she would never have. She felt as if she were hollow inside; just a vast nothingness filled with pain.

Her arms ached for the newborn child she would never hold. Her eyes ached with tears that would never ease her misery. Her heart ached for the bond a child created between a man and a woman.

Stay safe. That was what the swans had to do, and what she needed to do also. She needed to stay safe. And that meant stay careful. Stay alert. Stay apart.

Ollie stirred at her side and she bent over to hug him. Poor baby. It was getting cool and the bugs were starting to bite. It was time to go home. Even if she would be all alone.

Jack didn't believe that Cassie was as okay as she'd wanted him to think. All through dinner he fretted about her and stayed distracted as he played endless games of old maid with the girls. Finally, after they were in bed, Aunt Hattie frowned at him.

"It's not like your young lady lives in another county. And it's not like nine-thirty is all that late."

Jack stared out the window through the darkness. It was alive with the sounds of night. Just like the past was alive with the sounds of memories. But all he was conscious of was Cassie's house across the way. The lights were on, but it seemed to have gloom hanging over it.

Maybe he could help see her through this time of trouble. And no matter what she said, her heart was having some kind of trouble.

"I wouldn't mind checking on her," he said. "We ran into her ex-husband today and she seemed upset."

"Was he rude?"

Jack shrugged. "To be honest, he didn't seem like anything. He was pushing his kid in a stroller and stopped for about two minutes to exchange pleasantries. I don't know why she was so upset."

Aunt Hattie made a face. "He had a baby in a stroller and you don't know why she was upset? Jimmy Jack, I'm surprised you had sense to be born. No woman can see the family that could have been hers and not feel something. If nothing else, it makes a body pause some."

"She said she didn't care about him anymore."

"Don't matter if she wishes the man was roadkill. That baby could have been hers and her arms must be aching for loss of him."

Suddenly he saw the truth of Aunt Hattie's words and it seemed even more necessary for him to check on Cassie. His eyes sought her house through the night. The lights were on.

He would walk over. But first he stopped at the cabinet in the family room and pulled a few movies out.

It took him about two minutes to walk across his yard, two minutes of watching her shadow moving against the drapes. For a moment, he hesitated, wondering if she might have someone there with her, but then decided the hell with it. The worst she could do was throw him out and he'd end up watching Three Stooges flicks by himself at home.

"Jack?" She was surprised to see him at her door. "What are you doing here?"

He held up the movies. "Brought over some laughs for us."

She frowned when she saw the movie titles. "Don't tell me. Aunt Hattie and the girls threw you out and I had the only other VCR you thought you could use."

"You don't like the Three Stooges?"

"Name one woman who does."

"What an attitude." But she let him in. Other than Ollie, she was alone. "So does that mean you don't want to watch these?"

"Only if I can make popcorn."

"A real man never turns down popcorn." He followed her into the kitchen and watched as she put a packet of popcorn into the microwave. "I should have brought us some wine."

She made a face and pulled a bottle of wine from the refrigerator. "Just how many women have you rescued from the depths of depression before?" she asked.

"Who said anything about rescuing?"

"I see. This is just some meaningful Three Stooges anniversary and you wanted to share it with me."

"You're very suspicious." And he was more than a little irritated with himself for letting his motives be read so easily. But she didn't seem upset with him. "Supposing I was rescuing, would that be a problem?"

She just laughed and pulled the popcorn from the microwave. When she ripped open the bag, the kitchen filled with the rich buttery smell. "I think it's sweet of you," she said. "Not necessary, but sweet."

Jack frowned. She was talking pretty big, but he wasn't sure he bought it all. There was something about her eyes that said the world was not yet right. He wanted to take her in his arms, to hold her all night long and show her that happiness was all around her. Instead, he picked up the wine bottle and got two glasses from the cabinet.

"Come on," he said. "Curly, Larry and Moe await."

"Goody."

But in spite of her statement that she didn't like the Three Stooges, Cassie did her share of laughing over the next few hours. As they sat on the floor, their backs against her sofa and his arm around her shoulder, Jack could feel the tension slip away from her.

While a certain different tension was tightening in him.

"How about if I top off your wine?" he asked after he set the last tape to rewind.

She looked at the glass in her hand and then at him. "Are you trying to lead me down the garden path, kind sir?"

Her brown eyes were soft and glowing. Without guile—like a child's. Knowing—like a woman's. A hell of a combination, and it took a hell of a woman to pull it off.

"I won't lead you down any path you don't want to go," he replied. But neither would he refuse to follow her, if that made sense.

After taking a sip of her wine, Cassie snuggled back down into his embrace. She was so beautiful. It was getting harder and harder to just sit here, holding her. There were so many things his hands wanted to do, so many ways his heart wanted to please her. So many—

"I think after having to watch these stupid movies, I should get a reward," Cassie said.

"They're classics," he corrected. "And what kind of reward do you want?"

"I'm thinking."

Her voice had a teasing quality to it that had been missing for a while and he told himself it was good that he had come. Never mind his growing hungers, she had needed him here.

"You know, this house is almost seventy years old." She put her glass of wine on the coffee table, then moved away from him to lie on the floor. With her hands behind her head, the gentle swell of her breasts looked like two soft mountains, inviting him to rest his weary head on them.

"Oh, yeah?" Jack took a deep breath and tried to look at the television screen. He had no idea what was on. He couldn't even remember what she had just said a few seconds ago. All he knew was the essence of her, the womanly presence that was so close.

"In the early-morning hours, it gets to creaking and groaning real bad."

"Must bother Ollie," Jack said. He felt her nearness, sensed the soft movement of her breathing. She was so inviting. So tempting. But he would be damned if he would take advantage of her in her emotional state.

"He's used to it," she said. "I'm the one that it scares."

Jack turned to frown at her. It was hard to imagine her scared of anything, let alone a creaking house. "And you want me to stay?"

"Not unless you want to."

All he did was blink.

"I'm not going to lock the door and keep you prisoner," she said. "But neither will I throw you out in the street if you want to stay a little longer."

She stared at him and Jack looked deep into her eyes. Folks said the eyes were the windows of a person's soul. He didn't doubt that at all. He just wished Cassie would pull her shades up a bit higher.

There appeared to be a lot inside there. Love. Pain. And everything in between. But he was finding it hard to make out what the pieces were and what they all meant.

She reached out and stroked the back of his head, causing him to lay his head down on those breasts, but only lightly. It seemed as natural as breathing.

"Sometimes it's hard being alone."

Her fingers picked up their stroking intensity and Jack could feel his breathing quicken. He was being pulled toward her.

Like a positive ion to a negative, like a yin to her yang, like ketchup to a french fry. It was all so natural, a need implanted in the first living thing that was placed on this earth.

When her caresses slowed, he rolled over to his left—a little farther away from Cassie but where he could drink in the whole expanse of her beauty, from the top of her head to the bottoms of her feet.

Was she really asking what he thought she was asking? Or was it just his love-starved hormones sending fantasies to his mind?

He reached over and brushed a few errant curls back from her forehead. "I sense a certain tension in the air," he said.

She frowned at him. "What are you talking about? I'm not tense."

"You were earlier," he said, and let his fingers run lightly over her arm. Her skin was cool and smooth, and sent sparks into his heart. "And I don't think it's all gone."

"You think you can read my body better than I can?"

"I have powers," he said.

She caressed his arm, from his biceps on up to his shoulder. "I can see that."

"No, no. I mean real powers. A sensitivity. An ability to communicate at the most basic of levels."

"You must be talking about your silver tongue."

"It's not silver." He bent close, kissed her gently on the ear and then briefly flicked his tongue over it. "Silver is a metal, cold and unyielding. Mine is flesh and blood, moist and warm."

"I see."

Her eyes were dark and stormy but he could discern no other emotion. No excitement. But she didn't pull back, either. Jack bent down and put a moist trail under her ear and down her neck. A fire was growing in him, a need to do more than just touch her. More than just kiss her and play little word games. Then he pulled away again, looking into her eyes.

"I definitely see what you mean," she said.

"The eye, ears and tongue aren't the only vehicle of communication." He slipped his hand under her T-shirt. Her stomach was firm and flat yet as his fingers gently caressed, then moved higher and higher toward the soft swell of her breasts. "The fingers are also key."

They watched each other as he touched her. Her eyes were dark and moody, but still unreadable. They held secrets deep within; secrets that he desperately wanted to read.

"Where did you learn all these wondrous things?" Cassie asked. "Law school?"

"No," he said, laughing. "The law is like silver—cold and unyielding."

He kept moving his hand, slowly, very slowly; pausing often to listen, to feel, to absorb. Her breath had quickened; her skin grew flushed. Jack would have bet his life that buried beneath her tough exterior were vast pools of passion.

"Fingers can bring all kinds of joy." He curved them slightly. "To all concerned."

"You tickle me and you're dead."

"I wouldn't think of it."

He slipped his left arm under her head and, as she turned to face him, they snuggled into each other. It was comfortable and it wasn't. It was too little, far too little to satisfy him. Without a word, they came to each other with their tongues, with their lips, with their fingers.

Their embrace was charged with waiting thunder, like a storm building to a crescendo. Lightning was about to flash, fire was about to consume them. Yet he couldn't pull back. His heart was in her hands, waiting for her touch. He couldn't breathe, his need was so great; yet, neither could he stop touching her, stop letting his hands roam all over her delicious skin.

He finally had to pull back for air. "You know I never would have tickled you," he said. "I'd never do anything you wouldn't want me to."

"I don't do anything I don't want to do." She pulled him toward her again. "Not for as long as I can remember."

They slipped into a deep cave that was all their own. No one bothered them, no one intruded. There was nothing but the desires raging in their souls. Her hands were all over him as if she could drink him through her touch and when they parted for air, he looked into her eyes, now like chocolate kisses floating in vanilla ice cream. There was no need to guess at her feelings; her hungers were as strong as his own.

She drew closer to him, putting a smooth, firm leg between his. "Your fingers aren't the only things that speak with feeling," she said, her voice husky and raw.

"That's cruel." He wanted to devour her with his lips, to explore every inch of her with his hands; to own her, to have her, to be one with her. But he pulled back.

"Are you sure this is what you want to do?" he asked.

"I told you. I don't do anything I don't want to do."

"But..." He sat up, trying to make his befuddled brain work. "I wasn't planning on this. I didn't bring anything."

She frowned. "What should you have brought? Your teddy bear?"

"You know. Protection."

She laughed, the sound softening the shadows of the room and firing up his desire once more. "I think I have some condoms. They might be a little old, but they don't spoil, do they?"

She got to her feet and pulled him to his. Ollie lifted his head slightly from where he was sleeping when they passed the kitchen door, but then settled back down as she and Jack went along the hallway to a bedroom that was somehow sparse but filled with her personality. She dug in the back of a linen closet and found a partial box of condoms, which was their only concession to practicality.

Once loose in the semidarkness of the bedroom, passion ruled. In a fevered heat, they undressed each other, clutching at chances to kiss, to caress, to feed the hungers that could not wait for the slow passage of a shirt being removed. It was like they'd never known lovemaking. Like the fires that raged in their hearts were out of control. Like their desperate needs could only be answered by each other and only at this moment.

There was a bit of awkward fumbling at first, but desire overrode their lack of familiarity and then all inhibitions dropped away. He carefully entered her, trying not to hurt her, trying to be gentle. But her legs grasped him hungrily, pulling him within her.

"I ain't made for breaking," she whispered in his ear.

And like a wild beast unchained, he mounted her, plunging into the paradise that was Cassie. He went deeper and deeper. Her legs and her fingers grasped him, bringing forth that mixture of pain and pleasure that only the deepest desire could evoke.

The pleasure climbed higher and higher. They were racing toward the heavens themselves. And then, just before their hearts would burst, they clung together and exploded into the stars. They floated there for a moment—a long, precious moment—then slowly floated back down to earth.

They lay in each other's arms for half an eternity, waiting to be able to breathe, waiting for their hearts to settle. He was afraid to speak. He was afraid it would break the preciousness that lay between them.

"Oh, baby," she whispered.

"Thank you," he replied.

They had been on a long journey and could again feel the earth beneath their feet. Nothing was changed, everything was changed. Neither wanted to let go. Jack didn't. And Cassie didn't seem to. He was so happy that he could laugh and cry at the same time.

Cassie lay in Jack's arms, in that netherworld halfway between dreams and reality. It was so pleasant there, like lying on a cloud. From Jack's even breathing, she guessed he was dozing. She felt ready to curl up herself; just nod off and sleep until their passions awoke them. But instead she stirred and pushed herself up on one elbow.

His eyes flickered for a moment, then opened wide. His smile was totally satisfied. "Hi, beautiful," he said softly.

"You seen an eye doctor lately?" she asked.

"Why?"

Cassie ran her fingers through the mess on her head. "I'm afraid I'm a bit disheveled."

"Disheveled is good."

"Oh, yeah?"

"Well, it depends on how you got disheveled." He rolled over, putting his arms around her waist and his head on her stomach. "And a body couldn't get it better than you did."

She kissed the top of his head.

"I have to get going," he said.

"I know."

He'd only been on loan, not hers to keep. She watched as he got to his feet, gathered up his clothes and went into the bathroom. Once the door was closed behind him, cutting off the light, she rolled over onto her back and stared through the dark at the ceiling.

It had been wonderful to have him here. He'd made her feel all woman; there were no traces of her gloom left after seeing Ron and his child. She was fine as she was. More than fine when Jack was around. She closed her eyes and let the warmth of his love surround her once more.

"Cass?"

She opened her eyes. Jack was dressed, sitting on the edge of the bed with a frown the size of Indiana on his lips.

"What's the matter?"

"The condom split."

She smiled at him, at his worries. "That's okay. We didn't really need it anyway." She wanted to tell him about her problem, but just couldn't. She just couldn't bring a shadow into their perfect evening.

"You sure?"

She reached for his hand and brought it to her lips. "Positive."

He leaned over to kiss her lips one last time, then with visible reluctance he pulled away. "Sleep tight," he whispered. "I'll give you a call tomorrow."

"Yeah." She yawned, then reality started slipping back. "Oh, wait. I'll be gone all day tomorrow, I'm going into Chicago for a closeout sale at one of my suppliers!"

"Give me a call when you get back, then," he said. "Let me know you got home all right."

She shrugged, then realized he probably couldn't see it in the dim light. "It'll probably be late."

"I'm a big boy, I'll be up." He kissed her again and then was gone, but the touch of his lips on hers lingered like the promise of sweet dreams in the night.

With a soft smile on her face, she rolled over and went to sleep.

Chapter Eight

Cassie looked at her watch and sighed. She had only a half hour before she was supposed to meet Burt and hadn't covered even a third of the aisles she was supposed to. She would like to tell herself that it was because the plumbing warehouse's closeout sale had too many things she was considering buying, but knew that wasn't quite the case. Her list had barely a dozen items on it.

It was more because of a certain tall ex-football player who seemed to charge into her thoughts at the slightest provocation. She couldn't believe how stupid she'd been last night, how weak and pitiful she'd been. Just because seeing Ron had thrown her for a loop, she'd practically begged Jack to stay the night.

Where had her courage been? What about her common sense? She needed to stay clear of relationships—not throw herself into them headfirst.

She stopped to look at some ceramic pedestal vanities. They were used, but seemed to be in good condition. A lot of rehabbers were looking for things like this. Jack might even—

No. She was not going to turn every business thought into one of Jack. She was not some moony young thing.

"Hey, Cassie. How are you?"

She turned and saw Lou Macri, the owner of the warehouse, hurrying toward her. "Hi, Lou," she said. "Sorry to hear you guys are closing up shop. Hope we can take a number of things off your hands."

"You name it and it's yours," he told her. "We need more like you in the business. Fair. Up-front. Honest."

How honest had she been with Jack on Sunday night? She'd used him to soothe her shattered ego. But was he thinking they'd started some grand romance?

"I was hoping we could have lunch," Lou was saying.

"Ah, I—"

"Yeah, I know," he said with a laugh. "A pretty girl like you has more boyfriends than you can shake a stick at. You don't want to waste your time with a married man who has eight grandkids."

"Lou," Cassie protested. "Going to lunch with you would not be a waste of time."

"Sure, sure." Then he hugged her again. "Hey, you ever in Florida, you come see us. Martha and me, we got ourselves a little place in Naples." He patted her back as he stepped away. "But it ain't too small. Got a couple of extra bedrooms for friends."

"Count me in," Cassie said before Lou sprinted off to greet another customer friend. See? She had lots of friends. Lots of places to go, things to do. She didn't need to cling to a certain ex-jock. A stinging behind her eyes contradicted her.

Cassie shook her head sharply. Damn, she was in a teary mood today. And she didn't have a practice or game or anything tonight. No softball. No soccer. Nothing. Not even swimming lessons for Jack's twins.

Double damn. No matter which way she turned, that guy was sitting in her brain. Clenching her jaw tight, Cassie forced her feet down the aisle. There was no reason for her to let a one-night stand discombobulate her like it had.

Yes, she and Jack had made love to each other. They'd had sex. It had been exciting. It had been great. But there was no reason for her to act like a fifth grader after her first kiss. They were adults. And adults didn't act like children. No matter how much they wanted to.

What she really didn't like was how Jack was dominating her thoughts. He was like Godzilla sitting in the back of her mind. That could not go on.

She still had a business to run. She still had her sports teams to play with. She still had a life of her own. And she needed to keep it that way. If anything, that was certainly something she should have learned from the disaster that had been her marriage. Make someone else the focus of your life and you were in deep trouble.

"Hey, Cassie. How you be?"

"Hi, Marty," Cassie replied. Marty Daniels owned a plumbing-supply store in Kouts, Indiana, and had a family of four boys. "How's the family?"

"Eating me out of house and home," the thin, balding man answered with a laugh. "And how's that big mutt of yours?"

"I think he's stopped growing," Cassie said. "But he eats enough to feed a pack of wolves."

"Maybe you just ought to turn him loose. A beast that big can kill his own dinner real easy."

"I'll think on it," Cassie said as they parted.

Yes, she'd think on Ollie. She'd think on her business. She'd think on her sports teams. She'd think on her family. She'd think on all the damn pieces of her life—on everything but an ex-football player and his blown-out knee. Although that was the only thing in his body that wasn't perfect.

She growled through her tightly closed teeth. Damn it, she was still doing it.

It wasn't like she objected to giving Jack a piece of her thoughts, but that was all. They'd only spent that one night together, for heaven's sake. It wasn't like they'd pledged their troth to each other. He might be the marrying kind, but she sure as heck wasn't.

"Hey, boss lady. Thought you got lost."

She spun around, blinking at Burt and his frowning face. "No," Cassie said, looking at her list. "I still have a few aisles to look at. Did you find much in your half?"

"A few things."

She glanced at his list, then ripped off hers to go with it. "Why don't you settle up with Lou for this stuff while I run through the last few aisles?"

"Sounds good."

Cassie hurried through the rest of the warehouse, determinedly adding a few more items before meeting Lou and Burt at the front of the building. They got the truck loaded amid cheerful bantering that left no room for moping. Then there was nothing left but the drive home.

She had to get things back under her control, she told herself over and over again as she sped along the tollway. She had to stop all this moping and crazy dreaming, she admonished silently as she got off at the South Bend exit. She would have to make it clear that last night had been a onetime thing, she vowed as she pulled into the store parking lot.

By the time Cassie was driving home, she was feeling good. Feeling determined. Feeling strong. She could pull herself away from Jack. No problem.

Ollie greeted Cassie effusively when she stepped in the door, letting her scratch his ears. Then, tiring of that mushy stuff, he ran to get his leash. Apparently his energy level was on high.

"Hey," Cassie said. "I take it you missed me a whole lot."

He wagged his tail in agreement and Cassie realized how much she loved the big guy. She always knew where he stood. He didn't have mood swings, nor would he walk out on her. She put his leash on and they went outside.

"Jack said to call him as soon as I got in," Cassie said.

Ollie stopped as he checked out the scents on a clump of evergreen bushes.

"Like who made him boss, huh?" It would be a good place to start asserting herself.

Her dog grinned at her as he added his two cents to the string of messages that the neighborhood dogs had "engraved" on the bushes.

"I've been taking care of business for a long time now," she said as they moved to the next message station, a young locust tree in the parkway. "And I imagine I'm going to keep on doing that for an even longer time."

They reached the end of the block and Cassie turned around to head back home.

"So I don't think I'm going to call him tonight." She pulled on the leash to settle Ollie into a more sedate walk by her side. "No use starting something that'll just bring us all problems. It'll be better for everyone if we just leave things the way they are."

"Daddy's still grumpy."

Jack gave Mary Alice what he hoped was a properly stern look.

"I know," Mary Louise said. "Just like he was last night."

"I wasn't grumpy last night," Jack said. Maybe a little concerned since Cassie hadn't called, but that was all. "And I'm not grumpy this morning."

"Are too," the twins chorused, as they stuffed waffles into their mouths.

He wanted to shout "Am not!" but he knew better. His daughters were "Are too/Am not" professionals. Tournament champion material. There was no way he could compete.

"Eat your breakfast," he said, turning his attention to the paper before him. Cassie hadn't gotten in all that late last night—he'd seen lights on in her house by nine. So why hadn't she bothered to call?

Jack stared at the paper and tried to make sense of the ink spots on the white background. And he would have if it wasn't for the snickering that erupted.

"Girls." Aunt Hattie turned from the sink where she was rinsing off some dishes. "Settle down, please."

"Daddy's got his paper upside down," Mary Louise said.

"You can't read that way," Mary Alice added.

Jack squinted his eyes as he focused on the newspaper before him. Damn. No wonder he couldn't read the stupid articles.

The snickering turned into laughter. Jack just sighed and turned his paper over.

"Clean off your plates," Aunt Hattie said. "Then go upstairs and get dressed."

Jack watched glumly as his daughters did as they were told. If it weren't for his aunt, his kids wouldn't have a clue as to what adult authority meant. They gave him a syrup-sticky kiss before skipping off to their rooms. He sighed.

"You've got to quit arguing with them, Jimmy Jack. You're the father. And a father's word should be the law."

"I know."

"Although, I'll grant you, it is hard for a man to raise little girls. Girls need a woman's hand. Someone who won't be taken in by their little tricks."

Jack felt a heaviness around his heart. They'd had this conversation before. It was Aunt Hattie in her caretaker role—someone sitting in until he got things sorted out permanently. Except he didn't expect things to change.

"How's your young lady?" Aunt Hattie asked. "She feeling better?"

How would he know? He hadn't talked to her since Sunday night. Or rather, yesterday morning. "Fine, I'm sure."

"She suits you well," his aunt said, turning from the sink and wiping her hands on a dishcloth. "Right well."

"We're just good friends, Aunt Hattie."

His aunt snorted in an all-knowing, old-woman way. "If the Lord wanted men and women to be friends, he would have taught women how to spit, throw a baseball, and aim when they peed."

"Cassie can throw a ball as well as I can," he said and got to his feet. "I have to get to work. See you tonight."

"You're getting up on that high horse again, Jimmy Jack," she called after him as he sped out the door. "Ain't nobody won a lady's hand by letting their pride get in the way."

Who said he was trying to win Cassie's hand? he asked himself as he pulled the minivan out of the garage. Neither of them was looking for something permanent. And didn't he have the right to be a little miffed that she hadn't called? She'd said she would. He frowned at the traffic ahead of him. At least, he was pretty sure she had.

But Aunt Hattie was right about what she called his "high horse." He ought to find out what had really happened before he jumped to conclusions. He turned at the next corner and headed downtown. Her truck was in the store parking lot.

Jack parked his minivan and dropped to the ground, working on finding a smile. He needed to learn not to take everything so personally. Hell, she probably had a real good reason for not calling.

"Hi, folks," he said heartily as he stepped through the door. "A top of the morning to you all."

Ellen smiled at him and returned his greeting. Ollie appeared around the counter and bore down on him, but Cassie didn't even smile. He felt the hairs on the back of his neck prickle, but he forced down the irritation.

"Morning, Cassie," he said.

"Good morning, Mr. Merrill."

He frowned. Obviously, something was amiss. Jack moved to where Cassie was and leaned with his elbows on the countertop. A little part of him said to leave, that this was the part where he was supposed to beg and plead and grovel a bit. But he forced his feet to stay put.

"Get in late?" he asked.

"No." She shook her head. "I didn't think it was late."

"Oh." He looked around the room for a moment. A polar bear would sure enjoy the climate here. "I was just wondering."

She barely glanced at him, shuffling some damn papers.

"You know," he said. "While I was waiting to hear from you."

"I'm sorry," she said.

Jack heard the words but he figured they'd been spoken by another person. It couldn't have been Cassie. There wasn't anything sorry in her voice, expression, or eyes.

"I didn't realize that calling you was an order," she said. "I thought it was just a suggestion."

What in the hell was going on? What did she want from him? "Is anything wrong?"

"Should there be?"

Jack had always thought of himself as an adult. Someone who'd been back of the barn enough times to know that when a woman answered your question with another question, that meant you were standing knee-deep in a manure pile.

Obviously Cassie was having second thoughts about having made love with him. And only one thing came to mind—she'd measured him against her ex, and Jimmy Jack Merrill had come up short. A man didn't have to have an overload of pride to find that hard to swallow.

"Well," he said, grabbing on to a hundred-pound bag of cheer. "I see you made it back safe and sound."

"I always have, so far."

"Well, that's good." He straightened and took a deep breath. "I just wanted to make sure that the girls' swimming lesson was still on for tonight."

"I would have called you if there was a problem."

"Oh, right." He forced himself to look bright and chipper. "What was I thinking of? I mean, you're always calling. Keeping in touch and all."

The look in her eyes would have wiped out a division of elite fighting troops, dropped them in their tracks at two hundred paces or more, but it left him untouched.

"Is there anything else, Mr. Merrill?"

"No, not at all." He backed off toward the door. "Just glad to see that things are going well for you."

Her eyes stayed hard as steel, with not a single blink.

"See you tonight." He turned and was about to step out the door when he stopped. "Hey, feel free to call and chat anytime you want, now, hear?"

He stomped out down the steps and on toward the parking lot. He wished that he still played ball and that there was a game today so he could spend an hour or two whacking some three-hundred-pound monsters—maybe even getting into a few fights.

Opening the door of his vehicle, Jack threw himself in. He started the motor, then yanked on the seat belt, trying to fasten it before it spent too much time beeping at him. Unfortunately, the thing tended to stick. He gave it another pull.

"Son of a bitch," he exclaimed, looking at the torn piece of seat belt in his hand.

He threw the belt aside and sat there, staring out the car window. Aunt Hattie was right. Men and women weren't meant to be friends. And he and Cassie apparently weren't meant to be lovers, either.

Jack leaned back and pinched his eyes. It was almost eight o'clock. The kids would be home from their swimming lessons and done with their dinner, probably watching some reruns on television.

He hadn't made it home yet. This morning he had been a little down. This evening he was grumpy—extremely so. There was no need to subject the girls to that, so he'd called Aunt Hattie and told her he had to work.

And work he did—finished up two articles that weren't due for another month and started outlining one of the courses he would teach this fall. And he hadn't thought of Cassie. At least, not much. That was the major advantage of all those years of football. It had given him the discipline to concentrate on what he had to. Now that he was done with his writing, though, she came into his consciousness with a flying leap.

Damn. Damn. Why did she still have to be hung up on Ronnie the Wimp? What the hell had he done for her lately?

Jack's computer had gone into the screen-saver routine, electronic frogs croaking in an electronic pond. He stared at them.

He loved his girls dearly. He was financially comfortable and doing what he damned well pleased. Life couldn't be better.

Except along toward the wee hours of the morning, when the kids were fast asleep and the house was too silent for words. That was when he really noticed how lonely he was; how he just ached to roll over and hug a woman to himself.

"Oh, hell," he muttered. "Better get out of here and grab a sandwich before I get really mopey."

He was about to stand when he noticed a little mail sign flickering in the corner of his screen. Switching on his mail program, he quickly flipped through the E-mail messages that had come in during the day. The first three were just chitchat from friends. The last wasn't. It was a reply to his inquiry about Cassie's father.

Jack quickly read through the short message. It didn't hold a lot of information, but it was enough to start on. He wasn't sure he really wanted to see Cassie again, but he did need to tell her what he'd found.

He sent the message to his printer for a hard copy and, as the data was being printed, dialed her telephone number. Her voice came on the line and told him to leave his message. Jack hung up, deciding to drop by her house instead. She might just be out in the yard with Ollie.

He drove on home and saw her truck was in the driveway. Cassie was waiting at the door by the time he walked over.

"What do you want?" she asked.

Jack stopped in his tracks. Man, that was a fine welcome. "I just came by to visit my old buddy, Ollie," he said, indicating the dog and his wagging tail.

"I'm sorry I didn't call when I got home," she snapped. "But I was tired."

He didn't want a repeat of their earlier discussion. He was here on business and once that was over, he would be on his way. Sure, he'd enjoyed their time together, but he wasn't so hard up for companionship that he had to beg to be a substitute for Ron the Wimp.

"And then things turned busy for me when I got to work," Cassie went on.

"What's all this about?" he asked.

"I know that you feel you owe me," Cassie said. "And while I don't entirely agree with that, I sure as hell don't agree that you own me."

He could feel an aggravation growing and his stare turned into a glare.

"So I don't feel that I have to report my each and every movement to you."

Jack shook his head. "How about if I go back home, count to ten, and come back? Then we both can start over."

This time it was Cassie's turn to glare.

"I dropped by because I got some news about your father."

Her face paled and he forgot all his annoyance. Opening the door, he stepped in. "Why don't we sit down?"

"What did you—"

He didn't like the way she looked, so, taking her arm, he led her into the living room. "I want you to sit down first."

She chose the nearest chair, a straight-backed wooden one, to sit in, folding her hands in her lap and curling her bare feet around the legs. She looked so worried that Jack began talking fast.

"I don't have that much yet."

She nodded but still continued looking into his eyes. There was so much there—trust, worry, pain, hope. He pulled up a chair and sat down in front of her.

"He was in the navy like you said. Enlisted in Pierre, South Dakota."

A frown mixed into the worry lines creasing her face. Most likely the man had never told his family he'd lived in South Dakota. "And sometime while he was in the navy, he legally changed his name."

"Why?"

"I don't know. At least, not at the moment."

Something in her eyes caught his attention. Was it pain?

"But there's no indication that the change was made to hide a criminal record."

Ollie had ambled over and laid his head in her lap, and Cassie stroked him while she gazed out toward the street. "More lies," she said slowly. "Every time I try to find the real him, I just find more lies."

"I take it your father never mentioned South Dakota?"

She shook her head. "He talked about the navy but nothing about before that."

"Nothing about parents? Aunts? Uncles? Relatives of any kind?"

Again she shook her head. "He talked about his great-grandpa Horace. We thought it was Horace Waldo Fogarty. You know, the writer. But then we found out Fogarty didn't have any descendants."

They shared a long silence, Jack watching Cassie while she looked out her front window, appearing to be studying the street scene. She looked so vulnerable even as she seemed to fight for control. He forgot all of his earlier annoyance. She needed him and he had to be there for her.

She turned to him again. "What now?" she asked. "Can we find out more about him?"

"I can try."

Silence enveloped them again, but color was returning to Cassie's cheeks and her petting of Ollie became more vigorous. Jack wasn't surprised. She was a tough, resilient lady.

"I'm sorry I was so crabby." Her voice was quiet and held a trace of reluctance, making her sound like his daughters when they had to apologize for something.

He smiled at her. "It caught me by surprise."

She laughed and smiled back. "I had a nice time the other night," she said quietly.

"I had a great time." He'd hoped it had been better than nice, but nice was a start. "A super time."

"So did I." A beautiful flush filled her cheeks. "I just didn't want to sound like I was gushing."

"Nothing wrong with a little gush now and again. Helps keep a fella's ego up."

"I was kind of scared."

"Of what?" he asked.

"Everything. Nothing." A little-girl smile filled her face. "I was afraid I was getting preoccupied with you. Afraid I was losing myself to some guy again."

"I'm not trying to own you. Honest. I just like being with you." He grinned at her.

She laughed. "I guess my marriage left a few scars that I'm still having trouble with."

"You were young," Jack said. "You made the mistake of marrying a jerk."

She shrugged. "I guess."

Cassie looked so appealing that he wanted to just crush her to his chest, but that wasn't the way things were done in the nineties. You felt things out, first. You determined what the object of your affection really wanted. You—

He stared into her eyes. Soft, warm, loving. The hell with it. He stood and snatched her up, pulling her to his chest. And held her tight as he kissed the top of her head.

"From now on," he murmured into her hair, "don't have anything more to do with jerks. Understand?"

"Yes, sir."

He just held her, feeling a peace settle in his soul. Somewhere along the line, his life had been blessed with a touch of magic and he had the urge to never let go.

Chapter Nine

Cassie hurried up the walk, hoping that the girls had been able to keep their little secret. Not that she'd been too sure she would be dropping by here on Father's Day if you'd asked her a few days ago. But she and Jack seemed to have found a new understanding. She was no longer letting her fears rule her.

She knocked on the door and a few minutes later it was opened by Jack, a section of the Sunday newspaper in his hand and a surprised look on his face—a look that turned into a smile of genuine pleasure.

"Hi," he said. "This is a nice surprise. I thought you were spending the day with your dad."

"I'm on my way there. I just thought I'd stop by and say hello."

His smile grew, as did the spark in his eyes. "Well, hello, then."

"Hello, yourself."

They stood there and smiled at each other, their eyes saying all sorts of things that their lips seemed to be unable to say.

Suddenly the birds seemed to be singing sweeter and the sun seemed to be shining brighter.

"Cassie!" Mary Louise exclaimed.

The twins had bounced out onto the front porch.

"What are you guys doing out there?" Mary Alice asked.

The spell broken, Cassie laughed. "I'm not a guy," she said. "Can't you two tell?"

The twins groaned, causing her and Jack to share a smile.

"Land's sake, Jimmy Jack. Are you going to leave that young lady standing on the porch like she were selling magazines or floor brushes?" Aunt Hattie stepped out on the porch and took Cassie's hand, pulling her into the house. "Come in, dear. And please excuse my nephew's manners. I don't know where that boy's mind goes sometimes."

Cassie tried not to stare in astonishment as the suddenly friendly Aunt Hattie pulled her along into the house. Cassie glanced over her shoulder, wondering if she should call for help, but the twins were just giggling and hopping about like munchkins on an overdose of sugar. Jack shrugged and smiled at her.

"Please, sit down, Cassandra."

Nobody called her that, not unless they wanted a bloody nose, but Cassie wasn't going to rock the boat. She sat down without saying a word.

"Would you like some iced tea?" Aunt Hattie asked. "It's such a pleasant day. Just right for something cool."

"Yes, please," Cassie replied. She actually did like iced tea, although she would have drunk it no matter what.

The girls dashed off toward the kitchen with Aunt Hattie following at a more sedate pace, leaving Cassie alone with Jack. His smile held a world of understanding.

"So, how are you?" Jack asked, sitting in the chair next to her.

She knew it wasn't a generic conversation-opener. That look in his eyes said he knew about the demons haunting her.

"Okay." She looked away for a minute, not to avoid confiding in him, but to gather strength from the peace around them. "I've been thinking about him a lot. My other dad, I mean. I keep trying to come up with good reasons for his lies, but I can't. I just can't think of anything that justifies all the lies."

He reached out and took her hand. She found herself clinging to it shamelessly, but she didn't care if that broke her rules. She was tired of her rules for now.

"We may never find out his reason."

"Maybe I just need to find out something about him that isn't a lie."

"Here we are." Aunt Hattie came into the living room, carrying a tray, followed by the bouncy twins.

"Thank you," Cassie murmured, taking a tall glass filled with tons of ice. Jack took one after her.

"Now?" The twins sang out the question. "Can we do it now?"

At Aunt Hattie's nod, they dashed off upstairs but were flying back down in a matter of seconds. Their great-aunt just sat there smiling, not even bothering to correct the girls for running up and down the stairs. It must be that holidays were special to the woman.

"Here you are, Daddy." Mary Louise handed Jack a small gift-wrapped package.

"Happy Father's Day." Mary Alice gave him an identical one.

Jack sat there with a gift in each hand, smiling at his daughters, but his eyes held a touch of panic.

"If each girl held her gift for you," Cassie said, "you could probably open them together."

She knew it was silly, but Jack's grateful smile was better than winning the lottery. Maybe her heart was just flighty today. Maybe it was hungering to be part of something. Maybe it was just a weak moment.

After some initial fumbling, Jack got the hang of things and managed to work the wrappings off the little boxes. He even managed to open each box at almost at the same time.

"Cuff links," he cried, and hugged both girls to himself. "They're very nice. Thank you."

"We each had to buy one."

"Yeah, on account of that's all the money we had."

"Cassie helped us."

"She really did, Daddy. She made the store people give us two boxes."

He turned another smile on her but Cassie wasn't sure what it meant this time. His baby blues were no longer placid and peaceful. An indefinable tension had crept into the room. Her mouth went dry, her hands turned sweaty. Her heart began to race. It was either lean forward and meet those lips head-on, or look away.

Cassie turned so that her glance included Aunt Hattie. "We talked it over when I came to take the girls to their swimming lessons," she told Jack, keeping her gaze from meeting his. "Aunt Hattie didn't mind if I took the girls shopping."

"I thought it was a right sweet offer," his aunt replied.

Cassie hadn't been sure what the older woman had thought; she hadn't said much of anything. "I was glad to help," Cassie said as the girls dashed out of the room again. "And it was easy to run over to the mall after their swimming lesson."

"We appreciate your help, Cassandra. We surely do." Aunt Hattie looked sharply at her nephew. "All of us."

"Right. Thanks for your help." Jack quickly glanced toward the kitchen, from where some minor bickering floated out. "Although it wasn't necessary."

Cassie shook her head and laughed. He was just like her brothers. They liked doing for others but didn't like others to do for them. "The girls wanted to get you something."

"I know. But I don't really need anything."

"You may not need the gettin'," Aunt Hattie said. "But the children need the givin'."

Before Jack could reply the girls popped back into the room, carrying a plate of cookies between them.

"We got cookies."

"We made them ourselves."

"Mostly."

"Aunt Hattie helped."

"Those cookies were what you decided on," Aunt Hattie replied. "That's what matters."

Cassie took one when they stopped proudly in front of her. "Peanut butter. My favorite." She took a big bite. "And really good."

"Thank you," the twins said in perfect harmony and went on to offer the cookies to the others.

Cassie let her eyes wander back to Jack now that her heart was under control again. He was occupied with the girls and she was free to gaze at him all she wanted. Free to let her heart warm at the pride in his eyes, to wonder what it would be like to walk with her hand in his.

Free to realize it was time to go.

Cassie finished her cookie and got to her feet. "Well, I really need to be going," she said. "I need to get to my dad's by two to help Sam make the lasagna."

"Aw, do you have to go?" Mary Louise moaned.

"We were gonna play badminton," Mary Alice added.

"Cassie's daddy would be sad if she didn't come," Jack said, getting to his feet.

"But we're sad if she hasta go," Mary Louise said.

"Maybe your daddy will take you over to the park for a while," Aunt Hattie said.

The girls hesitated. "We were gonna help you."

"With Daddy's dinner."

"Oh, don't worry about that." The woman pushed herself out of her chair. "You know I work better alone."

"Can we go to the park, Daddy?"

Jack nodded. "If Aunt Hattie doesn't need our help."

"Go," she said, making a shooing motion with her hands. "Just get out from underfoot."

The girls looked at each other in their Sunday clothes. "We can't play in dresses."

"We gotta change."

"That'll be another three years now," Jack groaned as the girls raced upstairs. He put his hand on Cassie's back. "Gives me time to walk you to your truck."

They started toward the door. Cassie was aware of Aunt Hattie following along after them, but more aware of Jack's hand on the small of her back. And of how, if she leaned back just slightly, his arm would be around her.

"Always did work better alone," Aunt Hattie said suddenly, her voice sharp. "That's what happens if you aren't careful. You work alone so long that you don't think there's any other way."

Cassie turned and found the older woman's eyes on her. Their gazes locked for just a moment, then Aunt Hattie hurried off down the hall. Cassie stared after her, until Jack nudged her.

"Something wrong?" he asked.

She shook her head and hurried outside. Was that what was happening to her? she asked herself, though. Did she want to be alone only because she'd been that way for so long?

"Wish your dad a Happy Father's Day from us," Jack was saying.

"Yeah. I will." She shed her moody thoughts and smiled up at him. "Have fun at the park."

"It'd be more fun if you were along," he said. "Then maybe the girls wouldn't gang up on me."

"I see," she answered with a laugh. "That's what you want me *for*—for protection."

"Oh, not hardly." His voice had gotten hoarse as he slipped his arms around her. "I can think of a lot of better things that we could do together than protect me from my kids."

She looked up into his eyes and felt his heat surround her, engulf her in a fire of desire all her own. The green yard all alive with summer disappeared. There was nothing but the two of them. Nothing but the hunger that was growing between them. Nothing but the touch of his hands on her back and the nearness of his embrace.

She met his lips as they came down to hers and a rush of light swept over her. Her mouth tasted his sweetness, and she knew a yearning that she'd never known. Life could be so perfect, so magical, if she would just let it. His lips on hers whispered all sorts of promises that only her heart could make sense of, but she just cuddled closer into his embrace.

"We're ready!" two little voices sang out.

Jack let go of Cassie with a reluctance that matched her own. His smile was shaky as his eyes found hers. She smiled back, starting to believe that this might only be the beginning.

"Fiona and Alex's wedding is next weekend," she said. "Will you all come and protect me from my family's matchmaking?"

"Gladly." He kissed her lightly on her lips as if to seal his agreement.

"Would you believe I'm missing a softball game for this?" Cassie grumbled under her breath as the minister went over the instructions once more.

Jack just laughed, seeing through her gruff exterior. "You'd rather be here," he said.

"Okay, so I'd rather be here," she admitted reluctantly. "But enough's enough. Does he think we're idiots? We understood the first three times."

"Maybe he wants tomorrow to be perfect."

They were at Clements Woods for Fiona and Alex's wedding rehearsal. A rather unusual setting for the wedding, but apparently the place had special meaning for Cassie and her sisters. From Cassie's attitude, though, you would think it held only bad memories. She insisted on standing off to the side as if nothing here was touching her.

"Is the wedding going to be here because of you guys rescuing the swans?" he asked her.

She frowned at him. "How'd you know about that?"

"Your dad told me."

"He tell you about the old lady too?"

"What old lady?"

Cassie sighed, looking like she'd been backed into a corner. "After we cut Juliet free, we met this old lady. She said something about us fighting for Juliet's love, so some spirits would come back and fight for ours. It was dumb."

The minister seemed to feel they'd gotten enough instruction and dismissed them. After Alex reminded everyone to head for Adam's house, Jack walked with Cassie through the shade toward the parking lot. Her story nagged at him—not because of the improbability of it, but because something about it felt so inevitable.

"So you don't believe in spirits?" he asked.

She tugged lightly at a passing branch, pulling the leaves through her hand. "It's just all so unbelievable. That there's something out there that cares whether Fiona or Sam or I find true love. Or even that such a thing exists."

"Well, Fiona looks like she found true love," Jack observed. "Did any spirits come and fight for her?"

Cassie snorted. "No, they left Fiona to do all the fighting herself and that must have been a real sight from what Alex says—mousy little Fiona charging into this ritzy restaurant to tell Alex off."

"Maybe she was possessed," Jack suggested.

"Possessed?"

"You know. By spirits."

Cassie just gave him a look and climbed into his minivan. "Don't tell me you believe in that nonsense, too."

"Oh, I don't know," he said lightly and concentrated on pulling out of the parking space. "I hope the girls won't have been too much trouble."

"They'll be fine. Rosemary and Nancy have managed larger herds before."

Jack just drove on to Cassie's brother Adam's house in silence. He wasn't really worried about the twins. They generally behaved pretty well. It had been more of a straw to grasp at. Anything to avoid thinking about Cassie and her spirits.

Anything to avoid wondering why the whole idea didn't scare him like it ought to. What was it he wanted these days? He used to think he just wanted to be left alone, to wander in and out of light relationships like a kid playing hide-and-seek. He used to think that he was happy alone, that the kids and his work were enough. Now he felt as uncertain as a freshman at his first football practice. He pulled into Adam's driveway behind Samantha and her father.

"I'm going to change my clothes," Cassie said. "The kids should be around back if you want to check on them."

"Anything I can do to help with dinner?"

"Convince Larry that steaks don't have to be turned into ashes to be done."

He watched her hurry off into the house with Sam and then wandered around to the backyard. The kids were all playing some game with a ball that looked like nothing he'd ever seen before. They were all playing enthusiastically, though, so he guessed the name of the game didn't matter.

Just as putting a name to his relationship with Cassie probably didn't matter. He should just relax and enjoy it.

"Your kids are great."

Jack looked at the young red-haired woman who had come over to him.

"I'm Rosemary," she said. "Adam's wife."

"I knew that," Jack replied.

"Sure."

"But I do appreciate the hint."

"Missy loves having the twins around," she went on. "She's finally got someone close to her age."

A group of young girls, including the twins and, he assumed, Missy, had broken away from the game and had suddenly charged an older boy. He ran away in good-natured terror.

"Do you roughhouse with your girls?" Rosemary asked. "Like you would if they were boys?"

"Naw." Jack shook his head. "I don't want to get hurt. I've got enough scars from my playing days. I don't want to wind up a total wreck."

Rosemary shook her head. "Cassie said you were really funny."

"That's cruel," he told her.

"I mean humorous." She frowned at him. "You know what I mean."

Jack just grunted, still watching his girls. They really acted differently when Aunt Hattie wasn't around. That was probably normal, seeing as how his aunt was the one who did most of the civilizing tasks.

"That's good, you know."

"Huh?" He'd stepped out of the conversation again.

"We were talking about your sense of humor."

"Oh, yeah," Jack replied. "You mean my good one."

Rosemary laughed. "You can't survive in this family without it."

That should have scared him, should have made him feel claustrophobic. But it didn't. It filled him with a comfortable sense of rightness.

"Say, Adam and I are taking a bunch of the kids down to my folks' farm for the Fourth of July. Missy would love it if your girls could come with us."

"That's nice of you to offer," Jack said. "But they really couldn't—"

"It's not a big deal," Rosemary assured him. "They'd sleep in sleeping bags in the girls' room, maybe get a few rides around the barnyard on old Billy, and catch lightning bugs in the evening."

Jack started to shake his head and repeat his gratitude for the offer when his eyes stopped on the girls, whispering conspiratorially with Missy. They would love going to the farm. They would love the sense of family. Outside of him and Aunt Hattie, they didn't have anybody else. To go someplace with a troop of make-believe cousins would be their idea of heaven.

"Hi," Cassie said, coming up next to him and slipping an arm around his waist.

She'd changed into shorts and a bare-midriff blouse. The outfit was no doubt comfortable for her, given the pleasant evening breeze. But seeing as how it highlighted her smooth muscles, it didn't relax him one teeny-tiny bit.

"Well." Rosemary stood, grinning as if she could see his sudden preoccupation. "Guess I'd better get going."

"Good idea," Cassie said.

Rosemary stuck her tongue out at her sister-in-law. "I was going to take care of the desserts," she said. "But it looks like you already have yours."

"Oh, you're so clever." Cassie shook her head. "You've obviously been living with my brother too long."

"You think about the Fourth," Rosemary told Jack before getting on her way.

"What was that all about?" Cassie asked.

"She invited the girls to go to her parents' farm over the Fourth of July."

"Really? They'll have a great time. Her parents are just wonderful. They love having the kids there."

Jack looked away from her assumption that he had accepted the offer. "I feel strange about letting them go," he said. "It's not like we're part of the family or anything."

She laughed and tightened her hold on his waist. "What is this—your macho Merrill pride again?" she teased. "You don't know my family very well yet. They just love to share stuff. If you ask Rosemary and Adam, they'll tell you that you'd be doing them a favor by letting the twins go, that Missy would have somebody to play with."

"I just don't like to impose on anybody."

She sighed and leaned even closer, letting her tongue flick into his ear. "If they go to the farm, we could go away for the holiday, too."

He gripped her waist even harder. "I'll give you three years to stop that, lady."

"And if I don't?"

He pulled her to himself and kissed her. But not long. In fact, he was just getting started when it dawned on him that it was getting very noisy nearby. He looked up to see a gang of kids hooting and hollering at them. Some were rolling around on the ground, while others made gagging sounds.

"Can I kill them?" he asked.

"I don't think so," Cassie told him. "I think the parents prefer to do that kind of thing themselves."

"Hey, kids!" Cassie's father shouted. "Time to eat."

The screaming horde charged past their grandfather toward the food tables. His sweet little girls, pushing and shoving, were in the midst of them all.

"Where would we go?" he asked, his eyes still on the girls.

"How about one of the little towns along Lake Michigan?" Cassie suggested. "There are some great bed-and-breakfasts along the coast."

"You think we could still get reservations? The Fourth's less than two weeks away."

"Dad's joined some innkeepers' association. I'll see if he can find us something."

The idea of a weekend away with Cassie was more than tempting. It was proving irresistible. Just the two of them. No schedules. No dogs. No worries.

"Do you, Fiona, take Alex as your lawfully wedded husband? In sickness and in—"

Cassie's eyes were on Fiona, facing Alex in the dappled sunshine of the clearing. Behind them, garlands of roses had been draped on the lower branches of the trees to form a canopy over her and Alex and the minister. Fiona was the proverbial bride—so happy that she radiated like the summer sun.

Cassie looked away suddenly, blinking back a stinging behind her eyes, and stared out over the lake. She was happy for Fiona and Alex; she really was. But she was also scared. Somewhere deep inside she was so scared that she would never be as happy as Fiona was today. That she would never find someone she could tell everything and anything to and know that she would still be loved. That all her big talk of not wanting to be close to anyone ever again was just that—big talk.

Taking a deep breath, Cassie looked around at the crowd gathered in the woods. Everyone they cared about was here. Dad was looking so proud and happy that you would think he was going to burst, although he had to be wishing Mom was still here to share in the day. But in a way, she was. Fiona was wearing the same dress that Mom had worn when she'd married Dad. And so much of what she and Fiona and Sam were now, was due to her raising.

Cassie's gaze misted over and she saw their first mother and dad as they had looked in their wedding picture. Fiona looked so much like their birth mother and Alex somehow looked like their father—all eager and proud and happy. They had been so in love then. That love had to have grown stronger until it was big enough to include them all. It had to have.

"Do you, Alex, take Fiona—"

Cassie awoke from her thoughts to see Romeo and Juliet swim into sight, coming around a finger on the east side of the lake. Cassie's smile grew. The two swans would bring good fortune with them. She felt a peace, a sweet certainty wash over her, and brought her gaze back to the crowd.

Jack was off to one side with a twin in each arm, holding them up so that they could see what was happening. The girls looked enthralled. Jack's expression was harder to read. But then his eyes met hers and she felt his tenderness surround her like velvet, turning her brain to mush and setting her heart racing.

Even from a distance, even without words, he made her feel cared for. Made her feel warm and safe and secure. She could relax with him. She could be grumpy or tired or loving and he was understanding. They were friends. Equals.

Lovers, a little voice reminded her, and she felt her cheeks warm at the memory.

"You may now kiss the bride."

Cassie awoke from her thoughts and joined the others in cheering and clapping. Arm in arm, Fiona and Alex walked through the crowd. It was a good thing they'd opted for an outdoor ceremony. The way the brothers were carrying on, they probably would have brought the roof down if they'd been inside a church. She closed her eyes for a moment, feeling almost weak from all the emotion in the air, then followed along with Sam.

Cassie watched as their father wished Fiona and Alex well. They looked so in love. Cassie thought of all the hard times she'd given Fiona when they were kids and was glad her sister had finally found real happiness.

"I hope you guys are really happy," Cassie said, when it was her turn to hug them. "You both deserve the best."

"Maybe it'll be your turn next," Fiona replied with a glance that Cassie assumed was in Jack's direction.

Cassie's voice faltered slightly, but she tried not to let it show. "Oh, don't hold your breath," she said. "That dress would look terrible on me."

"It would look perfect on you," Fiona corrected, ever the older sister. "Stop putting yourself down."

"Yeah, well, the dress might be okay but the institution wouldn't fit," Cassie said and glanced back at the others waiting to wish the happy couple well. "Hey, my time's up. See you later."

She moved out of the way, following some of the others up the path toward the shelter where the tables had been set up. Everything looked perfect. The tables were covered with white cloths, and garlands of roses and greenery trailed down the center of each. At the far end of the shelter, the food tables were set up. The wedding cake had the place of honor. It somehow seemed such a symbol of the fragility and sweetness of love that Cassie had to look away.

Her gaze fell on the pile of dinner rolls at the end of the buffet table. She grabbed up a couple and slipped through the crowd toward the lake. No one was on the beach when she got there, but the swans were hovering just offshore.

"Hi, guys," she called out to them. "How you been?"

The swans swam toward her, taking a cautious zigzag kind of route. She tore a roll into pieces and threw them out onto the water. "Fiona got married just a few minutes ago. So you two aren't the only happy couple around here anymore."

The swans gobbled up the bread, which attracted a pair of ducks. Cassie tore up more bread and threw the pieces across a wider area. She found herself wandering back through the years, to all the times she'd come here. When they'd rescued Juliet. When they'd gotten adopted by the Scotts and Cassie was so scared that somehow she would still wreck it for everybody. When she'd been about to leave for college. When she'd gotten divorced. Whenever she was hurting or scared or uncertain. This had to be one of the few places where everything was always swell.

"Hi, Cassie," a little voice called out.

"Whatcha doing?"

Cassie turned to find Jack and the girls were walking toward her. She smiled, somehow feeling it was right for them to be here now.

"I tried to tell them you might be busy," Jack said.

"She ain't busy, Daddy."

"She was just standing here."

"I was so busy," Cassie said. "I was feeding the swans."

"Can we feed them?" they asked.

"Sure." She handed each of them half of her last dinner roll. "Just tear it into pieces and throw it out onto the water."

While the girls did that, Jack came over to take her hand. "Did I tell you how beautiful you look?" Jack asked.

She glanced down at her dress. It was plain, styled almost like a T-shirt, with short sleeves and a collarless neckline, but was mid-calf in length and belted. And made of deep red silk.

"Fiona promised I wouldn't have to wear lots of ruffles," she said, not knowing how to respond to his compliment, or to the look in his eyes. It sent a shiver of desire coursing down her back and made something in her long to slide up a little closer to Jack.

"I think you'd probably look great in anything," he said. "Or nothing," he added in a whisper.

Cassie felt her cheeks burn with a sudden heat and turned to watch the girls. Their tosses didn't get the bread anywhere near the swans, but the ducks were delighted. They rushed madly for each piece of bread as the girls squealed in delight.

Cassie had never been one to show her emotions that openly—either her hungers or her excitement. "Sam thought these dresses were great because we could wear them for other occasions," she said offhandedly. "I don't know where Sam hangs out, but I can't see me wearing it to work or to one of my softball games."

"Maybe you need to start going out to other types of places," he said.

Fudge cakes, she'd made a stupid remark. He must think she was hinting for him to take her to fancy places. "Or maybe I could just fancy up the places I go to," she added quickly. "You know, the store might be better off with a little classiness."

"Maybe we should plan something special for our little holiday," he said.

The fire in his eyes lit the kindling around her heart and for some reason made her nervous as a girl on her first date. It wasn't exactly a bad sort of nervous. In fact, it wasn't bad at all. It was more like the slow climb up to the top of the roller coaster—you knew the ride would be wild and fantastic, but the waiting tied your stomach up in knots.

Not that she wanted him to know that. "I already did plan some special stuff," she said. "I thought we'd do some biking and some hiking and maybe some sailing."

"That all?" His voice tickled a spot deep inside her.

She grinned at him. "We'll just have to see, won't we?"

Chapter Ten

"Okay, okay." Cassie stepped out of her kitchen, wiping her hands on a small towel. It was hours past dinner. Who would be dropping by now? "I'm coming."

Ollie was barking at the front door and wagging his tail at the same time, not that that meant it was somebody they knew and liked. The giant dog always wagged his tail when he barked.

Cassie flicked on the outside light and looked through the side windows. She felt a grin rip through her defenses. "It's Jack," she told her fuzzy companion. She quickly opened the door. "Hi. This is a surprise."

"A good one, I hope."

His eyes were laughing and his smile was relaxed. Any fear that something was wrong was quickly dispelled.

"Can I come in?" he asked.

"Sorry," she said, and stepped aside. "I was daydreaming."

Remembering back to that day just a month ago, actually, when Jack had walked into her life wearing a three-piece suit. He'd looked very nice in that suit, but he looked even better in the knit shirt and shorts that he was wearing now. There was more of him to see.

Though truth be told, Cassie thought he'd looked best about two weeks ago, back when he wasn't wearing any more than the Good Lord gave him on the day he came skidding into this world.

"Did I come at a bad time?"

"No, no. I'm just doing some refrigerator baking."

He blinked at her. "Science was never my strong suit," he said. "So this baking-in-a-refrigerator thing has me a tad confused."

"I'm making a cheesecake. You mix up some cream cheese and fake whipped cream, pour it into a pie tin with graham-cracker crust, pop it in the refrigerator and leave it there until it hardens."

"Sounds good."

"It's not bad." It was the kind of thing she did when moodiness descended on her—made something sweet and delicious to eat. Then she would run a few extra miles to work off the calories. Equal doses of self-indulgence and self-discipline. It wasn't long before she was pert and chipper again. Worked all the time. "And it's not that many calories, either. I use all low-cal stuff."

"It sounds good."

"Especially when you top it off with fresh strawberries."

"Stop it, before I start drooling."

"If you're good, I'll let you have some."

"What do I have to be good at?"

"I'm talking like morally good." She turned and headed back toward the kitchen. "Not good at something."

"Can we negotiate that?"

The slap of his sandals made a rhythmic sound, indicating that his leg was feeling good. Sometimes it stiffened up.

"Do you want iced tea or lemonade?" she asked.

"Lemonade, please." He sat down on a stool at the counter. "And no sugar."

She stopped at the refrigerator and opened the door. "Worrying about your weight?"

"No," he replied. "It's just that I'm sweet enough already."

"I've noticed that."

Cassie felt the tension leave her shoulders as she poured their lemonade. Although she wasn't really tense. She was just a little down.

Oh, who was she kidding? She had a case of the blues that was fixing to grow and she was glad that Jack was here. Every since the wedding, she'd been dancing on the edge of the dumps, ready to fall into the depths. Her life just seemed so empty, so pointless.

But Jack was like a magic wand. All he had to do was wave his smile around and the sun was breaking through her clouds. She put the pitcher back in the refrigerator and sat down next to him at the counter.

"We can't have any cheesecake, yet," she informed him. "It's too soft and would just slop around."

"I could lick my plate." He reached down and mussed Ollie's head. "Me and Ollie can handle that real good."

"Ollie and you."

"Whatever."

"I bet Aunt Hattie wouldn't accept that as an excuse."

He continued scratching Ollie behind his ears. "Boy, you women sure know how to play hardball."

Cassie smiled and sipped her lemonade. "I don't think it would look too dignified for a law teacher to lick his dessert off his plate. There must be something in your professional by-laws against that."

"Probably." He gulped at his drink. "But I never read them."

"Goodness. You're a bad little boy."

He gave her a wink and a smile. "What you don't know can't hurt you."

"Oh, is that right?" She tried for a teasing tone, but fell a little short.

Jack's smile faded slightly and he put his glass down. "I ran your dad's name through some of the computers in Pierre, South Dakota. I didn't really expect to find anything and I didn't," he said. "Most of the systems have computerized in the last ten years and haven't gone back to add people from before then."

"I guess that makes sense."

"I thought maybe I'd try some of the Internet bulletin boards. There's a missing-persons one."

"What's that?" she asked. "I missed the turnoff for the Information Superhighway."

"Just a way for people to exchange things—information, ideas, recipes, whatever. It works pretty much like a regular bulletin board. You post a message and wait for someone to read it and respond. Well, I posted your father's name and birth date and the navy info about him. And hope that somebody who knew him reads the bulletin board."

"Sounds easy."

"The posting is."

"But the waiting isn't."

"I'm afraid not."

He took her hand, holding it tightly as if he was telling her that she could depend on him, that he would be her anchor. That no matter what they found out—or didn't find out—nothing would change between them. She took strength from him, let it flow over her heart and bring peace. She felt so much better with him around, so much less afraid of the demons that seemed to come out after dark.

Suddenly their stools got moved back from the counter as if an earthquake had hit. Ollie was squeezing himself between their feet and the cabinet wall, snuggling down as if he were a little baby.

"Ollie!" Cassie exclaimed. "You're not a puppy anymore."

"That's okay," Jack said. "We all want to be puppies sometime."

Cassie smiled at him. Men were a lot like dogs. The bigger they were, the gentler they acted.

"That cheesecake could be a bit soft yet," Cassie said. "But it might be manageable."

"Won't know until we try."

She got up and went to the refrigerator, pulling out the pie tin. "Want some fresh strawberries with that?"

"Only if you want me forever beholden to you."

Cassie stood poised, cheesecake in hand, and stared into his eyes—dark blue, almost black. Turbulence ahead. She could hardly wait.

"Watch me, Daddy."

"No, watch me."

"I got two eyes, sweethearts," Jack shouted in exasperation. "I can watch both of you at once."

They were all at the university pool. Cassie and Jack were in the water while the twins were on the edge. Cassie had been reminding them for days that they were starting lessons at the YMCA soon and that their father might want to see what they'd learned so far. Yesterday the girls had finally agreed, though reluctantly. Now they were as loud and obnoxious as any six-year-olds, each trying to outdo the other.

"All right, girls," Cassie called out. "How about if you get in the pool?"

They jumped in together, creating a massive splash, then they frantically grabbed for the sides of the pool.

"Wow!" Jack cried. "I'm impressed."

Cassie moved about ten feet from the edge and looked back at the girls. "Okay. One at a time now, swim out to me."

"Me first!" Mary Louise called out and began doing a slow dog paddle toward Cassie.

When she got near, Cassie grabbed her and let her catch her breath before sending her back to the side. Then Mary Alice did the same.

"Boy," Jack said as the girls clung to the side of the pool. "You guys are doing just great."

They didn't reprimand him for using the G-word, so obviously they were pleased with his attitude.

"How about if we use the kickboards?" Cassie reached for some foam boards that the girls used to help them float.

For the next hour or so, the girls swam and splashed and played in the water. They really had conquered their fears, although as swimmers they weren't Olympic quality quite yet. It was obvious they were proud of their new skills, though, and anxious to show off for their father.

When family hour was ending and some local swim teams were coming in to use the pool, the girls reluctantly got out of the water and took their kickboards down to the pile at the end of the pool. Cassie got out and walked with Jack toward the locker-room doors.

"I'd thought maybe Aunt Hattie would come see the girls swim," Cassie said.

"This has all been real hard on her."

Cassie didn't know why. "It's good for kids to learn to swim," she said. "It could save their lives."

His blue eyes turned cloudy. "Aunt Hattie knows that better than most people. Back when she was about ten years old, she and her best friend were crossing a footbridge by their house. It was just wide enough for one person to walk and there were no side rails."

Suddenly Cassie could see the whole picture. "Her friend slipped and fell in."

"Neither of them could swim and the river was near to flood stage." Jack shook his head. "All Aunt Hattie could do was watch Betty Jean get washed downstream."

A wave of guilt washed over her heart. She took Jack's hand. "I'm sorry."

"You didn't know."

"I know, but I didn't give her the benefit of the doubt."

"In what way?" he asked.

"Oh, it's just being dumb on my part." She squeezed his hand. "But now I know."

"Ah." He cleared his throat. "I'd rather you didn't mention anything. Aunt Hattie doesn't like folks who fish for sympathy. She'd thump me good if she knew I told."

"Hmm." Cassie squeezed up to him. "Now you're in my power."

"I'm hoping you won't abuse that power."

She kissed him and they hugged. "I take it Aunt Hattie has never learned to swim."

"She's scared to death of water."

Cassie pulled back. "And she feared for the girls."

"All the time you guys were here, Aunt Hattie was on her knees praying."

"I should have been told," she said, scolding Jack.

"I just told you I couldn't tell," he insisted. "She'd have crippled me up. Worse than those two defensive linemen did back when I still played ball."

Cassie just shook her head.

"Whatcha guys doing?"

Two little munchkins stood staring at them, with two pairs of the clearest blue eyes this side of heaven. She'd been so engrossed in her conversation with Jack that she hadn't heard the patter of their bare feet on the tiles.

"We were just talking about how brave your father is," Cassie replied.

"He ain't brave."

"He's afraid of Aunt Hattie."

"He won't talk back, or sass her, or anything."

"That doesn't mean he's afraid of her," Cassie said.

"Does, too!" they shouted in unison.

Cassie shook her head and laughed. "I'm not getting into this."

Jack joined in her laughter. It felt so good.

"Let's go change," Jack said to the girls. "I'm hungry enough to eat a bear. Fur, guts, and everything."

"Eww," the girls sang out.

"Thank you for the dinner," Cassie said as she and Jack stopped at her front door. A cloud of pleasant expectancy surrounded them. Even Ollie—who the girls had insisted come over, too—was waiting quietly at their side. "The whole evening was wonderful."

Jack glanced over toward her house. "I owe you a lot," he replied.

"No, no," Cassie said. "You don't owe me a thing. We're even."

He looked down at Ollie standing between them and scratched his head. Her giant dog groaned in ecstasy.

"You're spoiling him rotten, you know," Cassie said.

"My kids aren't afraid of the water anymore."

"Any swimming teacher could have accomplished that."

She could see by the light from the streetlight that he was looking at her. And, although it wasn't bright enough for her to read his eyes, she was sure they were dark blue. Something in the air around them told her they were.

"But how many swimming teachers would have clued my kids in on Indiana law?"

Cassie knew he was laughing at her. "I never said it was the law that they had to go barefoot during the summer. They made that up."

"Hmm. This calls for some investigative work."

"Like what?"

"Interviews." He nodded. "Checking for inconsistencies. Determining who's telling the truth."

"I see."

They stood there, listening to the sound of Ollie panting.

"Would you like a glass of wine or something?" she asked. Maybe Ollie was using up all the oxygen. It certainly was getting hard to breathe. "Maybe it would give you a chance to start your investigation."

"Good idea. The girls are in bed so I've got a little time free."

After unlocking her door Cassie stepped in and threw her sandals in the corner of the foyer. "Sit down where you want," she said over her shoulder. "I'll pour us a glass of wine."

Ollie meandered over to his bed in the kitchen and plopped down for a nap as Cassie poured two glasses of wine and turned to find that Jack had followed her into the kitchen.

Without a word, he took her into his arms. His mouth moved against hers hungrily, like a thirsty man finding water. His tongue pushed at her lips; she opened them to let him enter, to feel the probing and pulsing of his desires. It hadn't been that long since they'd fed those needs, but it seemed centuries past.

There was no yesterday, no tomorrow. Just this night with all the secrets of the darkness.

When they parted, she had no breath left and lay in his arms trying to breathe, trying to think. Next to her ear, his heart was pounding—the rhythm of the race she was running. He slid his hands over her back, as if afraid she might slip away and disappear. No chance of that.

"I've missed you," he said into her hair.

She didn't bother to tell him how many times they'd seen each other in the past week or so. She knew just what he meant. "Me, too."

His hands moved up to her arms, as if they could not stop touching her. "You feel so good." It was a sigh. A prayer. A plea.

She slipped her arms around his waist, holding him lightly to her. "You feel like you have too many clothes on."

His eyes looked into hers, fiery coals delving into the depths of her soul, but she just looked back. His needs were alive and burning, threatening to consume them both if she let them. She let her fingers lightly run along the line of his jaw, then linger on his lips for just a moment.

Jack grabbed hold of her hand and brought it back to his lips, kissing each finger slowly. His gaze held her prisoner, not letting her eyes wander, not letting her heart escape his grasp.

"You are so beautiful," he whispered, his voice raw and hoarse.

"You're blind," she said with a laugh. "But charmingly so."

She tugged at his shirt, pulling it from his shorts so that her hands could roam over his back. His skin was covered with hair that was soft as silk, but was somehow like flint to her touch, sending sparks into the very depth of her. There was a trembling taking over, a tension that was tightening and twisting in her soul, stealing her breath, stealing her reasoning.

His lips came down on hers again, this time rougher, hotter, deeper. The fire was ready to ignite, to devour them whole. His hands were under her T-shirt, although she had no memory of it coming free. His touch was feverish—over her back, sliding down past her waist, coming up to cup her breasts. He knew just how to tease her nipples to make the fire burn stronger, to tighten that knot of pressure until it was ready to burst.

"Maybe we should go into the other room," she whispered.

"I think we'd better," he gasped. "Your kitchen floor looks inviting, but we don't want to disturb Ollie."

She just laughed and led him past her dozing dog, down the hallway to the bedroom. His arms were around her faster than she could take a breath, and together they fell onto the softness of her bed. It was like a cloud, like a little bit of heaven come down to embrace them.

She had never felt like this, with such raging hunger to lie in a man's arms. No, it wasn't just any man's lovemaking that she needed, but this man's. She needed Jack at her side, Jack inside her. Jack to make her feel completely alive.

It was a marvel that she could only wonder at, although not too long and not too hard, although thoughts were hard to find. A burning was raging in her soul, making coherency a thing of the past. She let her hands tug at his shirt, then, once that was gone, at his shorts.

But he must have felt she was getting too far ahead in the race, for he pulled at her T-shirt, then loosened her bra. For a moment, it seemed enough. His lips took each tender tip in his mouth, sucking at it until it felt as if he was drawing the very life from her. And she was only too willing to give it.

She'd never felt so beautiful, so anxious to lie naked before another. It was so right, this joining of their bodies and their souls. They were each halves of the same whole. Each part of the same heartbeat.

Jack helped push her shorts off, then her panties, so they could lie together as one. She was ready for him, needing him with an intensity that was almost pain. He took just a moment to slip on protection, then she took him in and felt her soul come alive. They danced as one. Climbing. Shouting. Soaring into the heavens to join the stars in all their splendor.

Then they clung as the world exploded—hearts joined, souls as one. That was all there was. It was more than enough. It was everything.

Ever so slowly, their hearts began to slow, slipping back to normalcy. They'd had their piece of heaven and it was time to return to earth. She just lay in Jack's arms and wondered how she had ever been happy before. This was happiness. This was living.

And to think, in a few days they'd have their holiday. No one but the two of them for two whole days.

Chapter Eleven

Cassie looked out the window again. No Jack. She guessed she had time once more to check to make sure she had everything. Just in case she missed something on her first few rechecks.

"Food, dish, cookies and your ball." She looked over at Ollie. "You've got everything for your stay with Grandpa and Samantha."

She resisted the impulse to unpack her case and double-check her things. "What I don't have, I won't use," she told Ollie and glanced out the window again. "It's not like Jack to be late."

Just as it wasn't like her to be late.

Not that his being a little late would have an impact on their plans. They were just going to drive leisurely up to their bed-and-breakfast in Union Pier, then have a late dinner. It wasn't like they were on a schedule.

Her lateness was different. It was a womanly kind of lateness.

"I don't know, Ollie." She scratched the top of his head. "I'm probably just worrying about nothing. A woman's got to be late once or twice in her life."

That was what was really bugging her. She could almost count on one hand the number of times since college she'd been late with her period. Her periods had been nothing more than a regular nuisance—that is, until she got married. Then it wasn't long before she began to dread them. Each one became another brushstroke on the sign that broadcast her failure as a woman.

"Damn it, Ollie." Cassie glared at her watch—six-thirty. "If Jack doesn't get here soon, then you and I are taking a little jaunt to Harbor Country. Ain't no use losing the deposit."

Back when she was a child, people just said that they were going to the lake. Now that the eastern shore of Lake Michigan was so popular, especially with the Chicago people, it was called Harbor Country. It hadn't changed. The lake and the big sand bluffs were still there. It just made the restaurants and other accommodations more expensive.

"Oh, man." Cassie wiped at her face with her hands. "I'd better get a hold of myself. Grumpy as I'm getting, Jack's gonna wish he never bothered to get here at all." She glared outside. "Assuming he gets here sometime before noon."

Her period being late was no more a big deal than Jack's being late. Yeah, there didn't appear to be a logical reason. But so what? Life wasn't all logic. And clocks were a human invention, not Mother Nature's. Jack would get here soon, she'd have her period any day now, and everything would be back to normal.

Suddenly Ollie perked up and ran to the window. When Jack's minivan pulled into the drive, Ollie's tail started going a mile a minute.

Just like she'd said, Jack was here and everything was getting back to normal. Truth be told, the only reason she was disappointed was that she knew her period would start sometime during their outing. They'd just have to get a quickie in and save up their passion for later. Cassie pushed herself up and strolled over to the door.

"I'm sorry," he said. "Not only did Aunt Hattie double-check the girls but she had to triple-check them and everything they were taking."

"They really don't have to take all that much," Cassie said. "Blue jeans, shorts, a lot of T-shirts and a couple pairs of shoes."

"Aunt Hattie knows that," Jack replied. "She just isn't accepting it."

Cassie let him inside while Ollie bumped him about the legs.

"Ollie," Cassie admonished.

"That's okay." Jack bent down and scratched behind the dog's ears. "Me and him are buds."

The blur that Ollie was making with his tail fully confirmed Jack's words. "You want to sit down and relax awhile?" she asked.

Jack's scratching eased down to slow motion. He looked up at her, his eyes dark like the sea in a storm. Cassie felt her stomach tighten and her heart quicken.

"We should get going. Your father's expecting us."

"Okay." Cassie thought of her period—the one that would come sometime this holiday. "But you may be sorry. Good opportunities don't come by every day, you know."

"I'll have to take my chances."

Jack picked up her suitcase and Ollie's bag of dog food while she picked up the odds and ends. By the time she got to the van, Ollie and Jack were already settled, so she had to crawl over her dog to get to the passenger seat.

"You take up a lot of room, dog," she grumbled as she hauled her feet over his back. The big mutt was looking adoringly at Jack, so, sighing, Cassie fastened her seat belt. Jack turned on the ignition and pulled away from the curb.

The traffic was light and they quickly covered the short distance to her father's house. Turning the corner, they could see him standing in his front yard.

"Don't worry," Jack said. "I'll take the blame."

"I'm not worried," she told him. "He's the gentlest man I ever met."

"How about me?"

"I don't want you too gentle," she replied. "You're not my father."

Jack smiled as they coasted to a stop. "I'm sorry," he called out as he stepped from the car. "I was late picking up Cassie and Ollie."

"You haven't trained him very well, Cass," her father said.

"Give me time." She climbed out of the van. "It's not even two months since I first met him."

"Slowing down in your old age?"

Cassie restrained herself from giving her father a punch, kissing him on the cheek instead. She must be getting old. Actually, what it really was, was shock. Shock at how fast things had gone with her and Jack.

"Hi, Ollie," her father said to the dog. "Ready for a few days of batching it?"

Ollie wagged his big tail, giving an enthusiastic yes.

"His food is in the bag," Cassie said, indicating the dog paraphernalia Jack was pulling out of the van. "And there's a small bag of cookies inside."

"I'll take that," the older man offered, taking the items from Jack.

"I can put it in the house."

"You guys are already late," her father reminded. "Get going." He turned around and walked toward his front door, Ollie walking alongside and wagging his tail.

"I guess he's saying goodbye," Cassie said, staring at her dog.

"He wants to get on with his vacation. And so should we." Jack took her arm. "Let's go. Time is running out on us."

In some ways it was and in other ways it was dragging. It was funny how different something could look, based on the angle you were looking at it from.

The sun was setting in spectacular fashion out over the lake as they pulled into the lot of the bed-and-breakfast, a quaint old home high on a bluff overlooking Lake Michigan. The reds and yellows and golds in the sky all seemed to be shouting in celebration, and joy was finally seeping into Cassie's heart.

"Makes you just want to stand here for the rest of your life and soak it in, doesn't it?" Jack said softly.

"Yeah." It would be nice if time could stand still, at least for a moment.

But standing out in the evening wasn't exactly what she wanted to last forever, and they eventually went inside. The bed and-breakfast was an old house with large bedrooms and furnishings that made it feel like a home.

"Did I tell you Dad's got another old house he wants me to look at?" she asked Jack as they followed the manager up to the second floor. "He's really serious about wanting to run a bed-and-breakfast."

"It's a lot of work."

"That's what I thought, but I figured he knew what he was doing."

"Ah, but do we?" Jack asked as they stopped in the doorway of their room. In the middle was a four-poster bed—which had to be three feet off the floor.

"Hope you're in the mood for cuddling," he said. "I don't want to get too near the edge. Falling out would hurt."

She joined his laughter, barely paying attention as the manager pointed out the bathroom and the closet. Once the man was gone, she went into Jack's arms. "I guess you'd better be a good boy, then."

"Didn't we have this discussion already?" he asked, his eyes darkening to match the lake at night. "And weren't you rather vague as to your definition of 'good'?"

"Complaints, complaints," she teased and moved out of his arms to look out the window. Below them the lake was turning a nighttime black. An uneasiness had come over her, a fear that some shadow was looming over them, ready to strike. It was crazy. Probably just the result of fretting about her late period and her even later dinner. She forced the gloom away.

"So, are you hungry?" she asked.

"Starving."

His smile was so sweet, so genuine. What was there to fear?

Cassie grabbed a jacket and they walked down the street, looking for a restaurant. They passed antique stores and art galleries, ice-cream parlors and tea shops. At the end of the street, they came to a small tavern with a deck out back that looked down over the lake. It fit their mood perfectly, so they went inside, taking seats at a wrought-iron table at the edge of the deck.

The air was cool, but the metal of the chairs and table still held the warmth of the sun. Just as their friendship—all right, more than friendship—held a warmth that kept her heart cozy even when life got a little chilly.

Once they'd given their orders, Cassie gazed down at the lake, lights reflected from the town glittering like diamonds on its surface. She felt her tensions seep away and peace take their place.

"I've got something for you," Jack said.

She turned toward him, ready with a joke, when she saw his face was serious. "Oh?"

He slid a piece of paper across the table toward her. "We got an answer from the posting about your father," he replied.

"What did it say?" Sudden fears surrounded her. She took the paper but was afraid to pick it up.

He shrugged. "There're not a lot of details, but it seems your father wasn't trying to hide something he'd done, just who he was."

She didn't understand; her eyes locked on to the little piece of paper before her.

"He grew up in eastern South Dakota," Jack went on. "Part Dakota Sioux and one-hundred-percent poor. He moved to the city, joined the navy and changed his name, leaving his old self in the past."

Cassie felt stunned. "That's it?" she asked and picked up the paper.

He nodded. "In essence."

She glanced at the printed copy of an E-mail message Jack had gotten earlier that day. It said pretty much the same thing that he'd just told her. She put the paper down and sighed. "So that was it? After all this worrying and fretting and stewing, he was just a teenager who was ashamed of his parents?"

"I don't know if that was it exactly," Jack continued softly. "I think he just hated the poverty and all that came with it. When you're young, it seems so easy to escape. Just run and don't look back."

She reached out for his hand, not certain what was behind his words, but knowing something was.

"It's what *I* did, to some extent," he said, and looked away for a long moment. "I tried to leave the hills behind."

"But you didn't change your name."

"Kind of." He shrugged. "It's really Jimmy Jack Merrill."

"My real name is Cassandra," she said. "I never use it, but that doesn't mean I'm hiding from anything. It means I have more sense than my parents did when it comes to names."

He just laughed and his hold on her hand tightened. "So you aren't upset?"

"About my father or about your real name being Jimmy Jack?" She looked into his eyes and knew that honesty would come easily with him. "I don't know what I feel about my father. It's not what I expected. I'm not sure what it all means to me."

Their dinner came just then. Jack made small talk as they ate, but Cassie found her mind wandering. She wasn't really upset, she knew that much. Mostly she was conscious of a sense of disappointment. Not because her father had kept his past a secret, but that learning all this meant nothing to her. She had been hoping that somehow she would find some message in it. Something she could hold on to. Something that would wipe away the lie she'd been living with for the past twenty years.

"Want to walk along the beach after dinner?" Jack asked.

"That would be great."

And it would be. That was just what she needed—Jack's gentle presence to let the past flow away from her and go back to its sleep. She would concentrate on now and tomorrow—on the special time they had together here—and not try to find answers in riddles posed by the distant past.

Maybe she was growing wise as she was growing older.

* * *

"There's a shelter at the end of this path!" Cassie shouted. "Let's go."

She was pedaling down the trail through the afternoon shower before Jack could get a word out, making him race to catch up with her. "What's the matter?" he shouted back. "You afraid of getting wet?"

Instead of answering, she just kept pedaling furiously, up the hill toward an open-sided building that he could now see. He was relieved at how playful she was today; more like her regular self.

After he'd told her about her father last night, he'd worried that her holiday would be spoiled. But it hadn't happened. She'd been pensive last night. Well, not all night. His heart raced as his mind replayed their lovemaking. Then this morning, she'd seemed chipper as ever. He wasn't fooled into thinking the news hadn't mattered, but felt that maybe it was something she needed to know. And he sensed that she was working on putting it behind her.

Jack was soaked by the time he pulled his bike in under the roof. "I still don't understand why you are so afraid of getting—"

Just then an enormous bolt of lightning flashed down at the shore, bringing a clap of thunder that sent him almost to the open rafter above him.

"Holy cow!" he exclaimed. "That's enough to scare the stuffing out of a man."

"Told you."

"You didn't tell me anything. You only said to pedal fast."

Cassie just gave him a look as she sat down on a picnic bench and began to untie her sneakers. "If I tried to explain things to you, we'd still be out there." She pulled off her sneakers. "You know how you lawyers are. Always asking questions."

"I thought we had an agreement to be nice to each other this holiday," he said. "I don't see where cracking lawyer jokes counts as being nice."

"I'm not telling any lawyer jokes." She pulled off her wet socks. "I'm just giving you the facts."

He shook his head. There was no winning an argument with this woman.

"Hey." She wrung out her socks. "You can't tell me that you guys don't badger a person to death with a zillion dippy questions."

"We're trained to seek the truth."

"Sure."

Cassie leaned back against the table part of the picnic unit and grinned at him—her well-shaped, muscular legs stretched before her, her elbows back on the table, enhancing the smooth rise of her breasts. Too bad this shelter had no walls. He sat down next to her.

"As an example," he said, "your feet are still wet."

"Yeah?" Her emerging frown lines did nothing to mar the beauty of her face. "And you think I don't know that?"

"Well, you took your shoes and socks off but you don't have anything to dry your feet with. So they're still wet."

"So what?" She wiggled both feet. "It's a pleasant kind of moist. With the wet shoes on, it was a clammy, unpleasant kind of wet."

"You rationalize very well."

"I cut through nonsense very well."

Jack smiled as he looked out over the lake. Ornery as a rat terrier. She'd been that way from the day they first met. And he hoped she would never change.

"Man," he said, looking at the sheets of water pouring off the roof. "It's really coming down now." And multiple lightning flashes told him it was a hell of a storm. "Damn thing came up awful fast."

"It's a lake squall," she murmured, staring out at nature's show. "That's how they usually work."

Through the rain they could see the lake surface boiling, with waves jumping high. Dark clouds hung out just at the horizon, serving as a counterpoint to the spectacular flashes of lightning. "Mother Nature puts on quite a show."

"It's a lot more enjoyable when you're watching from someplace safe."

"There's that," he agreed.

He turned away from the lake spectacle to look at Cassie. She wasn't big and loud, nor did she give off huge sparks, but in her own way she was quite spectacular herself. The wet T-shirt now clinging to her body certainly demonstrated that.

He shifted his feet, causing his shoes to make a squishy sound. Maybe it would be more comfortable to take the shoes off. He did a toe-to-heel on one, and then the other, before pulling off his socks.

"Well?" Cassie said, watching him wiggle his own feet.

"Much more comfortable."

"Told you."

He nodded and they watched the rain some more. It was hard to be certain, but he thought it was starting to ease up a bit. He did remember Cassie telling him that these lake squalls seldom lasted long. He pulled off his shirt.

She turned to look at him.

"Hey," he said. "If it works for my feet, it should work for the rest of my body."

Jack dropped the soggy shirt on the table behind him; Cassie kept on staring. "Boy." He waved his arms about. "That feels much better."

"Hmm."

"You ought to try it."

"Cute."

That wasn't quite how he would describe her smile. Cassie's grin was more like the one Miss Moorehead had given him back in third grade, the time she'd told him to come up and take his snake out of her desk drawer. Nature seemed to have given the female of the species a highly suspicious attitude.

"No, seriously. I was just thinking of your welfare."

"You're a true gentleman."

"I know you just hate that clammy kind of wet feeling."

"Not quite as much as I'd hate flashing my breasts at strangers coming up the trail."

He looked back out toward the lake and saw that the storm had passed over them, moving off to the east. They were left with a heavy drizzle that was obviously the tail end of the storm.

"Well, what do you want to do now?" she asked.

"My pants are wet," he replied.

She stared at him with her big brown eyes. They were pretty as a fuzzy puppy, but damn near unreadable. You could tell if they went hard or real soft, but hardly anything in between.

"Cold and clammy." He shook his head. "Very uncomfortable."

Cassie blinked, a slight smile growing on her lips. He used to think women's wisdom was an acquired thing. His daughters were showing him that that wasn't true.

"Of course, you have it worse," he said solemnly. "I'm only wearing my shorts. You have your shorts, shirt, and bra. That means more of your body is wrapped in cold, clammy stuff."

The ripples in Cassie's cheeks indicated she was fighting for control. The snickering indicated she had a ways to go. He wrapped her in his arms.

"You're very cruel," he said.

"I thought men liked that."

This time he had no trouble at all reading her eyes.

"Let's go back to the room," he murmured.

"And get these wet, clammy clothes off?" she asked, all innocence and passion.

"That's right."

Her arms went around his neck. "And get comfortable."

"Very comfortable."

They kissed. Long, but not long enough. Long enough so that he was gasping for breath but not long enough to be satisfied. Long enough to awaken all the devils of his passion, but not long enough to ease their hungers.

"Let's go back to our room."

Her eyes were open wide, the pupils swimming in a sea of white. For a moment, he wasn't even sure that she'd heard him.

"Cassie, I—"

"Last one there is a rotten egg."

She was up and gone before the words had registered in his brain, leaving him sitting there hugging air. Damn. That woman went from passionate to playful quicker than one of these Lake Michigan squalls.

She was almost out of sight down the path. He pushed himself up, grabbed his shirt and shoes, and hurried to his bike.

They were lying in bed, both on their right side, spooning. Skin against skin. Warm and cuddly as kittens in a basket.

Cassie's travel clock on the bedside table said it was almost three-thirty. It had been such a pleasant evening that they'd turned off the air-conditioning and opened the windows before they'd gone to sleep. Now, she lay there listening to the earthy blend of Jack's breathing and day birds discussing how they should greet the coming dawn.

Like in the Dickens novel she'd had to read in high school— it was the best of times for her, it was the worst of times.

Cassie wished that she could lie in his arms forever; and she wished the day would come so that she could get home and back to the normal life of her business, her family, and her sports teams.

She was deliriously happy, she was gut-wrenchingly scared. She wanted to sing, she wanted to cry. She was hungry enough to eat a bear, she was nauseous.

And her period still hadn't started.

She wanted to scream. And if Jack hadn't been wrapped around her, fast asleep, she would have.

The missed period was her agony and her hope. Hope that she could finally say that she was a complete woman.

But agony sat there in the dark reaches of her heart, like a man-eating tiger ready to spring out. Was her missed period something to talk about or something to carry as a silent secret?

Her clock blinked: 4:01 a.m. She wasn't going to get any more sleep. She might as well get up and do something.

Her body went into a warm glow. Actually they could both do something—something that a man and a woman could enjoy together. She toyed with awakening Jack but he was sleeping so nicely. They could wait another hour.

Another hour to lie here, quiet and still, like a mouse at a convention of alley cats. But, given the way they were entwined, that was the way it had to be. And he was sleeping so comfortably that she didn't have the heart to wake him up. So she would just lie there and worry.

Well, not really worry.

Yeah, she was late. But it wasn't that unusual. It had happened before. Her period would start sometime today, she was sure of it. It had to.

Chapter Twelve

"Ease up, boss lady. The big guy'll be just fine."

Cassie stared at Burt, leaning on the frame of the doorway to her small office. Big guy? She wasn't aware that there was anything wrong with Jack, especially since she'd just left him early this morning.

"What are you talking about?" she snapped.

Burt shuffled his feet and glanced back out into the store, as if he was looking for help. "Ollie," he replied, turning to face her again. "I'm sure your father took good care of him."

Cassie just stared at him.

"Hey, your dad likes dogs, right?" He twisted his lips into what he must have thought was a comforting smile. "He'll be just fine."

What in the world had inspired this stupid conversation? "Of course, he's fine," she retorted. "I just talked to my father not more than ten minutes ago."

Now Burt stared at her.

"We—I got back early this morning and didn't have time to pick Ollie up. Sam's going to bring him home tonight."

"Well, there you go." He shrugged, looking around again. "Like I said. Nothing to worry about."

"I never was worried."

"Well, you've sure been grumpy today." Burt wiped a hand across his mouth. "And when you're grumpy that means you're worried about something or other. Leastways that's the way it usually works."

Cassie could feel all her worries come bubbling up. Emotions that had been churning for days stood poised to explode. "I am not grumpy." She stood while Burt shifted from one foot to the other. "I might be a little tense, seeing as we need to do a complete inventory by the end of the week. I have a meeting with a guy from the state tax commission. And I have to put in a new hot-water heater at home."

She smiled at Burt, taking a perverse joy from the little worry lines forming on his forehead. "Aside from that, I'm feeling just as loose as a goose."

"That's good," he mumbled.

"So if you come in here again—" her voice was rising into the shouting range, but she didn't care "—and call me grumpy, I'll rip your heart out and nail it to the front door!"

"What's going on here?" Ellen marched through the door and took up a position between the two of them, as if to keep them from fisticuffs. "They could hear you guys bellowing up in Three Oaks."

"We weren't bellerin'," Burt snapped. "We were just discussing as how Cassie weren't grumpy."

Ellen looked sharply at Cassie, then put her hand on Burt's arm and tugged him toward the door. "Come on out back and dust the shelves."

"The hell I will." Burt went out with her, but then paused and looked back over his shoulder. "And I ain't doin' the windows, neither."

Cassie just threw her pencil down on the desk and leaned back in her chair, closing her eyes. This thing had to be settled before she went out of her mind.

What was she going to do if she was pregnant? What would Jack want to do? Things had been going so well between them lately, but that would have to change if she was pregnant. Would he be happy or angry or—

No, she realized. He would accept responsibility. Whatever his true feelings, he would keep them hidden and accept responsibility. He would do the right thing by her. Which would be almost worse than him ranting and raving. How could she bear being the recipient of him doing his duty? And how long would it be before he began to resent her, began to feel trapped by her?

She would rather be alone.

About a hundred years later, when five o'clock rolled around, Cassie took a spin up South Bend Avenue to the supermarket to pick up something for dinner and check out the drugstore.

As she pulled into the parking lot, she noted with satisfaction that it wasn't too much more than half full. That meant she'd be in and out like a bunny, which was good. Samantha was bringing Ollie home around six-thirty and she didn't want them waiting around outside. She needed her big, fuzzy Ollie. Needed him to bring things back to normal in her life.

Cassie parked her truck, hurried across the lot, and then dashed through the supermarket like a cartoon character. She picked up a package of stewing meat for herself and a package of Yummy Cuts—chunks of dog food that were colored to look like beef—for Ollie. The food was made by a local firm and it was even wrapped in the same butcher-shop paper that they used for her meat. Darn stuff smelled horrible but Ollie loved it.

The drugstore was right next to the supermarket and she hurried in, walking the aisles and looking for the pregnancy-test kits. She knew that there had to be a zillion of them. They were always advertising the darn things on TV. Always.

"Can I help you, ma'am?"

"Yes, I—" Oh, man. It was a high-school boy—all smile, ears, and acne. What had she done to deserve this? "I'm looking for aspirin. A big bottle. The biggest and strongest you got."

"Yes, ma'am. Aisle nine, to your left."

"Thanks."

"No problem, ma'am. We're here to help."

Cassie smiled and turned away. If that kid said "ma'am" one more time, she would have mashed his nose and tied it in a knot behind his head.

She found the aspirin, a hundred million varieties of it. Closing her eyes, she picked a box, then stepped out into the main aisle and checked both ways before hurrying off to find the pregnancy-test kit.

"Anything else, ma'am?"

Cassie screamed and did a five-foot vertical leap. "What the hell are you doing sneaking around on people?"

"I'm sorry, ma'am."

"And quit calling me 'ma'am.' I'm not your mother."

"Yes, ma'am."

His smile had faded to dust but he was standing his ground. Cassie wondered if she could get him a military burial after she killed him. He deserved nothing less.

"Anything else you need, mmm—"

"Vitamins." Cassie snapped the word out before the kid took flight. He sounded like a damn helicopter. "Just plain old vitamins."

"Aisle sixteen, right, mmm—"

"Thanks." She turned to find the vitamins but stopped and looked back. "Don't you have anything to do? Stock shelves, sweep the floor, chase little boys away from the girlie magazines?"

"Oh, no. This is what I do, mmm—" He swallowed hard. "I help people find things."

Swell. Cassie stared hard at his name tag. "Do me a favor, *Carl*. Don't help me."

"Yes, mmm—"

Cassie checked out the ceiling fixtures and held her breath. If she hung her little helper up there in the rafters, everything would be just fine. He would never be able to bother her again.

"Say—" his voice was filled with a joyful eagerness, enough to send shivers up and down her back "—are you related to Fiona Scott?"

Cassie closed her eyes. In her next life, she was going to live in some metropolis, like Tokyo or Mexico City. Someplace where every other person and their cousin wouldn't know her or her family.

"She's my sister," she mumbled, hoping that Carl would take his little nugget of information and run away, clutching it to his heart.

"She taught my oldest sister's little boy." He stood there, smiling like they were real buddies.

"Thanks for your help, Carl."

"He really liked your sister," he said. "He said she was the best teacher he ever had."

"Go away, Carl—" Cassie kept a pleasant tone in her voice "—while you can still walk."

Carl didn't say anything in reply. His smile flickered but didn't go out. He gave her a thumbs-up signal for A-okay, before hurrying off.

Cassie counted to ten, quickly glanced around for the ubiquitous Carl, and then hurried down the aisle to her left. She'd suddenly realized that the pregnancy-test kit should be with the feminine hygiene products.

That hypothesis proved true and, after another quick check to see that no one was following her, she snatched up the package closest to her and didn't breathe until she was safely home.

She carried her load into the kitchen, left out the package for Ollie and her pregnancy kit, and put everything else in the refrigerator. Then she picked up the kit and, frowning, began reading the instructions.

The frown grew as she finished the instructions and looked at her watch. Damn. Samantha was going to be here in a few minutes with Ollie. She should wait for them.

But she had to find out what was going on with her body. And who knew what her sister would want to do? Sometimes Sam had someplace else to go and would dash out. Other times she'd just want to sit around and talk. It could be midnight before Cassie would have a chance to run the test. She dashed into the bathroom.

The test was simple enough. Heck, lean it against some bush in the backyard and Ollie could take it. Making a face, Cassie stood and washed her hands. Actually, her dog might do better than she did. Males of any species seemed to have the inside track when it came to aiming their urine stream.

The doorbell rang as Cassie was wiping her hands, causing her to look at her watch. Another two minutes. Her sister would just have to wait.

Sweet, patient little Samantha quickly went from ringing the doorbell to banging on the door while Cassie counted down the last ten seconds aloud. "Three. Two. One. Zero." Gripping the edge of the sink, she slowly opened her right eye and looked. A single line meant just a late period, a double line meant—

"Ohmigod."

Her heart stopped, her stomach did a backflip and she wanted to cry. How could it be? Oh, boy. Oh, damn. Oh, Lordy.

She was pregnant.

Cassie slid down onto the toilet lid and, closing her eyes, leaned back. It sounded like Samantha was kicking the door now, and Ollie was helping her by barking.

But, hey. Nothing was set in stone. The test could be wrong. It was probably wrong a lot of times. Oh, wow. Oh, damn. Laugh or cry? Which should she do? Doing both would be stupid.

What she had to do was see a doctor. Right. That was it. Let a professional check her out. Not some stupid, two-bit drugstore kit. A real doctor would put things right.

"I'm coming." Shouting, she grabbed up all the test paraphernalia and stuffed it in a desk drawer, then hurried to the door. "Let's not wreck the house."

"Where were you?" Samantha demanded.

Cassie fought to catch her breath while fighting off Ollie's welcome. "I was in the bathroom."

"I knew you were home." Samantha pushed her way past them into the house. "Your truck's in the driveway."

"Why don't you come in, Sam? Sit down and rest a spell."

Before she could get a good argument started, Ollie was dashing into the kitchen. She and Samantha followed, urged on by his excited barking. Cassie smiled when she saw him eyeing the butcher-paper-wrapped package lying on the counter.

"Okay, big guy," Cassie said. "Just a minute and I'll give you a snack."

"Daddy's already fed him," Samantha told her.

"This is just a treat." Cassie unwrapped the package. "He really loves these things. They look like real beef chunks."

As she laid the now unwrapped package on the counter, Cassie remembered that Samantha still had Ollie's food dish and toys. "Sam," she said. "Get Ollie's—"

But it didn't matter anymore. Ollie had put his front paws on the counter, taken a deep breath and "inhaled" the whole pile of moist nuggets.

"Those things really look like beef," Samantha said as they watched Ollie lick the paper.

"I told you they did."

"I mean, dripping with blood and everything." Samantha made a face. "Yuck."

Dripping with blood? A cloud of dread circled Cassie's head and took her oxygen. She stared at Ollie, still energetically cleaning the paper, then pulled the other butcher-paper-wrapped package from the refrigerator. She ripped it open to find a load of Yummy Cuts, which went quickly tumbling to the floor.

She'd been building up for a cry before and now it was almost impossible to hold it in. But she did. She didn't cry. Not ever. Never.

"Ollie likes this stuff, too." Samantha bent down and picked up the wrapping paper. "Although the chunks don't look as moist as the other ones did."

Cassie glared at her sister. Samantha was good at that. From the day she'd started to talk, her sister was always trying to make everybody feel better.

"Why don't we go out and eat?" Samantha said. "Grab a quick sandwich someplace."

Cassie continued glaring, although she knew she had little choice. There wasn't much in her cupboard.

"All right." Cassie lifted her nose high. "But you are not to look at me or talk to me."

"Can I sit with you?"

Her sister never got mad about anything. She was just too nice. Cassie felt like drowning her in a cup of coffee. Unfortunately, that would have made it too sweet to drink.

"I don't know," Cassie replied. "I have to think on that."

Cassie lay flat on her back, her feet in the stirrups, and counted the dots in the acoustical ceiling. She hated these examinations. This damn position made her feel so helpless.

"Enjoying yourself down there?" she asked.

Dr. Maggie Novak straightened and peeled off her glove. "Purple," she said, as she stepped on the lever and dropped the used glove into the waste can.

"What's purple?"

"Your cervix."

Cassie closed her eyes for a moment. Breathe in, breathe out, she told herself. Breathe in, breathe out.

"My stick had two lines," Cassie said.

"You took one of those home tests."

"Why do you think I called you?"

Her doctor came over to the stool by Cassie's head and sat down. The doctor stared at her for a long moment, while Cassie fought a mixture of dread and impatience—wishing her doctor would hurry up and give her the news she didn't want to hear.

Cassie had been going to the same general practitioner since she was a kid, and when he brought in Dr. Novak four years ago to take over his practice so he could retire, Cassie stayed, taking an immediate liking to the young doctor. But given the fact that Dr. Novak had access to records of everything from the case of poison ivy Cassie had when she was eleven to her fertility problems, there was little the good doctor didn't know about her.

"That gives you two yeses," the doctor said.

Cassie's stomach did a jelly-like quiver. "What kind of reading did you get with the urine sample I gave you?"

"Ah, yes. I forgot. You have three yeses."

Cassie fell back and tried to finish counting the dots. They kept blurring and she quit, deciding to sit up instead. "I don't understand this."

"Almost thirty years old and you don't understand about the birds and the bees?"

"Ha, ha." She made a face at her doctor. "You're so funny. You should be onstage."

"I know. And the next one leaves in fifteen minutes."

Cassie didn't bother laughing. When you'd known one another for a while, all the punch lines were pretty well committed to memory.

"I thought we had determined that I could not have children."

"No, no, no. We did no such thing."

Cassie rolled her eyes toward the ceiling. The dots were still blurred. "When Ron and I were married, we could not conceive a child. Ron married another woman and he conceived a child. Ergo—"

"Ergo, schmergo." Dr. Novak gestured dismissively at her. "The only thing that we knew for certain is that you and Ron were unable to conceive a child. No more."

Cassie made a face and looked away.

"None of the tests indicated that you had a physical problem."

"But that's not—"

"Yes, it's very possible." The doctor shifted on her stool. "In about eighty percent of cases, the process of conception takes place without substantial effort on anybody's part."

All those women pushing baby strollers—whom Cassie had hated with an undying passion—certainly proved that.

"The other twenty percent have problems. Some physical. Some psychological. A few—total mystery."

Cassie searched her doctor's face, wondering if she was giving her all the facts.

"Yours was total mystery," the doctor said.

Actually, none of that mattered. What did matter were the two facts staring her in the face. She and Ron made love: no baby. She and Jack made love: bingo. One baby coming up.

"Apparently you and Ron were not physically compatible." A smile played on the doctor's lips. "Obviously that's not the case with you and—" the smile grew "—and Mr. X."

It was a small town and Cassie wouldn't have been surprised if the doctor had named Jack, but the woman had more class than that. They both sat quietly and shared the silence surrounding them.

"So," the doctor said. "Now what?"

Cassie shrugged.

"Does the father know?"

Cassie shook her head.

"That should be taken care of."

Her vision blurred even more and Cassie had to look away. Was this to be the end of her and Jack? Would he be genuinely happy or would he be quiet and controlled? One mention of "duty" or "responsibility" and she was throwing him out. Better now than later.

"You know," she said. "This is throwing my life into an uproar."

The next thing she knew was that her doctor's arms were around her. Slowly Cassie returned the hug.

"This is just the beginning, kid. Just a teeny tiny first step toward total chaos."

Jack raised his hand to ring Cassie's doorbell, but deep barking from inside the house told him not to bother. He stepped back and waited.

Within moments the door opened and Cassie stood there in all her radiance. Their holiday—spending just about every single second of the day together—had been as near to heaven as mere mortals could get. But she'd been in a strange mood since they'd come back.

He'd called her yesterday evening, but Sam had been over and they had only talked for a few minutes. Then today, when he'd called the store, she'd been out. It scared him, this inability to reach to her, but he told himself it was just his overactive imagination. She wasn't avoiding him. Their schedules were just out of sync, so once the kids were in bed he'd decided to take a walk.

"Hi," he said and whipped a covered plate out from behind his back. "Aunt Hattie sent over some peach pie."

She took the plate but there was no smile in her eyes or her voice. "How nice of her."

Maybe she just hated peach pie, he thought, and pulled open the screen door, bracing himself for Ollie's hearty greeting. As always, the big dog jumped up and put his front paws on Jack's shoulders, but Cassie just turned away and walked into her living room.

Jack frowned. Cassie usually scolded him for letting Ollie jump like that.

"Get down, Ollie." Jack spoke softly and followed Cassie. "Are you feeling okay?" Maybe she was just tired.

"Fit as a fiddle."

There was a strong edge to her voice. Jack could feel the tension tightening his gut. Something bad was coming down.

"Sit down, Jack." She grabbed Ollie by the collar. "Let me put him outside."

Jack's first inclination was to tell her to spit it out. Whatever was wrong, she should simply get it out in the open, but he just sat down. A definite smell of serious was hanging in the air.

Cassie returned from putting Ollie out in the backyard and sat down across from him, sitting forward with her hands on her knees. "I've tried all day to come up with a good and easy way to tell you this."

Jack took a breath and held it. It looked like he was going to have to play defense attorney—take the hit, then respond.

"But I never was a fancy talker." She took a deep breath. "So I decided to tell you straight out."

"Okay."

"I'm pregnant."

He was still, frozen even, as the words echoed around in his head. Pregnant. She was pregnant. A little part of him wanted to smile, to jump in the air, to sweep her into his arms. But another part—the part that was watching the stillness in her face—kept him from moving.

"I see" was all he was able to say. He saw her lying in his arms just a few weeks ago, assuring him it didn't matter that the condom had split, that it hadn't been necessary anyway.

"You're surprised," she said.

"Yes." Surprise didn't begin to cover it. Everything—joy, excitement, fear, wariness, amazement—were all churning in the pit of his stomach. But the look in her eyes was giving fear the upper hand.

"Well," Cassie said. "I was surprised, too."

Jack flexed his hands and swallowed hard. "I thought we'd talked about protection."

"I didn't think we needed it." She took a deep breath and stared at the wall behind him. "I was married before. Ron and I tried to conceive a child for over two years."

Something unpleasant was boiling in his soul—he could almost see it. He kept his mouth shut and waited. His suspicions were just part of a bad dream. He would wake up and everything would be all right. Cassie would be his Cassie once more and together they would plan for the birth of their child.

"We were never able to accomplish that little task."

"And you sought medical help."

She nodded.

"And the doctors said that you couldn't have children."

"Not in so many words."

Her face blurred and danced before his eyes. He looked away. He had no idea what she was thinking or feeling or wanting, but one thing was all too clear. She'd had a deep dark secret in her past that she'd kept from him. He'd told her all sorts of stupid stories from his childhood and his time with Daphne—half of them things that didn't matter a whit—and she'd kept something vital from him.

She hadn't trusted him, hadn't felt that they were growing close. Or hadn't felt that it mattered that he really knew her. Keeping herself apart while playing him for a fool.

He felt dead inside. No, not dead. That would mean the pain was over. A fist still had a hold of his gut, twisting and turning and yanking with evil pleasure.

"So where do we go from here?" he asked around the bitter taste of crushed illusions. "I'm not running out on my responsibilities, but—"

The lines in her face hardened and her eyes turned to stone. "I'm not asking for anything. I don't need anything from you."

Hadn't she already proved that? She hadn't needed—or wanted—his understanding, his support, his reassurance. Not one damn thing.

Except maybe his sperm.

"I can support a child," she said. "And I have a family that gives me all the emotional support I need. It'll be surrounded with love. I don't want a single, solitary thing from you."

"I know." His face twisted in pain as he stood. "You've already got what you wanted out of me. So now you can toss me aside."

"What?" She got to her feet.

He grabbed at the only thing he had left—his pride. He clutched it the way he clutched the football when he was about to be tackled. There was no force on earth that could make him let it go.

"You wanted kids," he said. "You wouldn't feel like a complete woman until you did. So you took a proven stud and bedded him. Suddenly everything is ginger, peachy keen. You've got all the slots in your ticket punched and you are now a full-fledged member of the society of women."

Tears overflowed and slithered down her cheeks. His hold on his pride slipped a little, but he clutched it even harder. Daphne used to be able to cry like a barfly drank whiskey—easily and often.

"I would never do anything like that," she said through clenched teeth.

"Right."

"You bastard."

Her fist swung out and suddenly pinwheels exploded in his head.

Damn, that woman could hit. She'd hit him a good lick. He'd gone up against three-hundred-pound tackles who couldn't throw a punch anywhere near that hard. He felt like snatching her up in his arms and never letting go.

And he would have. If it weren't for the fact that she'd used him like she had. Used him and spat him out like a piece of bubblegum. Like every other yahoo jerk in the world.

"Get out of here," she said.

"Gladly," he snapped.

Chapter Thirteen

"So how's everything?" Ellen asked, all bright and chipper the next morning.

Cassie felt like belting her one, but her knuckles were sore from last night. She just opened her carton of orange juice and took a long drink. She supposed, as a mother-to-be, she shouldn't be going around slugging people, anyway. It set a bad example. She doubted the kid would know what she was doing right now, but you never knew. Best to start as she meant to go on.

"I'm just fine," Cassie said stoutly and grabbed up her inventory sheet. "Thought I'd work on the inventory while you guys handle the customers."

"You sure? Burt and I could do it if you want to sit down."

Cassie just gave her a look. She was pregnant, not an invalid. "Call me if things get busy." She hurried down the end aisle.

The PCV piping was easy to count, in six-foot and ten-foot lengths and in various diameters. Then there were all the tee and ell joints. It took her about ten minutes to get really really bored and sink onto the step stool.

She'd done a lot of thinking last night. Since sleeping had seemed out of the question, thinking had been something to do to pass the long hours. She probably had told Jack about the baby all wrong, but then diplomacy had never been her strong suit. He had thought she wanted something from him. Maybe even thought she'd been trying to force him into marriage, which was the furthest thing from her mind.

But still, all she'd really heard was "responsibilities." He was willing to be responsible and she knew it was over. Although maybe it had all worked out for the best. Now, at least, she knew where she stood. No more fearing that he wouldn't be there in the long run.

"Hey, boss lady!" Burt called out as he ambled down the aisle. "Ellen said to help you with the inventory."

Cassie sighed, but didn't say any of the hundreds of things running through her head. This was getting scary. Was pregnancy making her mellow?

"Why don't you start at the other end?" she suggested. "I don't really need help around here."

"You sure?" Burt was frowning at her like a stubborn old bulldog. "Ellen said—"

"I don't care what Ellen said," Cassie snapped. "If you want to do inventory, do it down there."

"But Ellen said you shouldn't—"

"If you want to live a long life, do it down there!" Cassie shouted, immediately feeling better. She was herself. There was no need to worry.

Burt left with a great deal of grumbling about only wanting to help, but she wasn't left alone very long. She'd barely made a start counting the lengths of copper pipe when Ollie came wandering over. He probably wanted to go out, so she put her papers down and let him out into the tiny yard behind her store.

She sat down on the edge of the loading dock while he meandered around, sniffing at the scraggly scrub trees and bushes at the back. The sun was pleasantly warm, the breeze refreshing. She looked down at her knuckles, all scraped from when she'd hit Jack.

She felt like crying.

"This is so dumb," she said aloud, blinking away the sudden wetness in her eyes. "I am absolutely fine."

Ollie came trotting over to put his head on her lap. She petted his head slowly, trying to gather up the fragments of her emotions.

"Hope you weren't too attached to him," she told the dog. "I think I was always meant to be alone. I like it that way, actually."

She half expected a bolt of lightning to strike her or a sudden mass of dark clouds to cover the sun. "Yeah, I enjoyed being with Jack," she admitted. "But I knew all along it was only a temporary thing."

Ollie sat back, cocking his head to one side as he looked at her.

"Oh, I'm sure he'll be a father to junior, here. He's not the type to run off. But that doesn't mean he has to be anything to me."

Ollie tilted his head to the other side.

"We can still be friends. It's not like I'm going to refuse to talk to him ever again."

Ollie yawned and turned to watch a truck drive by. Cassie took the hint and got to her feet.

"Want to go back in?" She led him over to the door. "You know, I have to tell the family one of these days. You got any ideas how?"

Ollie just trotted by her, hurrying down the aisle to his bedding. Obviously he felt she'd gotten into this mess; it was up to her to get herself out.

Cassie just sighed and went back to her inventory.

"Would you guys like anything to drink?" Cassie asked as Fiona and Sam settled down in the living room. She was starting to wish she'd waited a few more days before calling them over. Or a few more months. Confession wasn't a concept she was very comfortable with. "Iced tea? Lemonade? Orange juice?"

"Let's get your news over first," Fiona said.

Cassie looked at her sister and couldn't help making a face. Even a year ago, Fiona was nowhere near as take-charge as she was now. It had to be the marriage thing.

"I don't know where to start," Cassie said.

"Start at the beginning."

What good would it do to go all the way to the beginning, back to when she'd first met Jack? Fiona and Sam didn't need to hear about all the fun she and Jack had had together. Or the way she seemed able to talk to him about anything. None of that mattered now. Fact was fact. And her biggest fact right now was—

Cassie took a deep breath. "I'm pregnant," she said.

There was a long, heavy moment of silence. Long enough for Cassie to worry that they wouldn't be as accepting as she'd assumed.

"Does Jack know?" Samantha finally asked.

Cassie considered arguing that it didn't have to be Jack, but only for a moment. She hadn't been going with anyone before Jack, and everybody knew that she wasn't a one-night-stand kind of a woman. She nodded.

"Are the two of you going to do anything?" Samantha asked. "I mean, together."

"Nope."

Pregnancy didn't have to mean marriage anymore. Certainly not marriage without love. And she was not in love.

She was fond of Jack. She liked him a lot. She cared about his welfare, wanted him to be happy and safe and healthy. She really enjoyed the time they spent together, liked the way his laughter sent shivers down her spine and couldn't think of a better way to go to sleep than wrapped in his arms.

But she was not in love with him.

She hadn't loved Ron. She'd been foolish back then, thinking that she had to be like everyone else—wanting to be paired off. She'd learned since then that love wasn't for her. So she couldn't be in love with Jack.

No way. Never. Not in a million years.

Cassie took a deep breath and went on. "I'm going to keep the baby," she said. "I'm going to be a single parent."

No one said anything. Fiona didn't even look at her.

"I have my business so I'm financially comfortable. And I don't have to worry about pregnancy-leave policies or day care. Since I'm the employer, I can make things up as I need them." Then Cassie shrugged and tried a smile, but didn't quite make it. "And I figured all the rest of you, including the guys, would be there to support me."

"Of course, we will, Cass," Sam replied. "You didn't have to say anything."

Cassie smiled, but her sisters' faces were a tad blurred. Sam had rushed in with her support—but she was always trying to keep everyone happy. Fiona still hadn't said anything.

Did she disapprove of what Cassie had done? And if she did, what was it that bothered her? The fact that Cassie was having a baby out of wedlock or the fact that she was keeping it? Did Fiona think that her actions would bring shame on the family? Things didn't seem to work that way these days. For the first time in her life, Cassie hoped that Fiona wasn't angry with her.

"You know, it's kind of funny—" Cassie shook her head. "I'm—the first one of us who's going to have a baby."

"You were always the leader," Samantha said.

"No." It was Fiona speaking, but it didn't seem to be her voice. It sounded like a timid, frightened mouse speaking from a great distance, and with great difficulty.

"Huh?" Cassie said, staring at Fiona. Her face was white, her eyes almost scared-looking.

"Your baby won't be the first," she said.

Cassie and Sam just looked at her. Neither of them said a word. Even Ollie had stopped pestering for attention.

"I had a baby when I was away at college." Fiona paused to take a deep breath. "A little girl."

Fiona's gaze went from one to the other, switching back and forth as if afraid to settle on either one. Cassie didn't know about Samantha, but she was stupefied. Shocked. She didn't know what to say.

"I can't believe that you, of all people, would have done something like that," Samantha said.

"You were always so perfect," Cassie added.

"Yeah, right." Suddenly a dark pain filled Fiona's face. "That's why I could never tell."

For a moment, Cassie saw into the hell that her sister must have faced, and took her into her arms. Fiona burst into tears and then Samantha was there, holding her, too. Cassie's eyes grew watery and she tried valiantly to blink it away.

"What happened to your baby, Fi?" she whispered. "Did you give her up for adoption?"

Fiona's tears slowed after a moment and Cassie could feel her sister trying to compose herself. Finally Fiona nodded.

"Did you know who adopted her?" Samantha asked.

"No. Not for a long, long time, anyway." Fiona straightened, pulling away from them both as if refusing to lean any longer. "You remember the girl I donated the bone marrow to? Kate from Chicago?"

Good Lord. Fiona had given her bone marrow to save her own child and still had never told them. Cassie felt so weak and wimpy.

"Alex was hired by her adoptive family to find me," Fiona went on. "Well, he did. And, as the old cliché goes, the rest is history."

"Does Kate know you're her real mother?" Samantha asked.

"I'm her biological mother," Fiona corrected gently. "Her real mother is the one who raised her. But no, she doesn't know. Not yet."

"When are you going to tell her?" Samantha asked.

"When she's ready." Fiona shrugged. "And I don't know when that'll be."

"Haven't you missed her?" Samantha questioned. "Wondered how she was doing?"

"Yes."

"Did you even think about keeping her?" Cassie asked.

"I was in college, Cass. I had no skills, no job. No guts." Fiona took a deep breath that made it seem like she was in the middle of an argument she'd already had many times with herself. "She has a wonderful set of parents who have given her far more than I ever could have."

"Yeah, but—" Cassie shut her mouth. Going over Fiona's decision was pointless. All it would do was cause her pain and Cassie didn't want that. "I guess I'm luckier," she said slowly. "I'm able to take care of my baby."

"It won't be easy," Fiona warned her. "I see kids every day in school from single-parent households and I know all the challenges they face."

Cassie found herself studying the split skin on her knuckles—she'd really whacked Jack a good one. Yeah, she knew raising a child alone would be hard, but she had a big family. A big, accepting, buttinsky family. So she would never really be alone.

Suddenly she noticed the silence surrounding her and looked up to see both her sisters staring at her, their faces wrinkled with question. A question that they didn't have to articulate.

"I'm presuming that Jack will be involved in raising our child." She studied the bruises on her knuckles for a long moment before looking up again. "But we're not getting married. No way, under no circumstances. Never."

"That's pretty strong, Cass," Fiona said.

Cassie got to her feet. All this emotion was making her thirsty. She needed some lemonade and disappeared into the kitchen. "Having a baby is one thing, getting hitched for a lifetime is another."

She turned from opening the refrigerator to find Fiona in the doorway. Frowning.

"So not getting married is your decision," Fiona said, sounding like she was looking to place the blame.

This new Fiona was definitely hard to take. Cassie straightened. "Yeah. He didn't offer, but even if he had, I wouldn't have accepted. I don't need another man to let me down."

"Ron was a jerk." Sam had joined them in the kitchen.

"And Daddy didn't mean to leave."

Cassie just busied herself getting glasses out of the cabinet. "I presume you all want some lemonade, too?"

"Cassie, it's time you let yourself trust somebody," Fiona said.

Cassie just closed her eyes briefly, then began to pour.

"You keep turning people away and pretty soon there'll be nobody left for you," Fiona went on. "You've got to stop fighting with everybody."

Maybe that was the way she wanted it, Cassie wanted to shout. Maybe she didn't want to share her life with anybody. Maybe she would rather stay alone than be left alone.

Maybe she was afraid that if she stopped fighting, someone would find their way into her heart—and she'd learned long ago that love only left you crying.

"Good night, Daddy," his girls chorused.

Jack paused at their bedroom door and flicked off the light. He'd already gone through the standard bedtime ritual—the story, a kiss for each daughter, and a how-was-your-day chat. He'd done the whole nine yards and now they were down to the wheedling-and-delaying stage.

"That's it, ladies," he said. "Settle down and go to sleep."

"I hope your face gets all better."

"Yeah. Don't walk into no more doors."

"I'm fine." That part about walking into a door was rather lame, but the kids had been peppering him with questions the other day and it had been the best he could come up with. "I'll be more careful next time. Now go to sleep."

"Daddy."

Their one-word chorus caught him just as he was about to swing the door shut. "Now what?"

"I hope Cassie gets all better, too."

"Yeah, we need more lessons."

Jack felt his hands tighten for a moment. "You're taking lessons at the YMCA," he reminded them. "The ones with Cassie were only to get you started until you could take the real lessons."

"But we want Cassie." Their wails filled the bedroom, bringing a tension to the air that he didn't really want to deal with right now.

How did he answer that? "No more talking. Sleep tight." He quickly closed their door and made his escape.

He should have been more careful these past weeks. After all, it wasn't just him anymore, but the girls, too. If he had stayed uninvolved, as he should have, he wouldn't have to worry about hurting them through his own stupidities. His hand went up to his face. Not to mention fewer bruises for himself.

"All right, what's going on?"

Jack almost jumped high enough to slap the moon. Walking along and studying the fibers in the rug as he'd been doing, he hadn't expected to meet anyone. Not even Aunt Hattie. "I thought you were in your room, reading."

"Normally I would be," she replied. "But things haven't been normal in this house the past few days."

Damn. He didn't want to deal with anybody. He just wanted to find himself a hidey-hole and crawl in. Talking about his personal problems had never been a strong point with him. As far as Jack was concerned, he was the one who got himself into them, he would get himself out. Period, end of discussion.

"What's the problem between you and Cassandra?"

"Why does there have to be a problem between the two of us?" he asked. "For all you know, I could be thinking about a paper I'm writing."

"Don't be ridiculous, Jimmy Jack," his aunt sniffed.

"I'm going to read for a while."

"You'd best fix whatever's ailing between you and Cassandra. Foolish pride don't keep a body warm at night."

Was he being foolish? He didn't think so. Realistic was more like it. Anyone with an ounce of sense would interpret Cassie's secrets the same way—that she didn't care about him.

"I'll be reading for quite a while," he said. "So don't worry about the light being on."

He hoped that his aunt would read between the lines and see what he really was saying. The emphasis with which she stomped her feet as she made her way upstairs was encouraging.

Jack went into his office and picked up the pile of recreational reading sitting on his desk. It was a good assortment—

newsmagazines, a few sports things, an investment newsletter, and a thick publication rating all the new cars that would come out in the fall. There was enough in hand to keep him busy until the owls called it a night.

After several minutes of staring at the pile in his lap, Jack determined that nothing was ever as easy as it looked. Now he had to choose which magazine to start with. Quickly growing aggravated, Jack sat up and let the magazines fall to the floor.

His problem wasn't which periodical to read. His problem was what to do about Cassie—the woman who was carrying his child.

Yes, he'd been hurt the other night—he rubbed his jaw— both physically and emotionally. But it didn't really change anything. Certainly not the fact that she was pregnant with his child and he had certain responsibilities. His pride had been hurt—still was, for that matter—but that wasn't his child's fault. They were adults and needed to work something out. He stood and, leaving the magazines where they fell, went outside.

He walked slowly over to Cassie's house, pausing at the edge of his yard to ponder the disadvantages of small towns. If he were living and dating someone in Chicago, the odds were high that it would have taken him at least a half hour to get to her house. That would have been plenty of time to think, to figure out what he wanted to say and how to say it.

For a moment he considered walking around the block a few times but he dismissed the thought. Merrills weren't cowards. And a delay wouldn't help him come up with any better words. He was here now and he was a man. There wasn't anything left to do but to do it.

He crossed over into her yard. There was no mystery to what he had to say. *Will you marry me?* should do it just fine.

He walked up on the porch. The truck in the drive said she was home; lights in the house said she was still up. A man couldn't ask for anything more.

Ollie announced Jack's presence and, within moments, the porch light turned on and the door opened. She was wearing one of those short little summer nightshirts—the kind that brought a wandering man home and kept him there.

"Evenin', Cassie."

"What do you want at this hour of the night?" Her welcome was hidden deep in her heart, but that was a woman's right.

"We need to talk," he said.

"We've talked enough."

"We did talk a good bit." Women were like racehorses, beautiful creatures but a little on the skittish side. A man had to show the agreeable side of his nature, lest they bolted. "We just didn't talk about the right things."

"I suppose you have it all figured out as to what we should talk about?"

"As a matter of fact, I do."

"Go to hell, you pompous ass," she said, slamming the door on her own words.

He stood there for a long moment. What did she want him to do, kick the damn door down? Wasn't it enough that he was here? But Daddy had told him doing right wasn't always a quick trip down the interstate. Jack knew he had to give it another try.

"Cassie, open the door, please."

"Go away!" she shouted. "Or I'll call the police."

"I'm just asking that you talk to me. They'll probably recommend that you humor me." He wasn't sure that they would, but it sounded good. "So, let's talk, please."

"I'll send Ollie out. He'll rip you to shreds."

"You know that won't happen. He and I are friends."

There was a long silence and he hoped that Ollie wasn't getting too bad a shellacking. But the dog was a big fella. He should be able to hold up under it.

"I have a shotgun!" she shouted. "And if you aren't gone by the time I count to ten, you're going to be splattered up and down the block."

"You wouldn't shoot the father of your child."

There was a short silence, then a rattle as the interior door was opened. The screen door stayed closed, which was just as well. Jack didn't really want her taking another swing at him.

"All right," she said, arms folded across her chest. "Talk."

"This would go easier if I could come in and we sat down."

"It would certainly go easier for you if I didn't shoot you."

Obviously, appealing to her softer side wasn't going to work. But she had to have some concerns for the child. Their child. Surely, being raised by two parents was better than being raised by one. That was the tactic he needed to take with her.

"We used some harsh words the other night," he said. "But we had some good times before that, didn't we?"

Her posture softened and she leaned against her door.

"We get along very well with each other." He shrugged. "At least, I thought so."

Cassie didn't exactly nod but her body language wasn't negative, either. Reading a woman was harder than reading a jury.

"I'd like us to try again."

She sighed and looked down at the floor.

"Cassie, I want you to marry me. For our child's sake."

Her head snapped up and it was as if somebody had dropped a hot coal down the back of her neck. Damn. What had he done now?

"Why, you big, overrated, insufferable egomaniac."

With each word her voice was rapidly moving up into the screaming range. "Now, Cassie, just—"

"I am not marrying you!" she shouted. "I'm not marrying anybody and never will."

The slamming of the door ended her tirade. And should have left him feeling that he'd done all he could. He hadn't crawled or begged or pleaded, but he'd asked her to marry him. He'd done the responsible thing. Why, then, did he feel like hell?

His heart was suddenly in about a million pieces and almost screaming from the pain. It felt like the sun had been banished from his life forever. That he would never hear laughter or feel the sweetness of a smile again. That he was doomed to watching life from the outside.

He loved her.

He was in love with Cassie. If begging or pleading or crawling or doing anything at all would make her love him, he would do it. He would beg until his voice gave out, plead until the end of time, crawl until his knees wore off. But he had no hope. She had turned on him.

His bruised face would heal but his soul never would. Not unless he could find a way into Cassie's heart.

"Holy cow," Dan Scott said as he came into Cassie's house. "Somebody die and I didn't get told?"

Cassie glared at him and grabbed up her keys. She knew her living room looked either like a greenhouse or a mortuary from all the flowers Jack had been sending over the past two weeks, but it would have been nice if her father had been diplomatic for once and ignored them.

"You been robbing florists?" he asked.

Obviously he wasn't going to be satisfied until he got an answer. "Jack sent them to me," she said. "I should have thrown them out but that seemed so wasteful."

She decided not to mention the fact that she had the only flower-filled plumbing-supply house in creation, that she had already dumped several loads at the two hospitals in town, or that she had about ten boxes of chocolates in her refrigerator.

"Are we going to see that house you're interested in or not?" she asked.

He just took another look around her living room, peeking briefly into the dining room, which he could see was also filled with flowers, before following her out the front door. Cassie was striding briskly over to his car.

"You and Jack have a fight?" he asked.

One thing Cassie had to say for her sisters—they kept their mouths shut. It was her job to tell and they respected that. "Sort of," Cassie replied. She knew she had to tell her dad about the baby soon, but wished she could put it off even more. "What's this house like that we're going to see?"

He gave her a look as they got in the car, but played along. "Built in the 1890s, but it's in great condition—eight bedrooms with a fireplace in each, four baths, tile roof, on an acre of land. It was rewired about ten years ago, the kitchen was redone at the same time, and it's got a relatively new furnace. Plus, it's on Clements Lake."

"Sounds good," she said and meant it.

Her dad had been talking about starting a bed-and-breakfast for years, now. He'd let his dream slip a bit when their mother died, but she was glad to see that it hadn't died for good.

"What will you do with the house you have now?" she asked.

He drove a ways without speaking. "Actually, Fiona and Alex want to buy it," he said. "If that's all right with the rest of you."

"It's fine with me," she assured him. "Why wouldn't it be?"

He just shrugged and drove on. "Didn't know if any of the rest of you would want it."

"I've got a house," she said. "And it's just the right size for me." Actually, it was a little big now, with its three bedrooms, but soon it would be just right.

"True."

The silence seemed to weigh down on her and she stared out the window. Clements Woods was on the east side of the lake, but the west side was residential. The houses there were always snatched up quickly, though. It was amazing that her father might get one there.

"I put a deposit on the house," he told her.

She had an eerie feeling that he could read her thoughts and vowed to be careful what she was thinking about. "Oh?"

"Pending a couple of inspections," he added. "And your approval."

"I don't have to approve it." She felt funny having that kind of responsibility.

"I trust your judgment. Always have." He glanced at her as he pulled into a long drive. "Always will. No matter what."

Cassie chose to look at the house ahead of them rather than to respond to his words. It was a huge wooden house, painted gray and white and deep red, with a wide porch and lots of gingerbread trim. Oak trees towered over it, giving it such a feeling of stability and welcome that she was ready to move in then and there.

"I like it," she said.

"Wait until you see the inside."

She followed him inside, through spacious room after spacious room. Apparently the owner had died at the age of ninety-five and his estate was selling the house, so no one was living in it at the moment, although it was furnished with wonderful antiques.

"I have an option to buy some of the furniture, too," he told her.

"It certainly has charm."

He led her into the kitchen where she got down and looked under the sink. The last kitchen sink she'd toyed with was Jack's—a fact that made her frown.

"Want to run some water through?" she asked her dad. This was nothing like that evening at Jack's. Nothing at all.

The pipes seemed adequate, so they moved through the bathrooms, checking those out, and then into the basement to do the same. All the while, she was conscious only of the secret hanging between them.

"The plumbing's old," she said. "But it seems pretty adequate. Some of the sinks could stand replacing and just about all the faucets need some upkeep, but nothing major that I saw."

"Great." He looked like a kid who was promised Christmas. "Want to go out by the lake?"

"Sure."

He led her out the door and down the sloping lawn to the lake. The shade was delicious. She kicked off her sandals and walked across the thick grass with pleasure. A group of pushy ducks was waiting for them by the time they got to the water's edge.

"I don't have anything for you guys," she told them.

"Here." Her father handed her a bag of bread crusts. "I brought it over earlier today."

She'd thrown out only a few pieces of bread when who should come into view, but Romeo and Juliet. She sighed as she watched the majestic birds come closer. Juliet seemed to be looking straight at her. Was she like Ellen—able to sense a pregnancy long before anyone else? Cassie tossed the bread into the water, then walked over to the bench where her father was sitting.

"Jack and I broke up," she said as she sat down. "He wanted to get married and I didn't."

"Maybe you needed more time."

She looked away at the birds searching for scraps of bread. "I'm pregnant," she told him. "He wants to get married. I don't think pregnancy and marriage have to go together."

"No, I guess they don't," he said slowly. "But it's a lot easier on the kids if they do."

"Not if pregnancy was the only reason for the marriage."

"But you two got along well."

The shadows were getting deeper as the sun was sinking. They seemed more threatening, more mocking of her insistence on being alone. "But I don't love him," she said.

"Ah." The one word held a volume of meaning, none of which she wanted to delve into.

"I don't," she insisted. "I like him. We have fun together. But I don't love him."

"What *is* love?" he asked.

She glared at him, but suspected she was too much in the shadows for him to even know. "How the hell would I know?" she asked. "I'm about as far from an expert on the subject as you could find."

"Then how do you know you don't love him?"

She leaned forward, resting her arms on her knees as if the slight distance she'd gotten from her father was enough to keep her safe. "Because I do."

"I see."

Cassie hated it when he was so calm. "Love is something different. Something big and flashy like fireworks on the Fourth of July." She swallowed hard when she realized they'd had fireworks on the Fourth—the private kind, in their room at night. "It's warm and cozy like a fire on the coldest night of the year." She bit her lip when she remembered how Jack had come over to hold her the night she'd seen Ron with his child. "It lasts forever."

She should have felt a sense of victory, the joy of triumph. She'd found the key that proved her point, but only felt the weariness of defeat.

"So you must be happy now that Jack's out of your life," her father said, getting slowly to his feet.

"I am," she snapped. "Overjoyed."

"That's what I thought."

"I'm delirious with relief."

"Uh-huh. I can tell."

"I'm ecstatic."

"Shouting your joy to the heavens, as it were." His tone was definitely mocking.

"Exactly."

Chapter Fourteen

"You sure you don't want another beer?" Bobby asked as he brought fresh cans for his two brothers.

Jack looked at his own glass, two sips down from full, and shook his head. "No. I'm fine, thank you."

The four of them—Cassie's three brothers and Jack—were sitting on the deck in back of Bobby's house, sucking on the occasional breeze that blew in from the west. It was one of those typical Midwestern, middle-of-July nights. Hot, with the humidity hanging heavy in the air, like hope at a lottery-ticket counter.

He was here because he needed help, but there was a certain protocol a guy had to follow in these situations. First you had to beat around the bush for a while. And that was what they'd been doing.

They'd discussed whether the Chicago Bears would ever have another winning season, how the Chicago Bulls would fare on their quest for a fourth NBA title, and the miserable state of professional baseball, especially the White Sox and the Cubs. From there they'd gone into Notre Dame football and Indiana

University basketball. The conversation had wound down by covering each of the kids' teams that the brothers' boys and girls had been on so far this year. Another sip of beer, and they would be ready to talk serious business.

"Nancy says they're really having fun at the line-dancing class," Larry said.

"They sure are," Adam agreed. "Rosemary says it's the best exercise she's had in a long time."

Jack groaned inwardly. Now they were talking about their wives' aerobic exercises. Looked like he'd better make a move. Another minute and they'd be lying about their golf scores.

"Boys." Cassie's three brothers stopped talking and looked at Jack. "I'm in deep trouble and sinking fast. Falling straight to hell, as it were."

Sympathetic murmurs greeted his words. "What's up?" Bobby asked.

"I'm—" Jack paused to watch the fireflies for a moment, trying to decide how much of his soul he had to bare. Somehow he couldn't tell them he loved her—not when he hadn't even told *her*. "I'm afraid Cassie's mad at me."

There were grunts and murmurs of sympathy.

"We had one hell of a fight." Jack took a deep breath. "She punched me in the jaw."

"So, what do you want us to do?" Bobby asked.

"I don't know," Jack said, shaking his head. "I guess I need to get Cassie off someplace by ourselves."

They grunted to indicate their understanding.

"Somewhere where she can't run off on me."

This time they were dead quiet.

"I was thinking maybe I could rent a room. You know, someplace nice." It was too dark to read their faces but he could feel them with him. "And then you guys can bring her over."

"Say what?"

"No way."

"She'd never go for that."

"By the time you'd open the door, she'd be madder than a nest of wet hornets and beating on us."

The silence again surrounded them and Jack was glad that it was night, making it hard for the brothers to see how disappointed he was. He had hoped for better but it was obviously not meant to be.

"You sure it has to be Cassie?" Adam asked.

"What?" Jack asked.

"Sam broke up with Marty a few weeks back."

"Now there was a real jerk."

"Took her long enough to see we were right."

"Anyway," Adam went on. "She's a heck of a lot more easygoing than Cassie."

Jack laughed, even though his heart was near to breaking. "No, it's gotta be Cassie."

Murmurs of disappointment mixed with understanding bubbled around the table. It was time to hit the road. He didn't know what he'd been hoping for, but he wasn't going to get it. He guessed he would keep on with the flowers and candy. Maybe someday she would talk to him. Eventually, maybe. Sighing, he started to push himself back from the table.

"I got it." Bobby slapped the table and they all looked at him. "We got to get Jack and Cassie up in a balloon."

Jack stared at Cassie's eldest brother. Normally Bobby was a down-to-earth, commonsense guy. Unfortunately, it looked like he was also someone who could not hold his beer.

"I have to get going," Jack said.

"Hey." Bobby held up a large hand. "Just settle down and hear me out. Cassie's a hot-air-balloon pilot."

No one said anything. Either everyone feared Bobby or they pitied him. Not sure which way to go, Jack decided to just quietly lean into the flow.

"We give ol' Rocky at Fire Dragons a call." He leaned toward Jack. "Cassie used to work for him. Tell him to call Cassie and give her a story about how she has to take up this paying customer for him."

No one agreed with Bobby's scheme. But then no one disagreed, either.

"Okay?" Bobby looked from one to the other. "She gets the balloon all blown up and ready to go. Then ol' Jack here, he makes like a jack-in-the-box and pops up out of the weeds."

"She's not going to take him up," Larry said.

"The man's a paying customer," Bobby insisted. "She has to. It's the law."

"I don't know," Adam said. "It's not like you have to go for a balloon ride for your health."

"Jack's a lawyer, he'll work it out," Bobby replied. "Anyway, he jumps in, the crew lets them go, and there you have it." He turned and looked intently at Jack. "That'll put you in a four-by-four-foot basket, about a thousand feet in the air. You take it from there."

Jack could only stare at Bobby as objections danced in his head. A thousand feet up in the air?

"Hey, the two of you are stuck up there."

"Right, she can't even run to the ladies' room."

"What if Cassie brings the balloon right back down?" Jack asked. "She can do that, can't she?"

"The lift-off area is surrounded by houses."

"Once the balloon is up, it starts drifting."

"Then she has to wait until you're over some open space."

Damn, it just might work.

"Of course," Bobby said. "Cassie might hit you again."

"And so what if she does?" Larry added. "He ain't afraid of her."

Jack wasn't sure about that, but wasn't about to admit anything. He was a man. He could take care of himself.

"Of course, she could throw him overboard."

Whoa. His anxiety level shot up—straight up.

"Cassie'd never do that."

"Naw. They'd take her license away if she did."

Jack swallowed hard. He wasn't crazy about the scheme, but it's not like he had one of his own to propose. And it might just work. He stood. "So," he said. "You guys'll set this balloon thing up, right?"

They grunted their agreement.

"We'll try for a morning run," Bobby said.

"Fewer witnesses," Larry added with a laugh.

Jack didn't ask what they didn't want witnesses to. He was sure he didn't want to know. "So what time should I get there?"

"Around five."

"Five in the morning?" Jack asked.

"Best air is at dawn and dusk," Bobby replied. "And Rocky's more likely to be booked up already for the evening flights."

He nodded, and said his goodbyes. Cassie's brothers were a great bunch of guys. This thing might not work out but it wouldn't be for lack of effort.

But by the time he was in his minivan, fear was riding heavily in his heart, fighting with the hope trying to take root. He wasn't afraid Cassie was going to throw him overboard.

No, his fear was just a common, ordinary fear of heights. The thought of a thousand feet up made his stomach lurch and his hands sweat. But he could handle it. If this was the only way to get Cassie back, he could handle it. Merrill men weren't cowards.

Cassie got to the park just before 5:00 a.m. It was going to be a perfect morning for a balloon ride. It was clear and still cool, with the sun just starting to peek over the horizon. She was going to enjoy this, she thought—until she thought she saw a minivan that looked like Jack's at the other end of the park and felt like bursting into tears.

Marry him for the baby's sake! That kind of thinking went out with the Hula Hoop and coonskin caps.

Irritation pushed all other emotion out of her heart as she parked her car at the opposite end of the park, near Rocky's truck. The balloon was on the trailer, but as Cassie came over, she saw it was Bobby who was unloading stuff.

"What are you doing here?" Cassie demanded. She knew Bobby had crewed for Rocky sometimes—after all, she'd met him through Bobby—but her brother had never crewed for her.

"Boy, that's some welcome." He nodded at the large wicker balloon basket and she grabbed the two handles on her side. "I should have let you set this all up yourself."

They hauled the basket out and set it on the grass.

"Rocky call you, too?" she asked, knowing it was a stupid question. Why else would he be here?

"Yep. Said you needed a chase crew."

"And you're it?"

They started pulling the balloon from the basket, laying it out on the ground downwind of the basket. The balloon was massive—seventy-five feet high and sixty-five feet wide—and getting it unfolded from the basket was a two-person job in itself. Getting it ready to inflate would take Bobby a good half hour if he didn't have help. And she had to get the burners hooked up.

"Naw, I roped Larry and Adam into helping." They heard a car pull up on the gravel. Larry and Adam.

"Have they ever done this before?" Cassie asked.

"What's to do? We just need their heft to hold the balloon down until we're ready to let you go. Other than that, we just order them around." He grinned at her. "Should make your day—all three of us having to obey your orders."

Cassie just glared at him. They'd gotten the balloon out of the basket and she wanted to start him on stretching it out flat. If they waited too long to take off, the wind could pick up. But there were four heavy propane tanks that she would never move on her own.

"Let's get the tanks in," she said, and went over to take one side of the first one.

"Hey, Larry, move your butt. Adam, get over here!" Bobby shouted, then waved Cassie away. "We'll get these in, Cass."

Cassie refused to budge from her place next to the tanks. "Take your side, Bobby, or you'll be wearing this around your neck."

Bobby just smiled at her. "Now, don't get hostile, Cass."

But he helped her move the first tank into the basket. While Cassie was maneuvering it into a corner, Bobby and Larry carried the others over.

Once she got them strapped in, she had Bobby help her put the cagelike burner supports over the basket and cotter-pin them in place. Larry and Adam were busy stretching the balloon out on the ground, but that was the only movement in the area. The houses that bordered the small neighborhood park were still and quiet. No cars were coming down the street.

"Where're our passengers?" she asked Bobby.

He looked around, then shrugged. "Not here yet."

She frowned. "We always used to verify the flight with the passengers on the morning of the ride," she said. "But Rocky never gave me a name or number."

"I think he was taking care of that."

"If he could do that, why couldn't he take the flight?"

Bobby got real busy hooking up the cables to the burner supports. She watched him in silence for a few minutes.

"I'm not sure we should do anything else until the passengers get here," she said. "We could be doing all this for nothing."

"He'll show up."

Cassie stared at her brother. "He?"

"I mean, the passengers." Bobby glanced over at Larry and Adam. "I'd better help them with the top panel. That's tricky."

"I still think we should wait."

"Hey, it's all paid for," Bobby said. "If nobody shows up, go up yourself. It'll do you good. You've been kind of down lately."

"I have not," she snapped, but the thought of a solitary glide over the countryside as the sun rose sounded so wonderful that she gave up the argument. She climbed into the basket and started hooking up the propane tanks to the burners that would heat the air in the balloon.

Once she finished that, she attached the instrument panel—setting the altimeter at zero so she would know how high they were once they started going up, and checking the variometer and thermometer.

"She's all ready to start filling up," Bobby said. "Want us to lay the basket on its side?"

She let them but refused to start the fan that would blow air into the balloon. "We really ought to wait," she said and scanned the neighborhood once more.

An older woman in her robe and slippers was standing on her front porch, newspaper in hand, as she watched them. A police car was driving by slowly; the cop at the wheel waved when they looked his way. A jogger jogged by, apparently oblivious to the balloon all stretched out flat in a yellow, red and blue striped silhouette in the grass. Cassie sighed.

"This is really weird. I've never had paying customers not show up."

"Means you get a free ride." Larry glanced at his watch. "Come on, Cass. Rocky said if nobody showed up by five-thirty, you could go up."

She stared at her brother, her eyes narrowing with suspicion. "When did he tell you that? I thought he called Bobby and Bobby called you."

Larry looked at Bobby, unable to hide the panic in his eyes. Adam coughed. "Bobby told us," he said quickly. "You know, that Rocky told him."

"What are you guys up to?" Cassie demanded. "This whole thing has smelled fishy right from the get-go."

"What do you mean?" Bobby was obviously going to try to bluff his way out.

Then, suddenly, she saw through it all and started to laugh. "This is all a plot, isn't it?"

They looked warily at each other.

"You guys wanted to treat me to a balloon ride and you made up this whole scheme to get me up."

Bobby smiled widely. "Yeah, that's it, Cass."

"We should've known we couldn't fool you."

"Well, I think it's the sweetest thing anybody's ever done," she told them, her eyes stinging suddenly. She blinked and looked away for a moment. "You guys are the best."

They just grinned at each other, then back at her. "Just trying to take care of you, Cass," Bobby said. "Want to get that fan started now?"

There was no reason to wait, no reason to chance that the wind might change. They brought over the huge fan and Cassie turned it on as Larry and Bobby stood on either side of the bottom of the balloon, holding the opening wide. Adam went across the field to hold the steadying rope that would keep the balloon from righting too quickly.

In a matter of minutes, the balloon was like a huge striped nylon cave—a seven-story building lying on its side—filled with enough air that she could walk in and check the Velcro fastenings at the top.

This whole scheme of the boys really astounded her. They'd always been good brothers—maybe a little overbearing at times—but always caring. This elevated them into the "great" category. She couldn't believe how nice they were being. Everything looked fine and she came back out of the balloon.

"Dad told you, didn't he?" Cassie said as she turned on the burners. The flames shot into the inside of the balloon and began to heat the air.

"Told us what?" Bobby shouted over the roar of the burners as he stretched to keep the skin of the balloon away from the flames.

"You don't have to pretend," she called out. "It's okay if you know. I was going to tell you all soon anyway."

The balloon rose slowly as the air heated, putting a strain on the rope Adam was hanging on to. She watched the thermometer on the control panel. A little longer and the air inside would be one hundred degrees hotter than the outside air. When it was one hundred and fifty degrees hotter, the balloon would leave the ground and she would be free as a bird for the next hour. She wished she could shed her thoughts of Jack as easily as she would shed the shackles of the earth.

"You were going to tell us what?" Larry bellowed.

"Well, it's not like I could really hide it for very long," she shouted with a laugh. "I mean, another five or six months and I think you all would be able to figure it out for yourselves. It's not exactly something a girl can hide."

"Hide?" Bobby yelled. "What do you want to hide?"

Cassie just laughed as the balloon slowly rose, righting the basket and rising majestically above it. She'd seen it happen dozens of times before, but the sight never failed to thrill her. She turned off the burners and climbed into the basket as Bobby and Larry clung to the sides, holding it down. Adam came running over with the rope. She tied it to one of the burner supports.

"Now what'd you say?" Bobby asked, his frown filling his face.

"We couldn't hear a damn thing with that propane burner going," Larry said.

"Just that I can't hide being pregnant," she said. "Sooner—"

"Pregnant?" Bobby shouted. He let go of the basket's sides for a moment and it careened wildly. He grabbed it again. "What the hell are you talking about?"

"How'd you get pregnant?" Adam demanded.

The three brothers looked at her, then at each other.

"That ass—" Larry snapped.

"Hey, none a that," Bobby said with a nod toward Cassie. "Pregnant lady present."

Larry and Adam paused a moment, blinking in a bewildered way.

"What the hell is with you guys?" she cried.

"You're right," Larry said with a nod. "I meant, that ... that ... scoundrel."

"That snake in the grass," Adam added.

Cassie just stared at them. It was like she'd stumbled into the Larry, Bobby and Adam version of the Three Stooges.

And if they weren't doing this because Dad had told them she was pregnant, why were they?

It looked like they were ready for him, Jack thought, and got out of his minivan. Bobby had said when the balloon was upright, he should hustle over. Then they would toss him into the balloon and let go. Well, the balloon was upright, like a medium-size office tower. No doubt about it, time to get tossed.

Maybe he could sit on the floor of the basket and not see how high it was rising. Better yet, he would just stare at Cassie the whole time, never noticing anything else.

Although there was always the possibility that she just might toss him back out. Then he would have no time to worry about his fear of heights. He would probably hit the ground before he could get focused properly.

Jack hurried across the grassy stretch. His heart sank a little as he got closer. It looked like they were having an argument. Great. That meant Cassie would already be aggravated. This was never going to work.

Still, Merrill men weren't cowards. He broke into a jog.

"Hi, y'all," Jack said when he was a few feet from the balloon. Larry was on one side, hanging on as the balloon fought to get airborne. Bobby and Adam, their arms wrapped around the corner posts, were anchoring the other side.

All three turned to look at him, friendly as a pride of lions toward a hyena who'd come upon them and their lunch.

"You reprobate."

"You vermin."

"What the hell are you doing here?" Cassie demanded.

Talk about your friendly small-town spirit. "I came for my ride," he said, choosing to address Cassie's question since she was the only one making sense.

"Your ride!" Her eyes went from sparkling to crackling as she turned to her brothers. "What's he talking about?"

"It ain't his talking that's the problem," Bobby snarled.

"This here's our little sister, you know," Larry told Jack.

"Yeah, she's not some helpless young girl all alone in the world," Adam warned. "She's got us to protect her."

Oh, Lord. It suddenly hit Jack like a five-hundred-pound opponent. Somewhere in between the planning meeting for this little outing and this morning, they'd found out Cassie was pregnant.

All three brothers looked ready to kill, or at least maim him. Probably the only thing saving Jack was the fact that if they let go of the balloon, it would go floating up, up, and away. Of course, once they figured out that that would leave them free to dismember him without Cassie's interference—assuming she would interfere—they would let go before he had a chance to blink.

"What the hell is going on?" Cassie shouted at her brothers. "Why is he here?"

He knew that he should be gearing himself up for the coming brawl, but Cassie looked so damn beautiful. The sparkle in her eyes put the morning sun—just visible over the eastern horizon—to shame. He couldn't imagine life without her. She would be his sun and his moon and his stars. She would be the air he breathed and the pulse that kept his heart beating.

If only she would give him a chance to slay the dragons that haunted her. To cut the bonds of fear that were holding her prisoner.

"I'm here because I love you," he told her. Jack was only watching Cassie. He knew her brothers wanted to stomp him good, but he couldn't worry about them.

"Fine way to show it!" one of the brothers shouted.

"Should've kept to talking, buddy. That's about the only thing a lawyer can do."

"Actually, he did a little more than that."

"This is a setup, isn't it?" Cassie demanded of her brothers. "He's the mysterious passenger."

"I want to marry you," Jack told her.

"You can bet all the gold in your trophies that's what you're going to do."

"Here and now, if we had a preacher."

"Hell, what're we waiting for? Let's go get us a preacher."

"Now, wait a minute!" Cassie cried. She was matching her brothers, angry look for angry looks. Except that one of hers was equal to three of the others' combined. "This wasn't some thoughtful little gift from the three of you, was it? It was a setup. A way to get Jack alone with me where I couldn't escape him."

"Just so we could talk things out," Jack explained. "I have no intention of forcing myself on you."

"Ha, that's a good one."

"Enough talking," Bobby said, getting a better grip on the bobbing basket. "Larry, go get a preacher."

"Wait just a damn minute," Cassie retorted. She grabbed Bobby's shirtfront and got right up in his face. "I'm not marrying him. You got that? I don't care how big any of you talk, or what kind of Neanderthal games you play, I am not marrying him."

She gave her brother a push and he staggered back a bit. But Bobby was a big fella and he kept a hold on the basket, keeping the balloon from floating free.

"You guys aren't exactly helping my cause," Jack reminded. He'd had bad feelings about this from the beginning. He should have just stuck with the flowers and the candy.

Sooner or later, she would have talked to him. Even if it was just to tell him to stop sending them.

"We should just let go and take care of this bounder," Bobby said.

"Good idea."

"Whoa," Larry said. "We can't let a pregnant woman go up in a balloon."

"Hell," Bobby agreed, his face falling in disappointment. "You're right."

Cassie just rolled her eyes. She looked like she didn't know whom to be angrier at, but Jack thought her brothers were ahead of him by a hair. It wasn't much but, at this stage of the game, he couldn't afford to look for a measuring tape.

"Leave while you got the chance, Jack," she snapped at him.

He smiled at her. "I'm not running." He turned to her brothers. "You boys think you can whup me, give it a try."

"Oh, for heaven's sake, Jack," Cassie cried, her voice sounding exasperated. "There're three of them."

"Merrill men never run from a fight."

"Swell. And how many Merrill men are left?"

"There might be one more than a few weeks ago." He caught her eye and thought there was a glimmer of softness there. He wasn't afraid of anything—not when she looked at him that way.

"We can take turns," Bobby suggested. "One of us thumps Casanova, there, and the others hold on to the balloon."

"Sounds good to me," Larry replied.

"Oldest gets first crack."

"Hell, I'm always last," Adam complained. "That ain't fair."

"Your home floor, boys," Jack said. "You call the tune and we'll dance it."

"This is stupid," Cassie insisted. "I can take care of myself."

"This won't take long, darlin'," Jack said.

Suddenly her hand whipped out and her fingers locked in his hair. Damn, she was quick.

"Get in here," she snapped.

"Hey!" Bobby yelled. "He can't go in there!"

"I ain't going no place," Jack yelled back.

"You get in here, right now!" Cassie shouted. "Or you're going to be as bald as a cue ball."

"Cassie, I—"

Her strong fingers twisted in his hair and he could see that it would be better to get in the basket and talk. It was a little difficult climbing in with her hand tangled in his hair but Merrill men never backed down from a challenge.

"Send him back out, Cassie," Adam said. "This is something for us men to settle."

"Shut up," Cassie retorted. Then she turned toward Jack. "Now, as for you—"

"Cassie," Jack said. "I love you."

"This is not the place for that kind of discussion," she snapped.

"You're right," he replied. "That's why I agreed to this balloon caper."

Her mouth opened but quickly closed. Uncertainty flittered about at the back of her eyes. Jack knew that it was now or never.

"I wanted to cut you free, Cassie. I wanted to be able to take you someplace where your fears wouldn't be able to follow you."

It was hard to tell if the uncertainty was fading, but he thought he saw her chocolate-brown eyes softening.

"We both have a lot of baggage," Jack said. "My stupid pride is keeping me from being happy. And you're afraid that love won't last. That I'll leave you like Ron and your father did."

Now he could definitely see the softening. In fact, her eyes were swimming.

"I wanted us to be alone someplace," he murmured. "Someplace where we could just talk. The two of us."

"There he goes with that 'talk' business again," Bobby said.

"I think I'll just get out and go home," Cassie said.

"If you do, they'll let go," Jack said. "And I'll float out over Lake Michigan and disappear, never to be found again."

"The wind will take you in the other direction."

"We're just going to thump him a little, Cassie," Larry said. "Nothing serious."

"All right, I'll go east. I'll disappear in the Atlantic Ocean. Never to be found again."

"You'll run out of propane fuel before you get anywhere close to the ocean."

"Fine." Jack threw up his arms. "Then I'll crash in some cornfield in Ohio someplace. Are you willing to face our son and tell him that you sent his father to his death?"

Her eyes rolled up toward the balloon above them. "It could be a girl, you know."

"And probably as ornery as you." He put his hands on her arms. "Cassie, I love it that you're pregnant, but my feelings would be the same if you weren't. I realized I loved you when you slammed the door in my face and all I could think of was how to win you back. Not worrying about if I'd look foolish."

He could almost feel her leaning forward. One step and he could put his arms around her.

"Cassie." It was Bobby's deep voice. "Send him out here. We want to put a few bruises on his body and some sense in his head."

"Turn that knob counterclockwise," Cassie said, pointing to a large black knob. "Now, Jack."

Without any hesitation, he turned the knob. The apparatus above them burst into an ungodly racket and shot a long blue flame up into the innards of the balloon.

"Hey!" Larry yelled. "Turn that off."

"Let go, you bums!" Cassie shouted and whacked at Bobby's hands. "Let go or I'll break your arms."

"Cassie!"

"Hey!"

But they all let go and the balloon glided slowly up into the sky.

"You better be married to my sister when you come back, Steeplejack!" It was Bobby yelling. "Otherwise you're gonna wind up more like a Quonset hut."

Jack was still pondering the Quonset-hut statement, when Cassie leaned over the side and shouted, "How are we going to find a preacher up here, you dummies?"

"You better be engaged, then."

The balloon rose slowly—above the housetops, then above the treetops. Jack swallowed hard and tried to keep his eyes on Cassie. She glanced over at a meter and turned the burners off. It was blessedly silent all of a sudden. His gaze wandered and he saw even the treetops were far down. Oh, dear Lord.

"They're really sweet guys. You just have to know how to talk to them." She leaned forward, her arms on the edge of the basket, and took a deep breath. "Isn't it beautiful up here? It makes a person feel so free."

He tried not to clutch the sides too obviously. Above him was air. Air caught in a flimsy piece of nylon with Velcro holding everything together. He closed his eyes for a moment, just to try to remember what it felt like to be on solid ground.

"So now that you've got me up here, what have—" Cassie stopped. "Jack? Jack, are you all right?"

He opened his eyes and forced a nonchalant smile. "Sure. This is great."

"You're white as a ghost." She pushed on his shoulders, and his unresisting knees gave way so he was sitting on the floor of the basket.

"This is humiliating."

His eyes drifted half-closed. Jack felt, more than saw, Cassie fooling around with a little bag hanging on the edge of the basket. Then, as she leaned close to him, he took a deep breath, trying to take a piece of her with him to his death.

"Oh, damn." He jerked his head back and hit it on the side of the basket. His eyes popped open and he could feel his sinuses clearing. Smelling salts.

"Better?" She stood again, glancing every few seconds at the instruments and over the edge.

He nodded slowly. "Yeah. Sure. Whatever you say. As long as you don't put that thing near my nose again."

"What'd you do, skip breakfast?" She reached up and turned the burners on for a long moment.

The moment of earsplitting noise gave him time to search for an excuse. A manly excuse. But the silence came back too soon.

"You might as well know all my faults," he said. "I'm tone-deaf. I need glasses to read and I'm scared to death of heights."

"What the hell are you doing up here, then?" she asked.

"Convincing you to marry me." He heard an airplane in the not-too-distant distance. "Are we going to be hit by that plane?"

She shook her head. "We have the right-of-way."

"Do they know that?"

"Don't change the subject. You could have asked me to marry you on the ground."

"I did that once and you hit me." He paused. The noise of the plane seemed to be fading. Maybe it wasn't going to crash into them. "No, you slammed the door in my face and threatened to shoot me."

"I was upset."

"You hang up on me when I call you." His voice sounded annoyingly weak. He wanted to be impressive, not pitiful. "You haven't responded to all the notes with my flowers."

"Yeah, I did." The world's most beautiful little smile played on her lips. "I tore them up and mailed them back to you. Maybe they haven't arrived yet."

"You know, this conversation isn't going the way I planned." He took another deep breath. "I'm supposed to be upright, coherent and persuasive. You're supposed to be charmed by my wit and passion, and fall into my arms."

"I see."

The burners went on again and Jack took the time to take deep breaths that he was sure would conquer his fear. By the time she turned the burners off, he would be able to stand and look her in the face. He could sweep her into his arms. The burners went off.

He pushed himself up to his feet—a bit wobbly, but upright. He looked only at her. At those eyes so full of fire and passion. At those lips that could drive him wild with hunger. At those arms in which he wanted just to rest forever.

"Are you all right?" she asked.

"Merrill men don't faint. And we propose on our feet." He paused, having a sudden thought. "No, on our knees. You'd prefer me to get down on one knee, wouldn't you? That's a hell of a lot more romantic."

"I'd prefer you didn't pass out," she said.

"You know, women really aren't romantic."

"Well, the romanticism of you keeling over and cracking your head open on a propane tank does escape me at the moment."

"If it wasn't for us men, there'd be no romance in this world."

"Sit down before you fall over again."

"I am not going to be the first Merrill man to let romance die on my watch."

"I'm not going to be the first Scott woman to have a man die of fright on her watch."

Ignoring her words, Jack went down on one knee—his reconstructed knee, which issued only a mild protest.

"Cassie, I love you more than life itself. I want you to be my wife. To walk side by side with me on this earth until the end of our days."

She sighed and looked down into his eyes for the longest time. Eons passed. Epochs, even. But she only turned to lean her arms on the basket edge again, and looked out over the hazy world below them.

"You just don't understand," she said slowly. Her voice was trembly and soft. It was full of tears. "I don't love."

He staggered to his feet and reached over for her hand, turning her to face him. Slow tears—like a knife twisting in his chest—were gliding down her cheeks. He wiped them away.

"No, you don't understand," he told her softly. "You love everything wildly and without restraint—your dog, your family, those swans."

He pulled her into his arms, where she lay unresisting against his chest. "You just don't believe that anything really loves you back," he whispered into her hair. "Well, Ollie does. Your family does, including your crazy brothers who I'm not too anxious to meet again. I do. I love you like no one's ever been loved before and I will never leave you. Not while there's breath in my body."

She started to cry again, sobs shaking her slender frame until he thought his own heart would break with her pain. "It's not that simple. You'll leave," she said. "They all leave. And I just couldn't bear it."

"It *is* that simple," he told her. "It's the simplest thing in the world. I don't want to live my life without you. I will never, ever leave you. I want to tell our grandchildren about you slugging me. I want to see you grow old beside me and know that you'll still care about me when I lose my hair. I want to know that I can make the bravest, most stubborn woman in the whole world happy."

"Jack—"

"Quiet." He placed a finger over her lips. "You're thinking too much. You have to feel. Just feel."

He just held her, taking a deep breath at the joy of having her there. He felt her breathing against him, felt her tears slow and stop. He felt the wonder and hungers of being so close to her again. Then gently, ever so gently, he let his lips touch her hair. He wasn't afraid of being so high anymore. The only fear he had now was that this was all a dream and he would awaken to be alone again.

She moved in his arms, but not to leave—to turn so that her face was looking into his. So her lips could reach up and touch his. He kissed her slowly, then slowly once more, willing all his love to flow into her and show her just how much they needed each other. She needed to see how much he loved her. How, without rhyme or reason, he would always be there because their souls were joined in some inexplicable way.

They pulled apart slightly and his gaze was snagged by a sight they were drifting near. He turned her slightly. "Look down there," he said.

She looked below and saw what he saw—Clements Lake with Romeo and Juliet gliding over its surface. The edges of the water were shadowed and blurry, but right in the middle, caught in the glow of the rising sun, were the two majestic birds.

"They're there because of the promise," he told her. "They're there to give you the strength to reach for love."

"That's crazy," she said, although her voice seemed to waver.

"What does your heart say?" he asked. "Not your head, but your heart."

"My heart doesn't do decisions," she said. "I never let it."

"You never admit to it," he corrected gently. "Your head would never have led you into the water to save the swans. Your head would never have let you offer to fix a stranger's sink. Your head would never have had me turn on the burners to get us away from your brothers."

"Oh, Jack." She sighed and fell back into his arms. "I'm just so scared."

"Actually, so am I."

Her wide eyes looked up at him.

"I'm afraid that once I let go of you, I'll fall overboard."

She started to laugh and he knew he'd won. "You aren't leaving, buddy, even if I have to tie you to the basket to keep you in."

"So you're admitting it. You do love me."

"Shut up," she murmured.

He frowned at her, and cupped his ear. "What did you say?"

"That's the problem with you lawyers," she said, her voice suddenly growing hoarse. "You always talk too much."

Cassie came back into his arms and touched her lips to his. It was a quick kiss, a kiss that promised much but that also still held her fears. She pulled away from him slightly.

"You promise?" she demanded, her eyes searching his. "I can't lose you. I just can't."

He just smiled at her. "On our fiftieth wedding anniversary, we'll go to The Royal House for dinner. Then on our seventy-fifth, we'll try Tippecanoe Place."

"What?"

"I still owe you two paybacks for fixing the faucet," he said. "They'll be them. Merrill men aren't welchers. I can't leave until I pay my debts."

"I'll hold you to it," she said.

"Just hold me to your heart," he said. "That's the only place I want to be."

Epilogue

"Hello, little mama," Jack said, an excited Ollie at his side.

Cassie turned from painting the garage door and smiled at him. "Hi, big daddy," she said. "What are you doing here?"

He scratched Ollie's head for a minute, then tossed a tennis ball that lay near the garage. The big dog raced off. "Checking up on you. Are you sure that you ought to be painting?"

She finished painting one panel before putting her brush down. "What's this? You copying the boys 'pregnant woman' weirdness?"

"I just thought paint was dangerous."

"That's lead-based. This is latex." She pulled off her gloves, then gave him a kiss for being so sweet. "Want some lemonade?"

"Sure." He followed her into the kitchen. "Going to be sorry to sell this place?"

She looked around at the kitchen she'd repainted and retiled in sunny, warm colors. The best thing about it, though—outside of the man standing next to her—were the flowers adorn-

ing the table and the counters. Jack's flower-sending had
slowed slightly but hadn't stopped.

"No, it was never really a home. Just another house I lived
in."

"We don't have to live in my place, you know," he told her.
"We can look for something together if you'd rather."

"We've been through all this before." She poured two glasses
of lemonade and handed him one. "I love your house. It's
great."

"I'm not sure it needs much work, though. And if you enjoy this . . ."

"I'll work on the garage apartment that Aunt Hattie wants."

They went out to sit at the picnic table in the backyard. The
sunlight captured the fire in her diamond so that it sparkled and
glowed. She could hardly believe that it was only two weeks
since that weird-and-wonderful balloon ride. Two weeks since
she and Jack got engaged. And only two months until their
wedding.

"I brought you a present," he said, breaking into her
thoughts.

She frowned at him. "You don't have to keep doing that, you
know."

"This one's special," he said, and handed her a small book.

She picked it up. It was slightly worn, with the comforting
feel of an old friend. She opened it up—a book of Indian tales
and legends. Her eyes lifted to Jack's.

"Look where it's marked," he said.

She turned to a page in the middle of the book. The story of
the Warrior Princess. "Jack?"

"Read it."

Her hands trembling slightly, she read the little story about
a beautiful young princess who loved a tall, brave warrior. They
were wed and lived very happily until one day when their little
village was attacked. The tall warrior fought bravely to keep the
attackers from crossing the river, but he was killed and his body
slipped beneath the waters. Although she was brokenhearted,
the princess fought in his place, turning back their foes when
it got dark. She mourned the whole night, crying for her love.
The next morning the attackers returned, but a fiercely beau-

tiful white swan was on the river and fought whenever they came near. No arrows could touch the swan and the attackers finally went away in defeat. For years, the fierce white swan stayed near the village, protecting it. The princess would feed the bird and talk to him, and when she grew old and died, the other villagers buried her near the river. The next morning, a young female swan appeared. Together the two birds swam down the river and were never seen again.

Cassie closed the little book slowly, not certain if she could speak with all the emotions churning in her heart. "Thank you," she whispered.

Jack took her hand. "You've got to believe now," he said. "Not only did the tall warrior's love last after his human death, but mine will, too. As did your father's."

She looked up at him.

"He gave you this story long ago, but you didn't know what it meant. Somehow his love has been here all along, trying to reach you, to tell you to love."

"And he found my line busy, so he talked to you instead?" she asked with a smile.

"You would have found the book eventually," he said. "It was in a box of old books in the apartment above the garage."

She stared at him, then down at the book. The strangest feeling was coming over her, a feeling of things being meant to happen. A sense of being watched over. A sense of peace. She didn't know whether to laugh or cry, but just grinned at him.

"Between my dad and your imagination, I think we've got it made."

He held her hand tightly. "Between your love and mine, we can handle anything."

* * * * *

The exciting new cross-line continuity series about love,
marriage—and Daddy's unexpected need for a baby
carriage!

It all began with *THE BABY NOTION*
by Dixie Browning (Desire #1011 7/96)

And the romance in New Hope, Texas, continues with:

BABY IN A BASKET
by Helen R. Myers (Romance #1169 8/96)

Confirmed bachelor Mitch McCord finds a baby on
his doorstep and turns to lovely gal-next-door
Jenny Stevens for some lessons in fatherhood—and love!

Don't miss the upcoming books in this wonderful series:

MARRIED...WITH TWINS!
by Jennifer Mikels (Special Edition#1054, 9/96)

HOW TO HOOK A HUSBAND (AND A BABY)
by Carolyn Zane (Yours Truly #29, 10/96)

DISCOVERED: DADDY
by Marilyn Pappano (Intimate Moments #746, 11/96)

DADDY KNOWS LAST continues
each month...only from

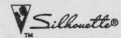

DKL-R

Take 4 bestselling love stories FREE

Plus get a FREE surprise gift!

Special Limited-time Offer

Mail to Silhouette Reader Service™

3010 Walden Avenue
P.O. Box 1867
Buffalo, N.Y. 14240-1867

YES! Please send me 4 free Silhouette Special Edition® novels and my free surprise gift. Then send me 6 brand-new novels every month, which I will receive months before they appear in bookstores. Bill me at the low price of $3.34 each plus 25¢ delivery and applicable sales tax, if any.* That's the complete price and a savings of over 10% off the cover prices—quite a bargain! I understand that accepting the books and gift places me under no obligation ever to buy any books. I can always return a shipment and cancel at any time. Even if I never buy another book from Silhouette, the 4 free books and the surprise gift are mine to keep forever.

235 BPA A3UV

Name	(PLEASE PRINT)
Address	Apt. No.
City	State Zip

This offer is limited to one order per household and not valid to present Silhouette Special Edition® subscribers. *Terms and prices are subject to change without notice. Sales tax applicable in N.Y.

USPED-696   ©1990 Harlequin Enterprises Limited

As seen on TV!

Free Gift Offer

With a Free Gift proof-of-purchase from any Silhouette® book, you can receive a beautiful cubic zirconia pendant.

This gorgeous marquise-shaped stone is a genuine cubic zirconia—accented by an 18" gold tone necklace.

(Approximate retail value $19.95)

Send for yours today...

compliments of ▼ *Silhouette®*
™

To receive your free gift, a cubic zirconia pendant, send us one original proof-of-purchase, photocopies not accepted, from the back of any Silhouette Romance™, Silhouette Desire®, Silhouette Special Edition®, Silhouette Intimate Moments® or Silhouette Yours Truly™ title available in August, September or October at your favorite retail outlet, together with the Free Gift Certificate, plus a check or money order for $1.65 U.S./$2.15 CAN. (do not send cash) to cover postage and handling, payable to Silhouette Free Gift Offer. We will send you the specified gift. Allow 6 to 8 weeks for delivery. Offer good until October 31, 1996 or while quantities last. Offer valid in the U.S. and Canada only.

Free Gift Certificate

Name: _____

Address: _____

City: _____ State/Province: _____ Zip/Postal Code: _____

Mail this certificate, one proof-of-purchase and a check or money order for postage and handling to: SILHOUETTE FREE GIFT OFFER 1996. In the U.S.: 3010 Walden Avenue, P.O. Box 9077, Buffalo NY 14269-9077. In Canada: P.O. Box 613, Fort Erie, Ontario L2Z 5X3.

FREE GIFT OFFER   084-KMD
ONE PROOF-OF-PURCHASE
To collect your fabulous FREE GIFT, a cubic zirconia pendant, you must include this original proof-of-purchase for each gift with the properly completed Free Gift Certificate.

084-KMD

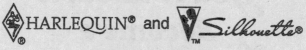
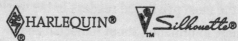

You're About to Become a

Privileged Woman

Reap the rewards of fabulous free gifts and benefits with proofs-of-purchase from Silhouette and Harlequin books

Pages & Privileges™

It's our way of thanking you for buying our books at your favorite retail stores.

PROOF OF PURCHASE

SSE-PP167

Offer expires October 31, 1996

Pages & Privileges ™

Harlequin and Silhouette— the most privileged readers in the world!

For more information about Harlequin and Silhouette's PAGES & PRIVILEGES program call the Pages & Privileges Benefits Desk: 1-503-794-2499

Silhouette®